BOLD PASSAGE

When Sam Cary and his bullwhackers set out on the Bozeman Trail for Fort Greybull, they knew they were riding into danger. Sam's arch-rival Mark Stockwell had been running guns to the Indians, a hot-blooded young warchief was stirring up the tribes and the cavalry had already pulled out.

But Sam was a fighter with a lot at stake—including a gray-eyed beauty named Gaybird. Besides, it was already too late to turn back. The first wagons were outside the sallyport when the thundercloud of warriors burst upon the fort . . .

Frank Bonham, in a career that spanned five decades, achieved excellence as a noted author of young adult fiction, detective and mystery fiction, as well as making significant contributions to Western fiction. By 1941 his work was already headlining Street and Smith's *Western Story Magazine* and by the end of the decade his Western novels were being serialized in *The Saturday Evening Post.* His first Western, *Lost Stage Valley* (1948), was purchased at once as the basis for a motion picture. "I have tried to avoid," Bonham once confessed, "the conventional cowboy story, but I think it was probably a mistake. That is like trying to avoid crime in writing a mystery book. I just happened to be more interested in stagecoaching, mining, railroading..." Yet, notwithstanding, it is precisely the interesting—and by comparison with the majority of Western novels—exotic backgrounds of Bonham's novels which give them an added dimension. He was highly knowledgeable in the technical aspects of transportation and communication in the 19th-Century American West. In introducing these backgrounds into his narratives, especially when combined with his firm grasp of idiomatic Spanish spoken by many of his Mexican characters, his stories and novels are elevated to a higher plane in which the historical sense of the period is always very much in the forefront. This historical aspect of his Western fiction early on drew accolades from reviewers so that on one occasion the *Long Beach Press Telegram* predicted that "when the time comes to find an author who can best fill the gap in Western fiction left by Ernest Haycox, it may be that Frank Bonham will serve well." In the *Encyclopedia of Frontier and Western Fiction* (1994) it is noted that "on even the shortest list of the finest... Westerns ever written would have to be included *Snaketrack* and *The Eye of the Hunter,* no little achievement when it is recalled that almost four decades separate the two books." *Night Raid, The Feud at Spanish Ford,* and *Last Stage West* are other Bonham titles which possess this same high standard of quality.

BOLD PASSAGE

Frank Bonham

GUNSMOKE

First published in the UK by Hodder and Stoughton

This hardback edition 2008
by BBC Audiobooks Ltd
by arrangement with
Golden West Literary Agency

ISBN 978 1 405 68222 0

British Library Cataloguing in Publication Data available.

Printed and bound in Great Britain by
CPI Antony Rowe, Chippenham, Wiltshire

Part One

I

CARY LEFT THE interior of the yellow railroad station and paused a moment in the doorway before stepping into the sunlight. He was a tall and limber-muscled man wearing a softly tanned leather shirt and old cavalry breeches with stripes of darker blue where the yellow slashes had been removed. His flat stetson was worn forward and to one side, a hat with its own casualness, the colour of deserts.

Glancing about him, he breathed the hot smell of the prairie town. Before him, tracks glistened fluidly under the sun. His handcar was drawn up beside the ties and at the corner of the station an Indian pony scratched luxuriously against a wooden sign nailed to the building. Cary's glance went briefly beyond it, to his own wagon camp a short distance away. A man on horseback rode into the sprawling square of wagons, dragging a load of mesquite roots by a rope. Bullwhackers worked stolidly in the dense morning heat, putting down the last of the freight for the haul from this railroad town of Cheyenne to Cary's trading post on the Montana border.

Cary turned to watch two of his teamsters back-and-bellying a crate from the loading dock, noting that four barrels still remained. Again he glanced at the camp, saw no one coming for them and stepped into the sunlight and crossed the tracks. Vaulting up on the high dock, he frowned at the words he had chalked on the tops of the barrels.

"Dunavan—repack."

His frown deepened. Then he saw his wagonmaster, John Silvertooth, coming from the camp, and he dropped to the ground and walked to meet him. The scorch of heated earth went through his bootsoles. The sun was like yellow glass melting in the sky. The thick, blackstrap odour of sage was in the air. Reaching Silvertooth, Cary asked off-handedly:

"Where's Dunavan?"

Silvertooth took time to fill his pipe, a big man in a red miner's shirt and smoke-tanned buckskin trousers. Deep grooves of displeasure pinched the skin between his eyes.

"Ain't seen him since breakfast," he said. "I hear it took six men to put him out of 'The Nations' last night. If he's got a hangover the size of his drunk, he'll sweat boilermakers for a week."

They walked towards camp. At the forge-wagon, a shirtless workman struck a rosy ox-shoe with ringing echoes.

Sam Cary stopped in the shade of a tall freight wagon. There was no sign of activity at Dunavan's faded blue Murphy wagon. Crates and barrels stood about and the tail-gate was down. Cary took a long breath of dissatisfaction. Silvertooth heard it and spat a mouthful of smoke.

"I say he's a troublemaker by trade. I could find a dozen better than him in any saloon."

"Soberer, maybe," Cary agreed. "But oxen and Oglalas don't set much store by whether or not a man's taken the pledge. Once we leave town, he won't be finding a saloon at every corner."

"*If* we leave town," said the wagonmaster.

"We always have, haven't we?"

"Up to now. But these bullwhackers are spoiling faster than pork, and the pork smells to high heaven. They had an edge like a Green River knife a week ago. They'd had their fun and were set to go. Now they've lost it."

Cary leaned by one elbow against a wheel a foot taller than he was. "They'll get it back fast enough, once they're standing night guard in Sioux country."

Disgruntlement did not leave Silvertooth's eyes. "Not with an Irishman like Dunavan bragging of what he's getting away with. Castro come to me this morning and asked could he pay back his advance and go out with Mark Stockwell's outfit. Stockwell got here three days after us, and he's going out before."

"What did you tell him?"

Silvertooth glanced at a cut knuckle. "I told him, no. There won't any more of them ask it, but I don't like the look of it. That Mick put him up to it. The same as he came to you and offered to sign on if you'd loan him the money to buy out of the army."

"Still a bargain," Cary stated. "He can't stand freedom: that's all that ails Dunavan. Once we stretch out, he'll pay his way."

"I don't like gambling on whackers. Not this year. This is the Sioux's year. The year of the big hunt. We should have gone out a week ago, when the men were standing on their hind legs clawing at the sky."

Cary smiled. "Don't blame me. I only own half this outfit. The other half will be here to-morrow sure—if the train doesn't get stampeded by a herd of buffalo."

He found a dipper on a nail and raised the lid of a barrel lashed to the side of the wagon. Pouring a dipper-full in his hat, he set it on the ground to soak. He drank a dipper, letting half the water slosh inside his shirt. It slid tepidly over his chest and puddled above his belt. Then he poured the water out of his hat and glanced up to see Silvertooth frowning at him.

"Are you going to let Gaybird go with us?"

For a moment Cary's mouth firmed. He regarded the other man flatly.

"What have I got to say about it? She's of age."

"She's your ward, ain't she?"

"At eighteen? She can sign cheques now, and pick a husband. Though of course I mean to throw the fear into her about the trail."

"I'd think so," said Silvertooth pompously. "If I was you, I'd say to her, 'Look here! That Bozeman road ain't no doings for a white man any more, let alone a woman. You get on that train to-morrow and go back to Cincinnati!' Though I don't expect she'll be fighting to live in a wagon anyhow, after the seminary."

Cary smiled. "You're talking about handling squaws and horses, John. Gaybird isn't quite either. She's cold-jawed as a bronc, and smart as a young squaw. She'll want to be handled cleverly."

Carefully he set his hat over his eye. They left the shade of the wagon.

"I thought of buying her out," he explained. "Her dad's half-interest ought to be worth fifteen thousand by now. I could give notes."

"She couldn't live on notes."

"I've got some cash."

"None you don't need. You owe Bill Orrum two thousand on those rifles." Then he looked startled and glanced about to be sure no one had followed, trade arms being banned on the Bozeman road this year. He referred to the code word, more loudly than was necessary. "I say, you need two thousand to pay for that hardware."

"God forbid I should ever need you for a spy," Cary chuckled. "I could give her some cash now and a thousand or so at the end of the summer. It's not right she should go into that Indian warren again. That was all right for her dad, and for a girl of thirteen. It was peaceful, then; part of the time, anyway. But she's no child, now. She'd find it rough."

Silvertooth tapped the hot, grey tobacco with his thumb. "She didn't find it rough last time she was out. She was riding everything in the corral. She learned to talk Oglala with the washwomen and shoot her own antelope."

"That," Cary pointed out, "was summer before last. She was sixteen. There's a difference between a girl of sixteen and one of eighteen."

Silvertooth thought and nodded, and said, "Yes, I reckon there is."

Cary had the nostalgic feeling that he would never see her again, the curious, laughing little girl-animal with black pigtails whom old Bob Phillips had left him to raise five years ago. A freighting accident had ended Cary and Phillips' partnership in Fort Greybull a year after they built it. Cary had installed the girl in a seminary in Cincinnati; summers, she visited the post.

On her last visit, two years ago, she had been a fascinating, half-civilized creature of sixteen. But Indian smokes had fumed too steadily last summer, and he had instructed her not to come out. He had again advised it this spring, but now it was June and he had her letter saying she would be out, and please wait for her in Cheyenne when he made up his annual freight-train.

He would wait, of course; but she could not make him take her. A man must go by his judgment, and Sam Cary himself was returning to the Bighorn country only because his business forced him to.

They crossed the camp through the jungle of trash, tarpaulins and tar buckets to Dunavan's wagon-and-trailer outfit. Silvertooth looked about. He said bitterly:

"Look at that!"

In the slovenliness of the wagon there was offence to a wagonmaster. The tail-gate slouched against a wheel and crates sat about in total lack of order. A rack of lead-lined yokes was overturned by the wagon. Silvertooth's hand angrily swept a heap of pipe dottle from the wagon-bed.

"Damned if he ain't trying to burn the outfit up, now!"

Cary recalled a conversation with Tom Braga, who ran "The Nations" saloon. He said thoughtfully: "Braga was talking about a shotgun the other day. Dunavan had been raising a little hell the night before. Pig's knuckles brine all over the nude behind the bar. A shame, at that. Braga was fond of that picture, and now the lady's left breast has run."

Silvertooth squinted with a tart blue eye. "A shotgun, eh? On one of our boys?"

Cary shrugged. "Talk. Dunavan didn't have any money, did he?" His glance went curiously to Silvertooth.

Colour invaded Silvertooth's face. "Not honest-to-God money, I reckon. I gave him four-bits for a pick-me-up after breakfast. He was shaking like a Cheyenne pup in February. But on four-bits he couldn't raise a smile."

Cary regarded him frowningly and began to walk back towards the tracks. After a moment Silvertooth followed.

"Listen," he said, "he couldn't get in trouble on four-bits."

"After last night, he could get in trouble by showing his face in 'The Nations'."

"He knows better than that. Don't he?" Silvertooth demanded.

"Maybeso. I keep thinking about that nude."

They reached the tracks and gazed up the dusty main street. Horses, turnouts and pedestrians briskly came and went through the rutted avenue cutting across the casual sprawl of tents, frame buildings and brick structures. "Well, we'll take a look," Cary said.

They crossed the tracks and passed the big trail outfit from Fort Stockwell, Montana Territory—Mark Stockwell's trading post in the Gallatin Valley. With dissatisfaction, Cary noted that a number of Stockwell's wagons were sheeted and ready to move.

Silvertooth observed this, also, and commented sourly: "He's worked the tallow out of his boys to hit the road ahead of us. If he takes out first, we'll live in his dust and camp trash and drink the brine he leaves in the waterholes all the way back to the border."

"Maybe his mules will all come down with the swinney," Cary said. "Not that I wish him bad luck."

They moved into town. A tall man with an easy stride, Cary kept to the thin slice of shade against the buildings. The sun, reflecting from the bleached ground, pinched his eyes. Freight outfits whooped and lurched along the shallow canyon of the street. Railroad workers were everywhere, hard-bitten Irishmen on their way to end-of-track or heading back from it. Soldiers from Fort Russell sauntered about. Distantly a smith's sledge shaped a tyre to a wheel bound for the wilderness.

This was still a town of primary colours and emotions, running more to tent and frame than to brick, more to fights than discussions.

In this vigorous emotional climate, gunsmiths out-throve haberdashers, and saloon keepers prospered above all others. Dunavan might be in any of twenty saloons, spending his fifty cents on beer or hunting whisky credit. They glanced into the "Shamrock," but the bullwhacker's bearish shoulders were not at the bar. They tried the "Copperopolis." Dunavan had not been seen.

Moving on they investigated the "Pawnee Bar." The Irishman was not at the bar, but as they went out the door a lean, dark-skinned man in stained buckskins collided with them. He wore a round-crowned stetson, from which pigtails descended, tied with greasy rawhide bows. Cary stared past him, but the newcomer said with a grin:

"Howdy, Cary! Are you early, or am I late?"

Cary said: "We're both early. I'll see you later, Orrum. In front of Bailey's."

Bill Orrum saluted and stood aside, a tall and indolent man with a fondness for rings and Indian tobacco. Silvertooth did not hide his dislike for the man as they passed; he failed to speak, and after they were on the walk he growled at Cary:

"You're not parading around with that offscraping in the open, are you?"

"He's got guns," Cary said shortly. "If the army won't let us buy them openly, we'll buy them in back lots and carry them under bolts of cloth. I don't know whether they're more afraid of the guns falling into the hands of Indians, or of honest traders making a dollar. We aren't going back into the Sioux country with the kind of blunderbusses the whackers are carrying."

Silvertooth grunted. "The smell of him will rub off on to you if anybody sees you talking to him. He ain't going up to the Bozeman with us, is he?"

Cary shuddered. "I take delivery on these guns in the brush. Like as not, he'll be freighting liquor to the Bannocks and bringing back gold bars they've plundered from Wells-Fargo. But Orrum's got the guns, and we've got to have them."

They had drinks at the "Shamrock," after failing to locate Dunavan in any of the larger bars. He had not been at "The Nations," and Cary found the edge of his concern dulling. Afterwards, Silvertooth went up the street on business of his own. Cary consulted his watch. It was time now for his meeting with Bill Orrum. Yet he did not hurry. He had another drink, wanting nothing to persuade Orrum that they had anything in common beyond a mutual interest in contraband weapons. Orrum was a shotgun trader; a smuggler of whisky into Indian territory, and the operator of a sporting house in Bannock. It was a demeaning thing to trade with him, but necessity had shaped many a man's ethics before Cary's.

In front of Bailey's Hardware, a collection of crates partially blocked the board sidewalk. Bill Orrum's crowlike shape was balanced on a crate as Cary approached. He was in conversation with another man. Cary hesitated. It would not do to seem to have an appointment with him: Orrum's trade was too well known. The army was lackadaisically inspecting all wagons going north on the Bozeman, but friends of Orrum's ran the risk of a more careful inspection.

Orrum's round-crowned stetson hung between his shoulder-blades by the rawhide lanyard. His black braids glistened with grease. His head obscured the face of the other man, so that Cary had approached to within twenty feet when the trader leaned back, exposing the face of Mark Stockwell.

Cary's inclination was to pass them up. But Orrum glanced around at a word from Stockwell, and his deep, slow voice said:

"You've kept me waiting."

Cary put a bootsole against a crate, a dry disgust in his eyes. "Well, you see I was up with a sick teamster," he said. "You seem to be in good company, anyhow."

Orrum smoked a Red Indian pipe and regarded Cary lazily. Smoking enough *shongsasha* in time wrapped a man in an aura of wildness, as his buckskins took on the wilderness stain of buffalo grease and woodsmoke. Orrum had acquired this fragrance. He wore Blackfoot moccasins and was sombre and sparing of humour.

"I could teach you things about freighting," he remarked. "One of them is not to hire a crew till you're ready to stretch. Whackers spoil faster than venison once they've taken the notion to travel. I hear your outfit's falling apart."

Mark Stockwell's pottery-brown eyes smiled. "Sam's in no condition to travel, anyway, Bill. He's expecting. Every year about this time he becomes a father for the summer. He's got a black-haired ward with a waist you could span with your two hands."

He laughed and punched Cary. Big and heavy-boned, durable as a Murphy wagon, Stockwell had a rough-cast countenance with a strong ledge of bone over the eyes. His shoulders filled his brown blanket-coat and his neck was short and strong.

"When's she coming in?" Orrum asked carelessly.

"To-morrow."

"Is she going up to the fort with you?" Stockwell demanded.

"Hard to say."

"If she were my ward, it wouldn't be hard to say. The Sioux are hunting early, like they had a big show planned for fall. We didn't lose sight of their smoke till we left the Bighorns."

Orrum sipped smoke from the pipe. "I reckon you boys could cut some throats in Washington for abandoning the Bozeman posts, eh?"

Stockwell shrugged. "They were blunderers; but they might have blundered in some time when we wanted them. Still—I keep the Injuns buttered up pretty well."

Cary regarded him quietly. "Ninety proof butter? You're new to 'The Nations,' Mark. I don't know how it was with you in New Mexico, but up here a man who buys the Indians' friendship with whisky is chiselling his own headstone. When you take it away from them you'll have a chivaree on your hands."

Stockwell smiled. "Maybe I won't take it away from them. I tease them: a bottle now, a bottle then. It gets me bargains when they come to trade. And I see to it that they do their drinking away from the post."

Orrum exhaled a greyness of bitter smoke. "I wonder how-come the army to pull out? They lost a hundred and fifty men holding the post last summer. Then they pulled out. Does that make sense?"

"Why do they wear winter uniforms until the men drop from the heat?" Cary said. "Because the head of the brute is in Washington, and the tail's in Wyoming. They'll let a trader build his post in the Sioux country on the proposition that he'll have protection. Then they walk out on him, and the trade dries up. Mark and I are the army, this season."

Black as currants, Orrum's eyes crinkled. "Or you might say you are, Sam. Mark had the good sense to build in Montana."

"Of course the Sioux are great travellers," Cary mentioned.

Stockwell's good-humour thinned to a pinch at the corners of his mouth.

"Don't hold it against me that the army pulled out on you." he said. "You talked it around that I was a fool to build my post where I did. You thought you'd grab off all the trade bound for the Montana mines before it ever reached me. For a while, you nearly did. The point is, I saw the time coming when the army would pull out, and the travel would steer away from the Boze-man. The Bighorns have been Sioux country for centuries. It's the last big hunting-ground, and you know and I know and the army knows that they won't give it up without a scrap. So—the army gave up."

With a gold cigar-cutter, he trimmed a cigar. He roasted it in a match-flame, and when Cary said nothing, merely watching him with a curious, half-amused light in his eyes, he said:

"So now the traffic goes north and east of us, by Missouri River packet. But they still come down from the mines to trade with Mark Stockwell. The lesson in it is—never trust the army."

"Isn't that the lesson for both of us?" Cary pointed out. "When they man the forts again you'll be swapping trade beads to squaws for coyote pelts. Just when you expect the army least—they'll come back."

Stockwell said dryly: "Let's all hope they come back. There's room for both of us. We can be rivals, can't we, without being enemies?"

"I've always thought so," Cary smiled.

The trader made a place for himself on the walk, moving unhurriedly towards the foot of town.

Cary then stared quickly and with rancour at Bill Orrum. "Where are they?"

"We'll come to that," Orrum said. "Walk up to my camp with me." Sam watched him strike his pipe gently against a crate. He was more like an Indian than Crazy Dog himself. He had the wild smell, the pigtails, the dark and greasy look.

They walked side by side to the north end of town.

II

ORRUN'S WAY WAS to bring in ten or fifteen wagons loaded with what he could sell quickly, dispose of it along with the wagons, and leave himself encumbered only with gold. His camp was in a coulee west of town, and consisted of a bedroll, a deerhide tent, one wagon, three spans of oxen and a riding mule. He had jerked venison drying on a line, and yanked off a strip and tossed it to Cary. Cary held it but did not eat it: it was easier to tell a man he was a liar and a thief than to say his food was filthy.

From the tent Orrum procured a rifle. He drew it and laid his cheek against the stock, sighting briefly and letting the hammer *snick*. "Springfield-Allin," he said. "Trapdoor Springfield."

It had a grand balance in Cary's hands. It was snug and compact and so new the grease had not all been rubbed off. He sighted and let the hammer drop. Quickly he re-cocked and threw open the trapdoor breech. The gun was at his cheek again in three seconds.

"This is the one," he breathed. "The rest are all the same?" His hand rubbed the brass lock-plate.

"One hundred Springfield-Allins," said Orrum, chewing the jerky. "Same price, forty dollars apiece, cash."

Cary's eyes snapped. "*Half* cash! The rest at the end of the season. That was the bargain."

Orrum blandly shrugged. "That was before we knew how bad things was. When they massacreed them miners last month I got to thinking all cash might be a better idea. I hear, too, they put an arrow in John Silvertooth's rump at Old Woman Creek on your way down."

"Did you, now?" Cary said.

Orrum recovered the gun. Putting it back in the tent he said: "No matter, Sam. I can sell 'em."

11

Cary's hand pulled him around and there was a meaty slap as his palm wiped across the gun-runner's cheek. "You're not going to hedge on me. I had the two thousand brought up from Denver. I've got a thousand here. You'll get the rest when I get the guns."

Orrum's eyes snapped blackly, but he stood under the pressure of Cary's hand. "I owe every dollar I'll get out of this to the bank. I can get the cash from somebody else if I can't from you."

"How much," Cary asked, "is Stockwell paying you to hold me up?"

"You wouldn't think much of me if I told my customers' names, would you, Sam?" Orrum smiled.

"I don't think much of you—put it that way. Where are the guns?"

Orrum grinned. "Where's the four thousand?"

His lack of ethics was of a highly ethical nature, Sam saw. He would submit to death by flogging before he would drop an advantage like this, for Bill Orrum knew Cary would exhaust every possibility before he killed him and let the guns rust in their hiding-place in the desert.

"I may leave to-morrow night," Cary said. "I keep all the post's money in a Denver bank. I'll give you a draft for it and you can send for the money or discount it to the local bank."

"I'm leaving town, too," Orrum said. "Major Drew had me over to the fort yesterday for questioning. I'm going up to Bannock, Cary. It'll have to be to-night. Talk to the bank. Transfer your account here. They ain't going to fold up."

He turned away and began to build a small fire under a black iron kettle. "I'll be around 'The Nations' till ten o'clock. After that I don't know where I'll be. But somebody else will have the map of where I left the guns."

Cary pulled a buckskin whang from the yoke of his shirt. His hands tugged on it a moment before it snapped. He threw the pieces in the fire. "For your own good, he'd better not have," he said.

At the camp, only a few whackers were about. John Silvertooth had a small fire burning. He was heating a mulligan. They squatted in the shade to eat, using shards of hardtack as spoons.

Cary said presently: "He's holding me up on the guns."

"You knew he would, didn't you?"

"He wants all cash. Where am I going to raise two thousand dollars? My account's still in Denver."

"We could work him over."

"If we got anything out of him, it would be lies."

Silvertooth pondered. "So it's got to be cash. Some men would go where they've got it, I expect."

"The bank? I've hardly said howdy to Henry Plummer."

"Hear he's square, though. He was in trading himself before he got too old. He had some money in the Pony Express, too."

"Is that right?" Cary was intrigued. A man who backed horses in any kind of enterprise could not be too conservative.

They washed their pans. A few whackers had drifted back from across the tracks, bored with town, bored with camp. They had lost their edge, as Silvertooth said. After a week a camp died, and a crew was living with its corpse. The men crawled under wagons to sleep out their excesses and boredom.

But Cary's worries crowded him. He had not moved his account up from Denver after the railroad came through, preferring to let things shake down in this brawling railroad boomtown before he took a chance on the local bank. And now he was in the position of wanting to cash a sight cheque for two thousand dollars, with a man who probably resented his lack of patronage.

He told Silvertooth: "Well, I'll see what I can work out." Settling his hat to shade his eyes, he left the drowsing camp and entered town.

Henry Plummer's "Miners' and Merchants' Bank" was jostled by two saloons. It was a narrow slab of a building with green-blinded upper windows. A section was railed off on the right by a glass enclosure with a single wicket. Within the enclosure were a double-doored safe, two desks and some chairs, and on the wall a calendar of the year 1868, furnished by the Cheyenne Brewery.

A gas lamp on an arm shed light on the desk of Henry Plummer. The banker thrust it out of the way as a paper-cuffed clerk admitted Cary. He leaned across the desk, half-rising, to shake hands.

"You've been boycotting me, Cary," he accused in a high, raw voice.

He was a squarish, truculent-eyed old man with a President Grant beard. He wore no coat, and his hand was hard as a board.

"Not boycotting—just watching," Cary contended.

"I take it I've passed muster, then?"

Cary took something out of his shirt pocket, regarded it a moment and with a smile passed it to Plummer. "Afraid you have."

Plummer inspected both sides of the cheque in the ancient rite. "Five thousand," he murmured. "I should think it was about time. A Wyoming bank for a Wyoming man."

"I've been thinking that, too." Cary sat down, balancing his hat on his knee. "That will start a chequing account. I'd like two thousand of it in cash."

Plummer glanced up sharply. "To-day?"

"Before ten o'clock to-night."

The banker uncomfortably hitched around in his chair. "Did you want to put up any collateral?"

"I'm cashing a cheque, Mr. Plummer. Not making a loan."

Plummer's eyes sought through the lowered tangle of his brows, watching Cary without seeming to. "I expect it would be unseemly of me to ask what you wanted it for."

"Business expenses."

"I didn't think it was to spend on women," Plummer stated. He pondered. "Look here. If I give you the cash, it will be on a purely personal basis. So you'll have to submit to some personal questions."

"Go ahead."

"You own this trading post—Fort Greybull—free and clear?"

"With a partner, Miss Phillips."

"How in the devil," asked the banker, "did you happen to pick a young woman as a partner?"

"I didn't. I picked her father. But he died and left me a new partner—as well as a ward."

Plummer moved a waste basket with his foot. "You know, we bankers regard a married man as a much better risk than a bachelor. Is there any understanding between you?"

Cary ran his thumb about the raw edge of his stetson. "Between me and this child, you mean? She was sixteen when I saw her last."

Disappointment brooded briefly in the banker's eyes. "I see. I hear you and Mark Stockwell are shooting at the same trade up there. Think you'll both make out?"

Cary met his eyes. "No. I think he'll go under, after the army reopens the trail. This year—next year—it's only a question of time."

"Time," Plummer said, "seems to be the big factor here. If they reopen the road next year, you may still be in business. If they don't—it will look like Mark Stockwell's the man to back."

Cary shrugged. "I suppose what I'm looking for is a gambler, not a banker. But I had the notion you were a little of each." He put his hand out for the cheque.

"Maybe I am," Henry Plummer agreed, his mouth suddenly easing. "Maybe if I knew what you wanted this money for I'd back you."

"To go back to the post on. I'm paying a manager and half a crew up there, but if they were doing any more than eat me into bankruptcy, I'd be surprised."

"How," asked Plummer, "will two thousand dollars get you there any faster?"

Cary said carefully: "Without it, I may not be able to go back at all. It's for—essential hardware."

Plummer's crusty eyes squinted. "Essential hardware. Is it the kind of hardware that kicks?"

"It might kick," Cary said, "if you overloaded it."

Plummer's grin squinted his eyes. "That's what I figured. You reckon this hardware will take the curse off the Indians?"

"It's been known to. I do know I won't go back with the kind of arms my men are carrying—forty-year-old Sharpses, leaky Harper's Ferry's—we couldn't stand up under a barrage of buffalo chips."

"And if you get back—then what? Are you going to go broke, or get rich?"

"I figure I'll get rich—if I don't go broke."

"Fine," Plummer said. "Now maybe you can show me where your success would do me any good. You said you figured

I was part gambler.'' He shook his head. ''I used to be. Dropped thirty thousand on the Pony Express. I haven't been much of a gambler since then. Assuming I collect from the Denver bank without trouble, will I be doing any more business with you, or any of the old freighting crowd that used to go through before the army closed the trail?''

''Mr. Plummer,'' Cary sighed, ''the day the army mans the posts again, they'll all be back. The traders have moved to Montana, and the freighters are following the Missouri. But they aren't travelling an extra two hundred miles to get to the mines just because they like desert scenery. They'll be back.''

''I hope so,'' the banker said. ''I know of one bank that may fold up if they don't get that Montana gold rolling down the Bozeman again. The railroad crowd will be moving along one of these days, and it'll be nip and tuck with me. If I could be sure of some mining and freighting trade, I'd even stick my neck out for a loan, to a man like you.''

He said: ''Are you sure you can get hold of any of this— essential hardware?''

''If I can get hold of two thousand dollars to pay for it,'' Cary countered.

Plummer grinned. ''Make it easy on me next time by saying what you want it for. Max,'' he called, ''Mr. Cary wants two thousand. While you're at it,'' he told Cary, ''why not transfer your whole account up here?''

Cary smiled and pulled out a leather poke as the teller brought a tray of coin. ''That is the whole account.''

It was mid-afternoon, but it had not cooled. The woollen heat made a man think of liquids. Cary let his glance travel downstreet. A burly figure in a red shirt approached through the turmoil of boardwalk traffic, moving quickly, and Cary saw suddenly that it was his wagonmaster.

They met on the walk. ''Kane just came in,'' Silvertooth said. ''He says Dunavan tried to borrow money from him.''

''Did he let him have it?''

''No. But Dunavan said he was going to have his liquor at 'The Nations' or wreck the place. He's downstreet.''

Cary frowningly hitched up his belt, beginning to walk towards "The Nations." They stopped across the street from the big false-fronted saloon. In the stifling afternoon horses crowded the unbarked hitch-racks. Now a great-shouldered shape of a man lounged from the foot of town and stopped before the slotted doors of the saloon. The sun burned in Dunavan's crisp red hair. Cary saw him glance down at his palm, toss a coin on it and with resolution move into the saloon. "The crazy Mick!" Silvertooth breathed.

Cary called out, but the doors had closed behind the freighter. They crossed the street. Cary stroked the slotted doors aside and glanced into the saloon. There was a feeling of lassitude to the huge, rough room with its mud walls and black-iron chandeliers. Customers were plentiful, but it was early for celebrating. Dice bounced, cards flashed, a soprano voice shrill with whisky was singing, *Oh, Willie, We Have Missed You*. Behind the bar was Braga's notorious nude, an opulent lithograph of a naked woman recumbent on a field of leopard skin. Brine of pig's knuckles had smeared her bosom.

Dunavan was moving along the bar, his figure wreathed in tobacco fumes. He was a black Irishman of rough make and blunt terra-cotta features. He shouldered into an opening and struck his coin against the varnished pine. A barkeep stopped and placed both hands on the bar.

"I'm hot, thirsty and broke," Dunavan said with desperate cheerfulness. "Give me a shot of the worst whisky in the place, and faith knows the best is bad enough."

The barman was glancing about for Tom Braga. Cary moved inside, seeing Braga come from the rear. When he swung past a table, Cary saw the bung-starter in his hip pocket. He was a grossly fat man with a body shaped like a sack of potatoes. Cary had no use for him. His anxiety to be catering to other men's appetites glistened on him like sweat.

Dunavan heard Braga approaching and turned to meet him. He did something which showed Sam Cary how desperate he was. He offered his hand to Braga. He said: "No hard feelings?"

Braga's hands rested on his hips. "No," he said. "But no whisky either." He smiled.

Dunavan turned resignedly to the barkeeper. "A beer, then."

He slowly turned back as Braga said levelly: "And no beer."

Cary said from the door: "Is this any way to treat an old customer, Braga? Who's drunk more of your rotgut than Dunavan?"

Braga's head turned. "Rotgut! My whisky is bonded. It—" He observed Cary's smile and amended, "anyway, it is good, for Cheyenne. Good enough for swilling."

"Then you can handle the by-products of swilling, such as ruined dispositions."

Dunavan's voice was a growl. "Do you let me handle my own affairs, Cary. I'm buying for myself, right?"

"Wrong," Braga said.

Dunavan's hand massaged the half-dollar. "I'm not a regular drunkard, man! I thought I was going out to-day and it would be my last drunk. But Mister Cary has decided to let us rot in Cheyenne a while longer. And the gods know I'm wanting a drink!"

Braga's glistening eyes savoured the situation. "That's fine. Do your drinking at the 'Copperopolis,' then. Or have they had enough of you, too?"

Dunavan made a gesture of wiping his jaws with his palm. "No liquor, eh?"

"Not a drop. Get out."

"Damn you!"

Dunavan roared it. "You'd let a man shake the hand of a pig like you and then deny him a drink!" The back of his hand smashed across Braga's mouth, rocking his head. He turned, took hold of a beer-cask in its cradle on the bar, and swung it about. Cutting the spigot open, he sank to his knees and let the foaming column spill into his mouth. Braga lunged back, the bung-starter in his hand. He swung at Dunavan's head, and Dunavan raised an arm and half-warded the blow. It landed with force enough to drop him to the floor.

Cary walked quickly into the room. They came from four points, the dish-towelled barmen armed with lengths of pool-cue. It was neatly planned, smoothly executed, and the only unplanned factors appeared to be Cary and John Silver-tooth.

"Braga!" Cary shouted.

Leaning over the whacker with the mallet raised, Braga halted. He discovered the stein Cary had thrown at him. He ducked. It smashed into his shoulder, drenching him with beer.

Cary lunged into him, his eyes on Braga's pulpy mouth. His fist collided with it with the good smack of a hand laid on a quarter of beef. Braga reeled into a table.

Cary heard a saloon-man slide in behind him. A lamp cast the semaphored shadow of an arm. A houseman, short and deep-chested and with a red, congested face, chopped savagely at Cary's head with a truncated pool-cue. Cary fell away, raising his shoulder defensively. The club struck painfully against the bunched muscle. Cary set his teeth and lunged into the man. He caught the thick, corded throat in his hands, jammed him against the tall bar and hacked at the turgid face with the edge of his knuckles. The saloon-man shouted and tried to writhe away. Cary gathered the power of his back and shoulder muscles into an overhand blow which smashed into the side of the man's jaw and turned it. He let the white face slide away.

The saloon crowd had shaped into a random crescent with Dunavan, Cary and Silvertooth in the centre and three of Braga's men carefully working in with pool-cue clubs at the ready. Cary looked at the ring of faces behind this shock-troop, thinking of loafer wolves. A tall man with a sallow, hairless face slanted in to chop at Dunavan's head. Dunavan caught the club in his hand, ripped it away and smashed the man across the nose. The houseman went to his knees, covering his face with his hands. Dunavan bent, seized him by an arm and a leg and lifted him over his head. He crouched and straightened, hurling the man across the counter and into the stacked bottles of the back-bar.

He took time to seize Cary by the arm, then, his face dark with anger. "Get out of it!" he said. "I can handle six of their likes alone!"

"Can you handle one with a scattergun?" Silvertooth panted.

Dunavan's bloodshot eyes comprehended slowly. He looked around for Tom Braga, but the saloon-keeper had disappeared. Dunavan stood slope-shouldered and puzzled.

Now Cary heard a man shout and saw him fall back in the crowd and turn to thrust to the rear. It was like a signal, splitting the crowd and folding it back to front and rear; men were shouting their terror, and one raised an arm towards Cary as if to ward off a blow. Cary suddenly brought his fist down at the root of Dunavan's neck, carrying him to the floor with him. He saw Braga's men fall back, getting out of line. It placed Tom Braga directly behind him, behind the bar, moving in with his double-barrelled shotgun.

Cary crouched there, his hand grasping at the sawdust. Dunavan was shouting curses and reaching for the edge of the bar. Cary rose suddenly and Braga was before him, a squat and greasy-faced man with a side-hammer shotgun prodding forward. Cary slapped his left hand down on the gun-barrel. His right flung sawdust into the saloon-man's face.

He felt the shattering roar of the gun through his hand and arm. The charge flashed between him and Dunavan. Overhead, the candles puffed out. Lamps burned at front and rear, and in the gloom men were lying on their bellies and clutching at the floor. Braga wrenched at the gun, his face distorted. Cary's hand slapped down on the hammers. He brought the gun-barrel up and around and Braga's grip was broken. Cary emptied the other charge into the ceiling. As he threw the gun aside, he saw Dunavan vault the bar and trap Tom Braga against the back-bar. He saw his fist come back and drive in; cock and drive again, his head held slightly on the side. He watched Dunavan release him. Braga turned and took one blind step towards the end of the bar, and collapsed.

Dunavan turned back. The saloon was quiet. Dunavan moved along the bar to the front, took a final look at the saloon, and moved on to the street. Cary and his wagonmaster lingered a moment and followed him.

Dunavan was waiting on the walk. He said: ''I suppose I should thank you, Mr. Cary?''

''I'd thank God, if I were you,'' Cary said. ''Did you get your fill of beer?''

''I got more than that. I got a fist into the middle of a face I've been aching to spoil. But it's too bad it had to end the way it did.''

''How's that?''

''With me beholden to you.''

Smiling, Cary watched Dunavan shoulder into the crowd gathering before the saloon.

Silvertooth had a puffiness under his eye and the shoulder of his calico shirt was ripped. Sourly he observed Dunavan's departure. "I could do with a whisky," he said.

III

THE DAY FINISHED out in a red and gritty dusk. Cary returned from Bill Orrum's camp just before dark, carrying in his hip pocket a thin slab of rawhide. On it, Orrum's pencil had traced a rough map of where the wagon with its load of rifles and ammunition was hidden. Supper fires puddled the dusk of the corral. A teamster was frying venison in a long-handled iron skillet, while another sliced potatoes into the sizzling fat. From south of town, the day-guard rode in from the dry task of herding stock.

It was all rough and casual, all utterly masculine. Cary remembered how Gaybird Phillips used to drink the strong liquor of whackers' yarns. How would it all seem to her now, a grown woman, after two years away from unshaven jowls, lumbering wagons, and dust—fine dust, coarse dust; red dust and black dust?

He regarded her dearborn wagon, standing spruce-topped among the burly freight wagons on the south line.

A thought came to him. Presently he walked to his own wagon and struck a match. He grubbed in the catchall box at the rear of it. He found something, and slipped it into his pocket with the map. Moving silently through the lazy camp, he reached the dearborn and mounted the ladder at the back.

As he stepped through the flap he heard a quick intake of breath. A man stood near the head of the bed.

Cary's hand dropped to the warm smoothness of brass and walnut at his thigh. In the gloom, John Silvertooth spoke quickly.

"Now behave! I was just checking around."

Cary struck a match and lighted the lamp. The light sparkled on a pair of beaded gauntlets in the wagonmaster's hand. "I see."

Silvertooth shrugged, glancing down at them. In an excess of casualness, he tossed them on the cot. "First of these I ever seen that anybody but a muleskinner could wear. Thought she'd like them."

Cary took a pair of moccasins from his pocket and laid them on the bed. "I thought the same when I saw these Blackfoot moccasins. She always did favour moccasins. I was wondering if that squaw got her sheets clean."

He pulled back the red-and-grey Indian blanket and inspected the stiff cotton sheets.

"What's the difference?" Silvertooth grunted. "She ain't going up with us."

"But she'll have a day or two in town, and the hotels ain't fit for whisky drummers."

They moved about, hunting dust and insects. The wagon contained a small chest, a commode, a goosefeather cot, a chair, and a mirror. Cary said quietly:

"I got the map. The guns are in Sweetwater Coulee."

"That's a hell of a ride for one night."

"And we've got to beat the sun. So let's find horses."

"Oxen with the wagon?"

"He said so. The wagon's only part loaded, of course. It's junk, and we'll leave it here."

He moved to the flap, and the wagonmaster said quickly: "She comes to-morrow, eh?"

"You know that." Sam put a leg through the flap, but Silvertooth said quickly:

"I thought you maybe had something to tell me."

"Dammit," Sam said testily, "why should I have?"

Silvertooth said: "Easy." He sat on the cot. "All right, I'll tell you something. The first summer she came out after you put her in the seminary, she told my missus something. She was fifteen, wasn't she? She said you and her was married. She said to keep it secret."

Cary's lips parted. He set them firmly together and his hand rubbed his thigh. "She did, eh?"

"She did."

"How many washerwomen has your wife told that to?"

Silvertooth grumped: "You know the answer to that. What I want to know is, what are you going to do about her?"

Cary found his pipe and packed it; but recalling how the odour of tobacco sank into blankets, he put it unlighted into his mouth. "I reckon you knew it, anyway."

He sat on the cot and scratched his neck. He took the pipe out of his mouth. "Well, just so you won't think it's worse than it is. . . . You see, I never figured we were married. It was just a contract, with me. Old Bob Phillips made me promise to adopt her if anything ever happened to him. After the Uncpapas did for him, I took her to Cincinnati, summer before you signed up with me. I figured to adopt her and educate her. But it seems I was twenty-two and a bachelor, and bachelors weren't adopting fourteen-year-old girls that year. So I tried to set her up in the seminary. But they reckoned that would make a kept woman out of her. All I could do was put her in an asylum."

Silvertooth made a profane observation.

"So all I could do was marry her. Then I enrolled her in the school as Mrs. Samuel Cary."

"That's about how I laid it out," the wagonmaster said. "Still, that was then. What about now?"

Cary gave way and lighted the pipe. "Contracts can be broken. She's a child. I'm a man—a Wyoming man, at that. Seminaries thin a girl's blood. I've heard some Eastern women wear bleaching towels over their faces to keep their skin white. Gaybird will be a real Eastern lady; but I hope not that Eastern. She'll take one look at the grease stains on my shirt and lose colour. It will be an annulment or a divorce. There won't be any trouble."

Silvertooth looked at the gauntlets and the moccasins, child-size, and bridled a sigh. "I reckon there won't. Well, let's git at it."

Cary followed him slowly, thinking nostalgically of a long-legged child with outsize eyes, like a young flicker. She would be gone; she would never come back to this wagon. He wondered what the new Gaybird would be like.

From the distant Laramie Hills, night sprawled across the prairie. Cary and Silvertooth ate camp bread and antelope steak and made a casual tour of the camp. Then, in the windy darkness, they carried their saddles to the line of saddle horses, Cary taking out a deep-chested pony and Silvertooth his calico mule. They rode into the stiff rabbit brush, walking their mounts until they were clear of Stockwell's camp, a hundred yards west, and then letting them reach.

Cary pulled his pipe from a pocket of his hunting shirt, considered a moment, and dropped it back, a tribute to the Sioux. They put ten miles behind them. The miles were as devoid of individuality as the ties of the tracks they followed. But as they rode they looked about oftener, holding their ponies in to listen. Farther north, anywhere beyond the Platte. a night ride would be suicide. Down here there was chiefly the possibility of encountering a band of Oglala Sioux out cutting telegraph wires.

A kangaroo rat bounded from the path of Cary's pony with a frightened chirp. The horse swerved; Cary hauled it around with an oath. He found he had flung his carbine up to cover the ragged head of brush into which the rat had bounded. He relaxed, giving his shoulders a settling shrug.

North-west he made out the flat bulk of a shaley range of hills. The landmark placed them a mile or so east of Sweetwater Coulee. According to Orrum's map, the wagon ought to be about two miles south of the tracks, hidden in the coulee.

Silvertooth glanced at him. "Am I gettin' womanly," he asked, "or do I smell Sioux?"

"You're gettin' womanly." Cary's horse bore him skittishly to the wagonmaster's side. They paced through the brush. The horse and mule had taken their restlessness. Cary's pony shook bridle with a jingle of coin silver.

The wind was redolent of sage. In the loose, gravelly earth, the animals' hoofs made a brisk crunching. They dipped into a wallow and mounted again the dead level of the plain, touched faintly with the light of a rind of moon.

Cary grunted. "Hope the fool left the oxen on a stout picket."

Silvertooth's arm went up. "Yonder they are!"

"Crafty like a fool-quail!" snorted Sam. "Hide the wagons and leave the oxen in sight! Hell, there's three span of them."

They made it to be about two hundred feet to the gully on the bank of which stood the animals. Cary was on the point of touching his horse with his heels when he suddenly brought his left fist to his chest, reins gripped tightly; his right arm extended to touch Silvertooth.

Silvertooth sat steadily in the saddle, staring. They saw one of the animals on the coulee's edge raise its head for an instant, scent, and quietly go back to pulling tufts of grass. It was light enough to determine that they were not oxen. Nor did they carry saddles. They were Indian ponies.

End of Part One

Part Two

IV

THEY TURNED SILENTLY and retreated. Dismounting, Cary thumbed back the heavy spur of the bronze-framed Henry. Big John Silvertooth moored his calico mule to a clump of black sage. He removed his hat and dropped it on the ground. A bare head was his fighting trim.

Cary stared at the Indian ponies in the far darkness. The wind carried the faint stir of hoofs and a sound of voices. "Damn the army!" he muttered. "Those rifles could have been set down in Cheyenne."

Except for the army, they would not have been under a responsibility to take on a patrol of buck Indians to recover a wagonload of destruction. Their responsibility was to themselves and every other man who lived north of Cheyenne. The tribe that got hold of a hundred breech-loading Springfield rifles could clean out every ranch and trading post on the Bozeman.

He stood close to Silvertooth. "Give me twenty minutes. I'll coyote around behind them. Try to belly up to where you can see them."

"If they've tapped the whisky," said the wagonmaster, "we can save our shells and tromp them out. Shoot, maybe they ain't figured out how them guns work, anyhow."

Cary walked north a quarter-mile to the tracks. He cut west to the coulee and crossed on the trestle. Standing there, he searched the coulee but found no pickets. He moved on. A night-hawk swooped low with a stiff rush of feathers. On a far ridge, a coyote yelped. He turned his head to seek the outlines of the ponies. Finding them, he went on more cautiously, leaving the trestle

27

and pacing carefully through the brush.

He was within a hundred feet of the ponies when he saw the Indian sitting cross-legged on the ground holding the reins. He sank down in a reaction of shock.

A full minute slid away. Cary knew that he was as visible to the Indian as the Indian was to him, but the sentry was watching what went on in the deep brush-choked coulee. He was a young brave with a prairie cock tail on his head. A dogskin quiver rode his shoulders. Cary read these signs and the clue of the pale bullhide hanging on the horses, and they told him, *Sioux*. A little gang of green Oglala warriors out hunting lonely stagetenders to murder or supernatural buffalo to kill, feats to make men of them in the lodges.

As he rose, he winced at the leathery creaking of his boots. He made out a sound of stone on wood, a deep-throated voice raised briefly in a laugh. The warrior rocked forward to look into the wash.

Sam raised his arm high in a signal. He breathed deeply, flexing his arms to ease the tautness out of them. He held the carbine lightly and began moving up behind the horses.

Now he could glimpse the action in the coulee through the tumble of boulders and brush on the stony slope. A tiny fire burned against the wind. Five Indians in hip-length leather shirts, breech-clouts and leggings were busy about a freight wagon. One stood on the wagon. Two others were attempting to yoke a span of oxen to the wagon. The rest were occupied in opening crates with rocks or in examining the guns. There was no sign or smell of whisky. A young buck raised a rifle to his cheek and sighted it, the barrel lining precisely on Cary. His heart exploded in his breast. But an instant later the brave lowered the gun and shook it as if to hear it rattle.

Cary settled his feet in the gravel, his left shoulder to his target, his right elbow extended. His finger painstakingly took up trigger slack. The gun-barrel lifted with a roar, the butt thrusting solidly against the packed muscles of his shoulder. He pulled the loading lever and sprinted forward. He saw the seated Indian lurch forward and sprawl out into the coulee, his arms reaching.

The tight huddle of ponies split open like a dropped melon. Two of the ponies plunged into the wash. A Sioux seized the mane of one and swung himself across its back. He turned and fired a carbine at Cary as his heels hammered the horse's ribs. The shot went through the brush with a rattle of broken twigs. The brave vanished in the dark.

A man was running along the bank with a thud of boots. A large and reassuring shadow, John Silvertooth sprawled at the lip of the barranca and lay in the brush with only his head exposed. His gun pointed like a finger at the Indian in the wagon, who was crouched in the deep bed with a gun thrust between the side-boards.

Sprawling opposite him, Cary heard the slam of the brave's gun. Grit exploded in his face, cutting his forehead in a wide and dull pattern of pain. He fired back and saw the splintered hole where the ball went through the wagon side. He could hear the brave moving in the wagon. Then the flash of Silvertooth's rifle illuminated the coulee and the Indian in the freight wagon moved convulsively.

Running low, an Oglala jumped the wagon-tongue, shot past the single yoke of oxen, and made for a break in the creek-bed. Cary fired. As the pouring echoes faded, he saw the brave writhing on the sand.

Somewhere, out of sight below the rim of the bank, two more coppery bodies moved, heard but unseen. Cary waited, thinking more about the man who had ridden up the wash. He lay still, alert for the tread of moccasins behind him. Then he heard a soft rush below. A hand came into sight on the rim of the wash. The Indian got his hold and vaulted up six feet in front of him, wide-stanced and stooped, a stocky warrior in a red breech-clout and long shirt. He searched the darkness for an instant before discovering Cary. He held a short-axe stolen from the wagon. Suddenly finding the long shape asprawl before him, he hurled himself forward.

Cary fired and rolled away. The Indian struck the ground, pinning Cary's legs. He moved spasmodically. A moment later, Cary became aware that the remaining warrior had lunged up the bank below John Silvertooth, a rifle raised in his hands like a warclub. Silvertooth fired once and the man turned and slid down the bank.

They lay there. There was a confused sound of oxen lunging about, chained to the wheels and unable to escape. Silvertooth's voice came:

"Sam?"

"All right. You?"

"Fit. Heard anything out of that other one?"

"I'm listening."

They waited twenty minutes before they descended to the wash. The Sioux were out of action, the guns unharmed, but Cary could not relax. "I'd give half the guns to have that one back. Did you see shields on the ponies? Those were Thunder Fighters, Esconella's blood brothers . . ."

Silvertooth halted in the act of searching out a keg of whisky. He straightened. "Hell!" he said. He thought about it solemnly. "Hell."

Cary unchained the oxen. "I'm not afraid of losing their love—but damn it! These breech-loaders were going to be a surprise."

"Maybe they hadn't figured them out."

A realistic man, Cary did not answer that. Silvertooth came to help him handle the oxen, and presently Sam threw off the whole notion of Indians with a shake of his head. "If we don't get back before sun-up and throw this one in line with the others, you can write off the rifles anyhow."

V

Bill Orrum came from the hot and windy night into "The Nations." The trader moved with a loose, easy slouch. He wore a leather shirt, leather breeches, and moccasins; his black pigtails were tied with greasy knots.

A crowd of railroad workers were hoorawing at the bar.

Orrum found a table near a chuckaluck game. He bought a bottle of whisky and poured his drink. He thought of Sam Cary.

Cary had come into camp that afternoon, paid him off and gotten the map. Then he had said:

"This is all the receipt I want." He had struck hard. The flushed bruise on Orrum's cheekbone was turning blue.

Orrum, the pigtailed, dark dweller of wilderness places, was not an overproud man, but he knew how to bring a resentment to maturity.

He thought about the trip up the Bozeman trail to the Montana mines, which was to think about Indians. For thirty years he had taken care of himself in this country. He had got along because he was like his hosts—silent, savagely practical, vigilant; not too hankering towards luxuries. Yet for the sins of other white men he must pay, also, and the price was smokeless fires and sleeping away from his camp. If trouble came, he counted on his pay-load to get him through. He carried a hundred and fifty ancient smoothbore muskets the army had abandoned in a warehouse twenty years ago. These could be sold decently in Butte—or traded for his scalp.

Darkness came and he was aware of Mark Stockwell in the doorway. Seeing him, Stockwell approached and sat at the table where Orrum drank whisky and played solitaire.

"Cary and Silvertooth just left camp," the trader said shortly. He was perspiring. A man of massive strength, he had a firm and compact make; his chest was deep and his neck short. He looked to Orrum like a man it would be easier to kill than to hurt, insulated from injury by the slow and easy power of his body.

"Watching Cary middling close, ain't you?" Orrum remarked.

Stockwell's eyes were sourly displeased. "You didn't sell him the guns?"

Orrum poured again from the bottle. "He raised the money. I hadn't got any choice."

Stockwell pressed the heel of his fist against the table with slow and bitter force. "Damn it! I'd have given fifty dollars apiece for those rifles. Why didn't you come to me first?"

"I didn't go to him. Cary came to me, six months ago, as soon

as the army said no guns. I tried to save them for you. When are
you putting out?''

"Can't say. Before Cary, I hope. You'll go back to Independ-
ence?''

Orrum turned a green glass ring on his finger. "Montana."

Stockwell's thick brows raised. "Up the Bozeman?"

"How else?"

"What for? You're traded out, aren't you?"

Orrum's eyes had a spark of humour. "You're full of wonders
about other people's business to-night."

Stockwell had a tenacious and unhumorous mind. He turned to
signal a bartender and again stared directly into the shiny, taut-
skinned features. "You may as well travel with me. You'd
damned well better travel with some train."

"I figure I'm better off alone than with somebody the Sioux
don't like."

"Such as me?"

"You and the younger set get along. The whisky drinkers.
The warrior societies. I've heard you and Esconella meet behind
the barn and smoke the pipe together."

Temper stiffened Stockwell's lips. "Is that what you hear?"

"I hear it direct," said Orrum. "I wouldn't trust him too far,
you know. Esconella may be a chief's son-in-law, and the old
man may be paralyzed, but—I wouldn't trust any of them. The
purtiest sight in the world is an Injun's back—in your rifle
sights."

"I don't worry about the Sioux. I'm north of their grounds.
But it pays to keep right with all of them." He received his
whisky from a waiter. "What are you taking along?"

"Trade goods."

"Beads and tobacco, eh—and guns?"

"No guns you'd like. A few old cannons the army gave up."

"Trade guns," Stockwell said. The suggestion of a smile
drew his lips

"Why, Mark!" Orrum said. "Trade guns for *Injuns*?"

Stockwell grunted, seeming offended that the idea had
been given words. "Don't be a damned fool. I live up there
too, you know. I don't want guns in their hands any more than
Cary."

"Of course the Sioux don't range about your post, though, if you wanted to get rid of some betwixt here and Cary's place. They've got gold these days, since they learned what it was for and Wells-Fargo put it in their way."

Stockwell's first reaction was a slowness to grasp it. Then his brows pulled in and he said softly: "You've rubbed up against too many of them. You've taken their ways."

Orrum said, "This is their country, Mark. You take their ways if you want to get along. And you ain't going to get along whilst Cary's splitting the business with you."

"I can get along without putting guns in their hands."

"If Cary don't shut you out first. The army will be back. Maybe not this year; likely next. He's a sharp trader, Mark. When the travel is going up the Bozeman instead of short-cutting him by going around, why, you'll see what I mean. You had a year of bucking him before the army ducked out, didn't you? Kind of slim tradin', I reckon."

A smoke of resentment fumed in Stockwell's eyes, as though he were angry at the trader for having brought something up which was better left unthought of. He finished his whisky and stood up.

"I'll be leaving to-morrow night. Meet us up the line if you want to go along."

"Thanks," Orrum said.

Cary awoke at sun-up, when the bugles at the Fort Russell began sounding their mixed glee of brassy calls. He heard his whackers turning out. Ironware clanged and burning mesquite roots sent their smoky incense about the corral. Lost sleep and reaction from the night's activity dulled him.

Quitting his blankets, which lay under a wagon, he stood in the harsh sunlight and pulled on his shirt. The arms-wagon occupied its place in the hollow square of freight-wagons. Neither the first nor the last, it was merely another great-wheeled Murphy with its tongue ran up under the wagon ahead of it. They had terminated the drive from Sweetwater Coulee two hours before sunrise.

Cary sombrely regarded the stork-like tank by the tracks, slowly dripping water into the salt-crusted puddle beneath it. He resented the trash about camp and the shirtless men yawning their way through pre-breakfast chores. This, thank God, was their last day in Cheyenne.

To-day Gaybird Phillips comes. There would be the difficulty of explaining to her why she must not make the trip to the border this summer. There would be the task of getting her back on a train to-morrow. And then everything would simplify, and he could slot his problems plainly enough—yoke the oxen and turn them north.

As he ate, he took notice of a buoyancy among the men. They were all as sick of the camp as he was. They looked forward to the trail, with all its dangers. Breakfast over, he gave the order to slip the wheels and tar every axle. Before the job was finished, the men were glancing up the tracks, anticipating the arrival of the passenger train. Work trains hammered through from the supply depot, heading west.

A little after noon, the telegraph's key rattled in the small yellow station with its two mud chimneys. The station-master came from the door to flap a sheet of paper.

"She comes! Forty-five minutes."

Cary killed some more time, his mind trying phrase after phrase. How to tell the girl without hurting her feelings? But better a hurt feeling than a lost scalp.

He started to move to the station to await the train, and then something caused him to glance at the loading dock across from the yellow railroad shack. In the bleached yellow sunlight, Dunavan's barrels still stood awaiting removal. Silvertooth had come up beside him. Cary was conscious of his testy gaze as he, too, regarded the barrels. Cary removed his stetson and sliced perspiration from his forehead with his finger, and then replaced the hat and said, "I reckon Dunavan's forgotten these barrels."

They crossed the corral and stood by the rear of Dunavan's lead-wagon. The two trailers were packed, but the gate of the main wagon was down and from the half-packed interior drifted a vapour of tobacco. Cary looked at the big man sprawling against a stanchion. Suddenly discovering him, Dunavan casually swung his legs overside. He regarded Cary with a shallow mask of respect.

"You've got four barrels on the dock," Cary said.

"Sure, no one told me," blandly said Dunavan.

"Someone's told you now. Silvertooth will help you move them. Unpack them all and repack the goods in the wagon."

The Irishman tucked a thumb under his belt. "I've heard it said Mark Stockwell is the best freighter in Wyoming. He carries his goods in the barrels they come in. Why can't you?"

"I'm not selling barrels. Why should I carry them?"

Dunavan frowned, but after a moment, his hazel eyes not leaving Cary's face, he began to smile craftily, and from his pocket he brought a small handful of coins. He glanced down at them. There was still the fifty-cent piece Silvertooth had loaned him, but there were, in addition, glints of gold. He looked beyond the men, at others of the bullwhackers who were within earshot. His expression subtly changed.

"Mr. Cary," he said, in bluff and artificial good-nature, "you can do what you damned please with your barrels. I'm quitting."

"You can't quit," Silvertooth snapped. "You're into us for sixty dollars."

Dunavan turned Cary's palm up and triumphantly dropped six gold pieces upon it. "I got on to that a week ago. You wouldn't shanghai a man, but you'd let him drink himself into your debt before he found out what kind of a circus he was into. I say this evens us up. I talked with Mark Stockwell on the way back. He advanced me the money to pay you off. I'm going to Montana with him."

Cary tossed the coins on his hand in mild wonder. He looked up at Dunavan and saw him braced for trouble. He chuckled and set the coins on the wagon-bed.

"You're a quick-headed Mick. Only you can't buy out of my army, the way you did Uncle Sam's."

"Can't I?" said Dunavan. "I reckoned I already had."

Cary's eyes ran over him, as they had that first day the Irishman came looking for work, hunting flaws and not finding any. His shoulders were sloping and massive, blotched with large freckles. The smell of him was of whisky gone sour and sweat upon sweat. He was a testy and tough man, something for the wilderness to bruise its knuckles on. Dunavan's eyes doggedly met his for a moment, and then slid down to a point on Cary's buckskin shirt and held there.

Cary asked quietly, "What's the matter, Dunavan? Do we make the coffee too strong for you?"

"No," Dunavan growled. "You set a man to do a boy's chore—repacking a wagon that's sound as a knot. We've been ready to move for five days. But we police and cook and stand guard until a man'd think he was back in the army. And we'll keep on doing it, until Mr. Cary's young lady comes on the train. You'd let ten tons of pork rot rather than miss the chance of hauling a hundred and ten pounds of young female to your post."

Cary heard the careful silence of the camp. A man casually walked between Dunavan's wagon and the next, stopping where he could watch. A muscle rippled under the smooth mahogany of Cary's jaw.

"We can leave the young lady out of it," he said mildly. "Are you afraid of the Sioux? Or of me?"

Dunavan's eyes lighted. He stood before the trader, a strapping man with a splayed nose and protruding ears. He stood taller than Cary and outweighed him. Cary saw in his eyes that he had been long at the brawler's evil of comparing. Dunavan's thumb gouged at the bowl of his pipe. "I don't fear the Sioux," he said, "and I ain't yet met the man I fear."

"That's fine," Cary said. "It doesn't do to fear Indians: They smell it on you, like a dog. And I like a man that will stand up to another. That's why I'm glad you're coming with us."

Dunavan looked puzzled. "I told you I was going with Stockwell. I had the advance so's I could pay you off."

"Did Stockwell know how you were going to use it?"

"It's my say how I use it."

"Not when you use it to put a man in a hole. No trader worth a damn would lend you money to leave another short a hand. Nobody but a trader like Stockwell. You'll take it back to him."

Dunavan grinned maliciously. "You weren't afraid of leaving the army in a hole when you loaned me the money to buy out, were you?"

Cary's eyes puckered thoughtfully. "Maybe they knew what

they were doing, at that. Maybe they'd already tagged you, the way they do a blown-out musket. '*I. & C.*', eh? Inspected and Condemned . . ."

Dunavan's weight leaned forward on to his toes. He put his hand up to tap Cary's chest; but it hung there and he pointed a scarred forefinger. "I done two hitches, Cary! I seen Fetterman throw his command away to Red Cloud, and after that anything in brass made me sick. The army never condemned me: I condemned them."

"Then you should like my army. Not an officer in the lot." His hand curled the brim of his hat. "Get on to the barrels as soon as you've returned the money."

Dunavan's boots stirred and his shoulders made a settling shrug. Cary looked into his corded red face without emotion, until Dunavan's eyes moved away again, and he said:

"A man might as well be in the infantry." He picked up the money, tossed it once in his hand, and sauntered off through the wagons.

"A rebel!" Silvertooth snorted. "A copper-bottomed rebel! There'll be trouble with him, I tell you."

Cary breathed deeply. "He won't make trouble. He's just letting me know he leads better than he pushes."

Silvertooth strolled to the barrels to await the bullwhacker's return. Cary walked up the tracks, stepped on to the splintered platform and sat on a bench, one leg extended, the other cocked across it, letting his muscles take their ease.

He looked up as a short, toughly made man in buckskin pants and a spotted calico shirt crossed the tracks and vaulted carelessly on to the platform, recognizing Cary with a lazy hand-salute. The man took a place on the bench, sopping perspiration from his forehead with a handkerchief.

"I wish some Sioux outfit," he said, "would whoop up a rain dance and break this weather."

"Any time the Sioux break the weather for us," said Cary, "it will rain arrows."

He kept his eyes on this good-nature from Coy Mullan. Mullan was Mark Stockwell's wagonmaster, and that was enough. He was also a transplanted Texan who wore one pant-leg in his boot and one out, and that was too much. He affected a knife in his right boot and wore a Dragoon pistol deep on his right thigh.

Mullan lighted a cigar. "I hear we've got important company coming on the train. Envoy from the Great White Father to Crazy Dog. Man named Merritt."

"God help us, then!" Cary said. "We'd almost lived down the trouble the last envoy made."

"It's time for a peace talk. The Piegans raided down into the Gallatin Valley last month, before we left. If they team up with the Sioux, we're both finished."

"I thought Stockwell kept them all happy with stick candy and Forty-Rod whisky?"

Mullan smiled. "He could show you some tricks, at that. He smokes the peace pipe with them with one hand and steals their buffalo robes for a dime apiece with the other."

"He'll get his scalp tanned in the bargain, one of these days."

Mullan chuckled, a calm and hard-featured man not easily roused. He was a sort of middleman in the distaste of these traders one for another. He grinned around his cigar. "What's the real trouble between you and Mark? You don't either of you talk much."

"Some people claim that's a virtue."

Mullan took this impassively. He let his eyes drift off towards the wagon camp. "What's different about your outfit to-day?" he frowned.

Cary's eyes touched him quickly. Then he shrugged. "Maybe the trash has been picked up."

". . . Twenty-four wagons last night, twenty-five to-day. Breeding them?"

"I picked up a wagon from an emigrant outfit last night," Cary said. "They'd quit it. Oxen broke down and I bought it for the cost of the goods."

"Washtubs and churns and wimmen's fixings?" Mullan inquired.

Cary's eyes went to his face. "What are you getting at?"

"Do I have to be getting at something?" Mullan winked. "I was going to say that if you wanted to park any of your wagons in our camp to-day, Stockwell says it would be okay. We've already stood inspection. There's a sergeant named Casner that can smell powder and ball through six layers of duck.''

"Am I carrying powder and ball?''

Mullan rose unhurriedly, pulled on the cigar and removed it to regard the smouldering tip. "You're cagey to-day, Sam. But Mark and I figure we've got to lend each other a hand in this trade, if we're going to get by at all.''

"Help me by keeping out of my way, then. How much was he going to charge me for this helping hand? Half the arms he thinks I'm carrying?''

Mullan looked at him and kept most of his anger out of his flat, ruddy features. "You figure you don't have much to learn about freighting, eh?''

Cary saw the raw end of Mullan's patience, and pleasantly pinked it again. "One of the first things I learned was never to trust a man who wore one britches leg in and one out.''

"Go to hell,'' Mullan snapped.

Cary began to chuckle. "I forgot about you Texans, Coy. Proud and sensitive as a fat Comanch' full of corn beer.''

Mullan's eyes flicked and his hands formed slowly into fists. Then he said brusquely: "Good luck with the army. I hope I'm around when you take 'em on.''

Cary's laughter followed him across the tracks.

Afterwards Cary's face sobered. It was plain enough that Stockwell knew of the gun transaction with Bill Orrum. He was in a position to put the army on Cary, and if he did not, it would not be ethics which restrained him. Cary was not sure what the commandant at Fort Russell would do if he had the report of the rifles. He was not sure what he would do himself.

Then he heard a man bawl three words: "*Yonder she comes!*''

VI

DOWN THE STRING-STRAIGHT filaments of steel Cary discerned a smudge of smoke. He heard his bullwhackers running up the platform and felt the sting of Silvertooth's palm on his back. Silvertooth said as he passed: "She's eighteen now, Sam! Hard candy and pacifiers won't work no more."

The train acquired colour and form and sound—a chunky little diamond-stack drawing six cars, breathing dust and smoke, alkali crusting the dented boiler jacket and brass steam dome. The locomotive coasted past the station and halted, exuding heat and rusty water, a snowy feather of steam dissolving into the deep blue of the sky. From its black iron bowels escaped strange digestive noises. Trainmen dropped to the ground and a wagon-load of cordwood whipped up to the tender. Passengers began slowly to appear. A conductor in a linen duster, his face bloated with heat, swung from the observation car. Mail bags were tossed to the ground.

Suddenly, down the line of coaches sitting unevenly on the tracks, through the crowd and an abrupt cloud of dirty steam, Sam saw her. Behind a bulwark of three black india-rubber bags stood a winsome figure in a bottle-green gown and a white basque, a frilled parasol over her shoulder. She waved at him, but he still stood there, astonished. What had happened to her, the girl in pigtails? She was gone, and in her place stood a young woman he had never seen before. Cary went forward.

He took her hands as he reached her, smiling as she laughed up at him. "Sam, it's so wonderful!"

He felt the small fingers through the starched mesh gloves. "So a stage isn't good enough for you any more!"

She wrinkled her nose at the train, floury with alkali. "Those things! Shake you to pieces!"

"What's a dearborn do?"

"Rocks me to sleep," she declared. ". . . Sam, about here you used to kiss me."

"Godfather's privilege?" He bent and kissed her cheek. She was a small and animated presence, bell-shaped with her full skirts and snugly fitted summer basque. He straightened, half-ashamed of himself; but he found the girl in pigtails slipping away from him, taking with her his own attitude towards her. His tendency was to regard her as someone new and desirable.

Gaybird's hair was as black as ever, lustrous with brushing. In the way the grey eyes, black-lashed, looked at him there was something more personal—as though they were focused on him instead of the whole, bright world.

He turned, feeling colour in his throat, and weighed the bags. "Travelling heavier. You can thin it out to-night, unless you want me to put a couple of bulls in the traces. I took a room for you at the Rollins House."

Gaybird inspected him curiously as they moved along the platform. "Didn't you bring my wagon?"

"Sure. But the camp's pretty rough."

"I was brought up to consider hotels an affectation. We'll cancel the room." Then she caught his arm. Before the station stood an attractive red-haired girl with a dour-looking man of middle age who wore a talma cape over his shoulders. "See her?"

The girl was looking at them. He saw her smile, and a moment later the red-haired girl called:

"Don't forget! You're to look us up."

"The Rollins House? I won't," Gaybird promised.

Cary met the girl's eyes for a moment. They were sage-green, and not shy. Neither were they bold, but with a quality of challenge in them. The man in the talma did not acknowledge them. He was absorbing the hot and dusty panorama with a stricken look. "He's a government man," Gaybird said. "An envoy to the Indian Nations. She's pretty, isn't she?"

Cary considered. "Not to say provocative. Is the name Merritt?"

"How did you know?"

"I heard he was coming. I hope he likes it up there in the Bighorns. He doesn't look like the type that would."

They met Silvertooth. He had a hug and a kiss for her. "Hard trip, lassie?"

"Those trains!"

Silvertooth chuckled and looked the girl over. "Will she toughen up to it again, do you think?" he asked Sam.

"She hasn't decided for sure that she's going. Either way, we leave at sun-up. Let the men go. Give Dunavan five dollars, but don't let him out of your sight."

As they crossed the tracks, Gaybird archly stared up at him. Cary's shoulders were nervously taut under the leather shirt, but his randomly sketched face did not give him away: All his practice skirmishing was nullified by the total femininity of this girl.

They passed a coal-yard. "So I haven't decided whether I'm going?" Gaybird remarked.

"Gay, we've got to talk about it."

A change came to her face, a thoughtfulness that firmed her lips. ". . . All right, Sam."

They made a perilous crossing of the street through freight outfits grinding by with the hard language of whackers and the sour stench of buffalo robes. A man in a derby and striped jersey was wrestling beer barrels from a dray. He stopped to look at her; Cary was obliquely flattered. She was a dainty and memorable spectacle for Cheyenne.

They reached the hotel. He had a wish deeper than a sigh: That they might have been meeting for the first time to-day—that for them it did not go back to a time when she was thirteen and he was her father's partner.

Spurs jangled on the sheet-metal floor of the dining-room. At red-and-white ginghamed tables, train passengers were gulping down their food, alert for the train bell. Gaybird made herself comfortable before giving him her attention. She disposed of the parasol and then, linking her fingers, looked soberly at him until she laughed.

"Sam, you're so funny!"

"What do you mean—funny?"

"So stern. What's the matter? Are you wondering how to make me drink my milk?" Cary scratched his neck. She watched him in amusement. "And what's this about my not going up to the fort?" she demanded.

"It's the same trouble as last summer, only worse. I wrote you that the army had pulled out. I saw the ashes of Fort Phil Kearny a week after the troopers rode out. How many emigrants and miners do you think are going up the Bozeman this year, without even the protection of a few hundred green recruits?"

She tried to be serious. "Why, I don't know, Sam. How many?"

He tapped the table. "An outfit went out last week. Those were the first wagons this summer. They may be the last. There's a reason. The Bozeman road may be two hundred miles closer than any other route, but no road is a short cut when you die on the way."

"But we've always been friendly with the Oglalas, haven't we?"

"With Crazy Dog's Oglalas. He's got a crazy son-in-law named Esconella, now, who's spoiling for fight. And Crazy Dog's sick—sick in the legs. How big a chief is a paralysed chief? If Esconella can tie enough yellow scalps to his lance when he goes out to proselyte warriors, then Crazy Dog is out of it. And we've got a war on our hands."

With devious feminine logic, Gaybird pointed out: "But he can't take scalps if the trail isn't used, can he?"

Sam smiled. "No, and we can't make money. But he'd have nothing against bullwhackers' scalps, and there's a couple of trains I know of going out to-morrow."

Her chin lifted. "You're not frightening me, Sam Cary. We built the fort when the Indians were unfriendly, and we can certainly hold it against them now."

"Suppose they besiege? Fifteen hundred braves piling logs against the walls could cause a lot of damage."

He saw the hurt in her eyes, and he laid his hand over hers.

"I'm sorry, Gay. It's not much of a welcome-home, is it? This kind of talk never built anything. But that's the situation,

and I'd be second cousin to a murderer to take a woman into
it. That's why I said what I did to Silvertooth. And that's why
I say I want you to take the train back to Cincinnati to-morrow.''

Gaybird's hand was at her throat. She pulled a thin gold chain
from the bosom of her dress and showed him the wedding band
laced on to it. Her face was very young and very pretty and very
solemn.

''I don't want to embarrass you, Sam, but—do you want this
back? Is that what you're trying to say?''

Sam had not seen the ring since that day four years ago. He
turned it briefly in his fingers. He saw that it had been engraved
inside.

''*Sam and Gaybird, August 12, 1864.*''

He looked quickly at her, but she pulled the ring away and
dropped it back into her bosom. ''I was a sentimental child,
wasn't I? I did that after you left.''

''I suppose we've got to do something about it,'' Cary
sighed. ''It's going to be awkward if somebody comes to ask me
for your hand, and I have to tell them you happen to be my
wife!''

She laughed, but the moment was stiff.

''I think we ought to remember what your father wanted for
you,'' said Sam. ''He wanted to make his stake out here and go
back East. He didn't want you to have to pick a man from a
couple of dozen bullwhackers and buffalo hunters. He used to
talk about the streets in his home town. Shade trees, and painted
houses, and galleries like the decks of a steamboat.''

Her grey eyes watched his lips while he spoke. ''How do you
know I want those things? I've just come from white houses and
shade trees. I'm dying for mountain meadows and snow creeks.
They're *my* idea of home.''

Cary frowned. ''I'm the wrong man to tout the East and run
down the West. But let's not forget Esconella and his Thunder
Fighters. And the Sand Creek Desert.''

''You forget those things when the danger is over,'' Gaybird
stated. ''But you remember the mountains.''

A waiter came. He took their order and departed. They did not meet each other's eyes. Something simple, thought Cary, had been made into something complex by a mumbling parson. She was essentially someone he had never met before. Yet a backlog of memories kept him from treating her like a charming stranger.

Suddenly she asked: "Sam—do you think marriages are made in heaven?"

"I think this particular marriage was made in a preacher's parlour," he smiled wryly. "I remember you were so tired from the train that you almost went to sleep during the ceremony. If God entered this one in the book, he must have entered it in pencil so it could be rubbed out."

"But it was still a marriage. And we can't just ignore it. That would be sinful."

"Sin," Cary conjectured, "is for preachers." He said pointedly, "If any notion of responsibility to a certain bullwhacker who needs a haircut and a clean shirt is on your mind, forget about it."

She raised her brows. "Oh, but I don't feel obligated! Only, I think you ought to decide what we're going to do."

What needed to be done was perfectly clear, thought Cary. Yet he could not make himself use the word. He found himself hedging from his bound duty. He was saying:

"The first thing is to settle the fort business. I'm prepared to buy you out. I wish I could give all cash, but I can't. I thought of a price of fifteen thousand for your share. I'll give you—"

Her eyes fascinated him. They were grey as a winter sky, but in no way cold. They were bright and noticing and alive. They watched him hesitate over the figures.

"One thing we can agree on right now," she declared. "Indians or no Indians, I'm going back to Fort Greybull. It happens to be my home. If I'm selling my home, I want to see it again first, if only to appraise it. That's reasonable, isn't it?"

Cary leaned back, his eyes unaccountably warm. "It would seem reasonable to a woman, I expect."

Gaybird gasped in astonishment.

"Why, Sam! That makes it practically an anniversary after all! It's the first time you've ever admitted I was a grown-up woman!"

VII

UNTIL DUSK, CARY escorted her from shop to shop, searching out luxuries Fort Greybull would not afford. Loaded with parcels, they started back to the wagon camp. Sunset gun boomed down the wind from Fort Russell. Invaded by a strong northerly breeze, the town began to cool. Cowboys rode in from outlying ranches. Soldiers off-duty from the post jogged in on well-curried cavalry horses. Freight wagons began to clear from the pulverized roadway and turnouts and saddle horses came and went briskly.

Gay suddenly squeezed his arm. "There's my redhead, from the train!"

Cary saw them entering the Rollins House—the gaunt-eyed man and the red-haired girl from the station platform. "The temperance deacon is her father?" he asked.

She scolded him quietly. "Her husband! And very distinguished. And he's not a deacon, he's a doctor, and a diplomat. He was ambassador in Mexico, or something, and now he's come out to talk with the Indian tribes. I don't think he's keen for it. He seemed a little gloomy. A man of *his* prestige."

"I'm a little gloomy about it myself," said Cary. "Prestige is what somebody else thinks of you, not what you think of yourself."

Now he discovered the walk blocked by three men. Without enthusiasm, he saw Mark Stockwell among them. The Montanan stood casually, thumbs under his belt and his coat thrust back to expose a pair of Dragoon pistols. A trooper in cavalry blues stood with him and Coy Mullan, the wagonmaster. It was too pointed an encounter to be casual. They had moved out in anticipation. Nothing about it was accidental.

Stockwell smiled as they approached, removing his stetson with flourish. "This must be the Miss Phillips I've heard about?"

Cary presented her, and Stockwell's hand enveloped hers. A big man, his hair brown and crisp, he showed a vigorous but disciplined interest in the girl. He presented Mullan and the trooper, a long-faced sergeant with pocked, coffee-brown features.

Cary said, "Excuse us. We leave in the morning. There's still much to do."

"You're stingy," Stockwell accused. "We haven't seen a girl without feathers in her hair for a year, and you hurry her off!"

"And the next time you see me," smiled Gaybird, "I'll have feathers in my hair. I grew up out here, Mr. Stockwell. Don't be surprised at anything." She gave Sam her arm. Stockwell and Coy Mullan stepped aside, but Sergeant Casner stood in the centre of the walk, his eyes on the girl. He seemed to have forgotten everyone else. He was a lank, deep-chested man with shallow black eyes. The moment grew awkward. Still relishing Gaybird, his eyes came to Cary.

"Before you leave I'll be going over your load with you."

Cary regarded him stonily. "Why?"

"Regulations. We aren't putting any more arms in the Sioux's hands *this* summer."

"You could have done this before. I'm loaded, now."

"That's too bad," Casner said. "Because I've got my orders."

"You've had them since April, in fact. I won't strew freight all over Wyoming now for you or anyone else."

Casner tapped Cary's shoulder. "Some advice. Don't try to handle the army the way you do your whackers. Does anything make you an exception to rules?"

"Until the army decides to re-man the Bozeman posts," Cary declared, "I'll decide what I need to maintain a post. I'll work with you or against you. It's your choice. But no inspections the night before I leave."

Ridges moved along Casner's jaws. "You'll buck me, then?"

"I don't think I'll have to," Cary said. "I think my quarrel is with somebody who picked you for a job—not with the army."

He nodded and moved Gaybird past the trooper. Casner put a hand against his shoulder. Cary halted. He looked into Casner's face, and then at Mark Stockwell. "What's the price for clearance, Mark?"

Casner suddenly lashed at Cary's face with the back of his hand. Ducking, Cary lost his parcels. There was a pallid print of knuckles on his cheekbone. He swerved back, but heard Gaybird's cry:

"*Sam!*"

Stockwell had moved quickly to her side and was attempting to pull her into the vestibule of a store. Mullan stood with a warp of anticipation in his mouth. The anger in Cary's eyes was full and strong: he poised there, toe to toe with the trooper for an instant. Then he stepped back.

He said: "That was a fine start for something I think I'd enjoy. Will you come to the camp after Retreat?"

Casner slowly gouged his fist against his palm. "I will," he said, "and with pleasure."

In the windy evening they moved on to the wagon camp. Gaybird carried her ribboned straw. She looked at Sam in pique. "I don't remember that we used to handle the army that way. This will mean trouble, won't it?"

"Depends on where he got his orders. I think he had them from Stockwell. Maybe he could still pull coals on our heads. But when he and I finish our rendezvous, he won't make trouble for anyone for a while."

Gaybird said petulantly: "I think you brought this fight on deliberately."

"If I did," Cary said, "it's worked in nicely, hasn't it?"

She held her skirts above the rough ground as they approached her wagon. He gave her a hand while she put her foot on the ladder. For an instant she looked down at him. "I—I hope you can handle him, now."

Cary chuckled. "So do I."

He saw in her face, before she entered the dearborn, the expression of a girl just beginning to discern the details of a picture she had not examined for two years.

End of Part Two

Part Three

VIII

IN THE DEARBORN, closely warm, and smelling of dust and creosote, Gaybird removed her basque and vest, unpinned the glistening dark *couronne* of her hair and stood before the mirror. Gaybird Cary—Gaybird Phillips, that was—had never looked so before this mirror, she thought. She felt like a young matron visiting a niece's room. Everywhere were the tokens of girl-hood—small treasures of her life in Wyoming. They seemed in surprisingly bad taste, some of them; all of them marvellously young.

Pleased, her hair hung in two braids coming across her shoulders. Her bosom was small but not too small. Soon her skin would darken with the stain of weather. Her eyes would appear lighter. Her lower lip was deep and rich, and she remembered what had been whispered about women with full lower lips being passionate. She wondered whether she was passionate. Certainly she was romantic.

Remembered impressions touched her . . . fragrant camp suppers in the heart of the squared wagons. A French harp singing in the prairie darkness; ungainly teamsters being awkwardly attentive. She was glad to be back.

She could hear Sam kicking up a fire and Silvertooth setting a dutch oven and coffee-pot on it. Their voices were low, but she remained quiet, and presently they forgot to be careful and she could hear them.

"Takes up where she left off, don't she?" That was Silvertooth.

"About Sand Creek, Cincinnati may begin to remember pretty fine," Sam contended.

"You couldn't talk her out of going with us?"

"She's set on it."

"Well. This country needs women, of course," said Silvertooth.

"You talk like a breeder," Cary told him.

"Who takes better care of his stock than a breeder? We need women, and she'd got her old man's toughness. No, I reckon you don't see it. You see 'seminary' all over her. But you'll see what I mean. Heat and sand won't change her none. If she's for Wyoming, you've got a pardner for keeps."

Silvertooth yawned, then: "I'll git uptown and keep an eye on the boys. A reg'lar brawl would set us back another forty-eight hours. *'Noches.*"

Gaybird smiled, poured water in a basin and washed. Then she dressed again, left the wagon and joined Sam for the rude camp meal.

She was washing the dishes when they heard boots stepping casually through the darkness towards them. The sergeant was on time for his rendezvous. Gaybird straightened and I looked at Cary, where he knelt, folding a tarpaulin. "Sam, I wish you hadn't done it!"

Cary came to his feet. "I tell you this is the best way. You'd better get in the wagon."

The boots came closer, and she was drying her hands as a man came into the firelight. But it was Mark Stockwell. Hatless, Stockwell's crisp hair was ruddy in the light. He made Gaybird a nod and faced Cary after a moment's idle scrutiny of the camp.

"You look trim. Pulling out to-morrow?"

"Maybeso. You?"

Stockwell smiled. "Maybeso. I was just talking to Major Drew, at the fort, about you."

Cary stared slowly at him. "You know we're in this together, don't you? If I get inspected, I'll see to it that every last scrap of gear you're carrying is set down."

The trader raised a glowing branch to start a cigar. "This wasn't about freight. It was about taking some passengers. This man, Merritt—the envoy—needs escort to the Bighorns. It seems Drew can't give escort, because the trail is off-limits. He wanted my advice and I suggested you, your place being close to Crazy Dog's grounds.''

"That's fine. Only I don't guide. Not for the army.''

"Then here's your chance to get right with the army.''

Cary picked up his coffee-cup and swirled it. "What's this fellow expected to do? Arrange a treaty single-handed?''

"He's a sort of flunkey to lay down the rug for the real treaty parley. He'll feel out the Oglalas. If they're amenable, he'll arrange for a full-scale parley at Fort Laramie this fall—feathers and brass and medals, all the usual la-de-da.''

"What's he like?''

"Cold as yesterday's dishwater. His wife's a beauty. Too bad she isn't the envoy. She could pacify me, I'll bet. They're waiting in the major's office right now. I said I'd send you up.''

Cary finished the coffee. "They'll have a wait, then. I can't leave Gaybird alone.''

"That's the part of this mission I like best,'' Stockwell smiled. "I'll take charge of Miss Phillips until you come back. I'd like her opinion of some dress goods I'm taking up, anyway. If she likes it, there's a bolt for her.''

Annoyance shaded Cary's face, but Gay spoke quickly. "Sam, you must! Could anyone guide him better than you?''

Cary sighed and pulled his hat from the bug where it rested. "Nobody could guide him more reluctantly. All that will come of it is slow travel, and sunburn for Merritt. The army will nullify whatever he accomplishes. But I'll talk to them.''

IX

THE COMMANDANT'S OFFICE was a low-ceilinged cell with un-plastered adobe walls mortared with grout. The walls were fitted with two maps and several photographs. A small pine desk rested in the centre of an Indian rug in a corner opposite the door. Standing in the doorway, Cary saw Major Drew rise from the desk, laying down a rifle which he had been examining. The envoy lounged in a chair near a window open to the night-sounds of the parade. Mrs. Merritt sat in an armchair near a hanging lamp; Cary wondered if it were part of a woman's strategy to sit where lamplight could burnish her hair. Mrs. Merritt's was lustrous as new copper.

Major Drew offered his hand. "This is Mrs. Merritt, Cary— and Doctor Merritt."

Cary looked into Merritt's dry, bored face. The envoy shook his hand with cold scrutiny. He had a long chin and pallid grey eyes, and his teeth barely showed in a smile. Long, down-curving creases of discontent enclosed his mouth.

Mrs. Merritt had a smiling regard for Cary. She wore a dark gown with a provocation of lace over the bosom. Her hair was parted and brought back to a large knot low on her neck. Cary had never before seen eyes which were actually green—glass-green—and he remembered things he had heard about green-eyed women.

"Stockwell told you why I wanted to see you?" Drew asked. Ruddy and grey, he was a jowly badger of a man buttoned tightly into infantry blues.

"Afraid so. Do you think I can give the kind of escort Doctor Merritt will need? We're bullwhackers, not soldiers."

"North of Laramie," the commandant said, "a bullwhacker *is* a soldier. And often better material than what we have to work with."

"It doesn't make the danger any less. I don't know how I could give Doctor Merritt proper escort into the mountains. Crazy Dog is holed-up where a loafer wolf would get lost."

Mrs. Merritt moved slightly; the light ran richly on her hair. "Are they really so ferocious?" Her eyes widened a bit, but a smile was tucked in the corners of her mouth.

"I've seen them when a mad dog wouldn't have associated with them," Cary assured her.

Doctor Merritt's lean hand made an impatient gesture. "Yet they'll send a man out to reason with them!"

"Well, they're reasonable people," Cary said. "Sioux like Crazy Dog are the last men to break their words. They don't violate a treaty until we've kicked it to pieces ourselves. This is your first assignment to the Sioux?''

"To any tribe. I was in Chihuahua City last.''

Moving across the floor, Cary glanced out the window. In the rich darkness, a lantern swung in striding arcs beyond Laundry Row. A trio of officers moved along the walk with its wand-like trees, cigars glowing. A vast sigh seemed to go up from the garrison, punished by day-long heat.

"How much can you offer for what you want to gain?'' Cary asked Merritt.

Tartly, the commandant came in. "Suppose you declare yourself before we take you into our confidence, Cary. Will you take them?''

Cary turned. "I can't tell you that until I know how Doctor Merritt is going about this peace mission of his. I won't be responsible for bringing in another like the last. Indians aren't our slaves; they're our hosts. This man didn't understand it.''

There was a silence. Doctor Merritt broke it.

"All right. Treat this as confidential, whatever your decision. My orders are to arrange for a treaty commission to visit Chief Crazy Dog this fall. The army wants to reopen the Bozeman Trail and occupy the forts. In return for this, we mean to guarantee that only essential hunting is done in the area.'' Grey and bitter, his eyes canted a sidelong glance at the trader. "Does that make me important enough to guide?''

Cary distrusted this moment. He distrusted what Merritt was saying and his own eagerness to accept it. It was what he and every Wyoming outlander had prayed for, but the gift came in the care of a man with obvious contempt for his job, with no recommendation for it other than correctness of deportment.

"Does the army intend to live up to those terms?'' he asked.

Toying with the rifle on his desk, Drew let the leaf sight fall with a snap. "It isn't only the army that forgets its obligations. Sometimes traders and hunters forget theirs.''

"I don't. And Crazy Dog knows it. I restrict my hunting and I give them fair value in trading with them. But I suffer with everyone else when a treaty is abused. This crazy-headed buck, Esconella, wouldn't have gathered all the lances he has if the Oglala Sioux had been treated fairly. That's why I insist on knowing whether this is *the* treaty, or just another pompous scrap of paper.''

''As far as it's in anyone's power out here, it's the treaty,'' Drew insisted. ''It's got to be, or the next thing will be the war we've been dodging for eight years. My information is that Esconella means to clean out every trading post between Cheyenne and Bannock. If it comes to that, how are you going to handle him? With more promises like the ones you've kept?''

''No,'' Cary said. ''Not with promises.''

They waited, but he did not enlarge. Presently he said: ''I think it would be wise for Mrs. Merritt to stay behind.''

''Oh, but I never stay behind!'' Mrs. Merritt exclaimed, her eyes teasing. ''Besides, I understand there's already a young woman in your train?''

''The daughter of my former partner,'' Cary admitted. ''Which makes her my current partner, so that I had nothing to say about her going. But she's used to sand in her victuals and scorpions in her bed. I'm sorry to say we can't even promise room service.''

Mrs. Merritt laughed. ''You won't frighten me off, even with scorpions. Not after Chihuahua City.''

''Then you'll take us?'' Merritt asked closely.

''For better, for worse,'' Cary sighed. ''You'll have to ride on a freight wagon and live in a tent, unless the major can give you an ambulance.''

''They'll have an ambulance.''

''Sun-up, then,'' Cary instructed. ''I'll send a man to drive you down. From there on you're your own skinner.''

Merritt gave his hand again. ''We're obliged, Cary.'' His dry smile came briefly. ''We'll try not to disrupt your train completely.''

Drew saw the door close and came around the desk, carrying the rifle. ''He'll need all the help you'll give him,'' he said doggedly. ''He'd hoped for a post in Mexico City. This is a comedown for him. Or so he thinks. Help him, Cary, and you help yourself.''

Sam had ceased to hear him.

He was regarding the rifle, which was a new Springfield-Allin, a trapdoor Springfield, in the army vernacular. The lock-plate of this gun was twisted from the stock and the breech had been blown out.

Drew was observing him. "Odd one," he said. "A patrol picked this up by the body of an Oglala warrior, north of the tracks this afternoon. He'd got hold of one of these army rejects somewhere. They found two thousand defective muskets after one of the big battles, you know. Apparently a lot of this stuff is being passed off on unsuspecting emigrants and the like. I'd guess the Indian had taken a shot at some game, and the charge came out of the breech."

Cary inspected the gun. He marvelled. "The junk they passed off as guns!" He handed it back. "I'll take care of your people, then. But I'll bill you for rations and nuisance cost."

"The latter," said Drew agreeably, "is likely to be the larger item. Good luck, Cary. Good luck to us both."

In the darkness Cary mounted and rode past the sentries at the gate, turning to jog townward. He came to a low, flinty divide and crossed it, the lights of Cheyenne on his left, hard and brilliant in the black desert night. He reached the coulee where Bill Orrum had his camp. Abruptly the heel of his hand smacked the saddle-horn.

"Damn the trash peddler!"

He saw where the sand was disturbed by wagon ruts and the hoof-pocks of a pony. Something slipped noiselessly into the darkness. He started. But it was only an animal quitting a spoiled quarter of venison; and Cary thought of the gun-runner, furtively forsaking his camp. Orrum had departed, leaving nothing but his trash, and a stark uncertainty in Sam Cary's mind.

X

AT NINE-THIRTY MARK STOCKWELL entered "The Nations."

He had left Gaybird at her wagon in the deserted camp. He was still warmly stirred by the contact with her, and sitting at a table where a chandelier would not drip candlewax and crisped

insects on him, he slowly drank a whisky and thought of
the girl's piquant beauty and the light-limbed grace of her
body.

She had wakened a gusty emotion in him, a headlong desire
not entirely like the disproportionate woman-need of distant
trails, and not totally dislike it.

He was not pleased with his hour with her. He resented the
impression that she had let him squire her to his camp merely to
make Cary jealous.

He was acquainted with the gossip that they were married.
Somehow he was inclined to believe it. But why try to make a
husband jealous?

Once in camp, she had become cool, hardly looking at his
bolts of delaine and calico, and in a short time she had asked him
to take her back. Then she said, pleasantly enough:

"You don't really need to stay. I'll be all right."

"Cary wouldn't like it. Everyone else is in town."

"Cary," she smiled, "should know by now that I keep a gun
in my wagon."

Stockwell poured a second drink from his bottle. It came to
him that he was drinking more in need and less in pleasure; he
put the liquor down stubbornly, at a draft. This last night before
taking the trail, he felt an unaccustomed queasiness. He thought
of the arid, bloody Bozeman, of the two-hundred-mile desert
between Cheyenne and the pine country, of the buttes which
could hide a thousand Indians, of the gaunt ruins of Fort Fetterman, near which a hundred and fifty men had died in one
blinding ambush.

There were the uncertainties which made getting his goods
through to his fort on Big Rosebud a perilous matter. But they
were also the factors which were making him rich. In two or
three more seasons, he could abandon the post at a profit.

The risk was that the army might reopen the Bozeman road
and throw the balance back to Cary.

Stockwell looked up. In the dingy mirror behind the bottles on
the back bar, he saw Sergeant Casner enter the saloon. The
trooper drifted down the bar, his campaign hat worn over one
eye, a tough, wedge-shouldered figure in trim cavalry blues with
a face as brown and durable as wood. He discovered Stockwell

and came to sit with him. A barman moved in to take his order. Casner glanced sardonically at the trader.

"I'd order Mountain Brook if I was sure this was still on you."

Stockwell said crisply: "It's not. You won't find it in a bottle anyhow," he added.

Casner took his glance to the barman. "J. H. Cutter," he said. Then he looked again at Stockwell. "I won't find what in a bottle?"

"What you came here to find. You were outmaneuvered, Sergeant."

"I don't think so. I've never liked traders, anyhow."

"I thought the idea was to inspect the wagons?" Stockwell chided. "You're not fighting to show off before the girl, are you? If you are, I ought to tell you you'll probably be whipped."

Casner palmed his drink. "He calls himself to be a handy lad, don't he? I've managed those handy lads before. Who was the girl?"

"His wife, I've heard. His partner, at least."

"I never heard he was married."

"That's the story. They were married four years ago."

Casner's fingers rubbed his long chin. "Why, she'd a' been a pigtailed kid! The damned cradle robber!"

Stockwell shrugged. "Put yourself in his place. If anybody else had married her, he'd have had a partner to check on him. And this way he owns all of Fort Greybull, instead of just half. I'd call it good business."

Casner drank slowly and steadily for fifteen minutes. Once he said: "What she needs is a trooper to give her some lovin', eh, Mark? A woman don't know what lovin' is till a trooper's showed her."

Stockwell perceived that a train of thought had been started in the trooper's head. Paying for his own drink, he struck Casner lightly on the shoulder. "Good luck. But don't get so interested in romance that you forget about your inspection."

Cary left his horse at the line which served as a hitchrack. The camp was silent. He had stopped at "The Nations" to instruct Silvertooth to round the men up: he wanted no heads to soak before taking off in the morning. He paced thoughtfully across the pounded earth of the corral, thinking of how this loose scatter of equipment and wagons must be pulled together in the last hour before sun-up. He reached the far line of wagons. There was a light in the dearborn. He reasoned that Gaybird must have returned from Stockwell's camp. Yet there was no indication of the trader, and an uneasiness that was displeasure stirred in him.

He inspected the shadowy lines of wagons and trailers. No sign of Sergeant Casner; nothing to be seen but the glowing canvas tilt of the spring wagon.

As he was about to move forward, he became aware that a man stood on the ladder of the wagon, his hand touching the rear curtain. Suddenly, then, the light gasped out and he heard Gaybird's voice:

"Sam?"

A man grunted: "Yes." The hand rose and quietly descended, with a silken tear of cut canvas. Cary heard her say, with the half of a laugh in her throat:

"Why—why, Sam Cary!"

Cary ran across the last dark reach of ground. As the man put a leg through the opening into the wagon he called:

"*Casner!*"

Casner's long body pivoted on the ladder. For a moment he was painted against the dark sky, one hand still clutching the canvas, the other half-raised with a dark glitter of steel. Without warning he plunged forward from the ladder.

The writhing weight of him bore Cary back in a sprawl. He caught Casner's wrist, but the knife slashed through his buckskin sleeve and bit deeply into his forearm with a feeling of cold fire. Landing heavily, Cary rolled away, his hand groping at the holster worn deep on his thigh. The pouch was empty: the gun had been lost in the fall.

He heard Gaybird come into the opening of the wagon and cry out sharply. "*Sam!*"

Cary watched Casner lunge forward in a rising crawl, a desperate, blind urgency in his face. Sam came to his feet and backed away. Suddenly Casner feinted, closing quickly as Cary raised his hand to block the slicing down-swing. A fluid spark of light slipped along the blade. With an expulsion of breath, the trooper drove the knife straight and clean at Cary's groin.

Cary fell away, nimble as a girl, but the blade took him in the hip. It slipped with cold haste into the muscle. He slapped his hand over Casner's and locked it there. His fist smashed at Casner's face. He saw the warp of the man's broken nose and the dark sheen of blood on his mouth. He struck again as Casner hauled violently at the knife. The sergeant's face was full of his terror—the horror of being taken in the act of a violation against a woman.

Viciously, Cary gouged at his face with his fingers, driving him back. Suddenly he brought his elbow against the trooper's jaw. Casner fell away and Cary freed the knife. Hot and dark, the blood came with it. Cary held the knife low and close, the wet blade waiting.

Casner, catching himself, came back with sobbing desperation. Cary swerved in smoothly.

The trooper brought up short with a hoarse exclamation. He pulled his hands in against his belly. The knife had found the softness just below his ribs. He stared at Cary, still with that stubborn mix of fear and hatred, his features slick with sweat. But Cary saw death in his face. He watched Casner's mouth loosen and saw him go to his knees and then sink forward.

He realized Gaybird had cried out. In stupefaction, he heard someone running across the corral. He turned slowly to confront the man.

The newcomer entered the tight square of wagons, looming against the dull backdrop of town lights as he halted a short distance away. Cary stood slowly rubbing his palms against his thighs. He was aware of sounds: the creak of wagons and the wooden squeal of axles from Stockwell's camp; a bullwhacker how-ing a team into a tongue. Stockwell's train was making up.

The man came forward. "Sam?"

Cary felt a weakness of relief. It was Silvertooth. He answered, and the wagonmaster ran forward. Silvertooth saw the dark shape on the ground and squatted to strike a wax match. He choked the flame quickly against the ground and stared up.

"*Him*, of all people!"

Gaybird with a moan knelt at the back of the wagon. All at

once Cary reached to steady himself. Silvertooth seized his arm. Cary breathed deeply a few times, his eyes closed. Somehow it was worse that a man's body should be violated by a knife than by a bullet. A bullet was cleanly masculine, a knife a savage perversion. It had gone into his body, coldly curious, and had achieved its destruction there and writhed away.

He blew out his cheeks, Gaybird was coming down the ladder. "Stay in the wagon," he told her. "John and I'll have to fix this up."

"You aren't going to move a yard from me, Sam Cary! I—I'll scream!"

"You already did," said the wagonmaster. "I was crossing the tracks when I heard you." He prodded Casner's body gently with his boot. His long, wooden features were melancholy.

"Get the medicine box," Cary growled. "And get me some pants and a clean shirt."

Silvertooth hurried after the box of rude frontier remedies. Gaybird retreated into the wagon and a moment later a lamp burned against the grey dusk. Cary dragged a tarpaulin up, cautiously lowered his cavalry breeches and lay on his face as Silvertooth hastened back. From the wooden box Silvertooth selected bluestone and sweet oil. He cauterized the wound with bluestone while Cary groaned.

"Lay still, now. I'm going to set the bandage."

Afterwards, clad in a clean shirt of stiff buckskin and fringed leather trousers, Cary limped over and looked at Casner.

Gaybird asked uncertainly: "Shouldn't we get the marshal, or—or Major Drew, or someone?"

"I wouldn't say so," Silvertooth drawled.

Cary tried to drive his thoughts like a team of horses. "Listen, John," he said, "we weren't fighting . . . At least this wasn't the fight we were supposed to have. I came across him trying to get into the dearborn. The fool pulled a knife on me."

Silvertooth listened with melancholy attention to the sprawling shape between them. "Well, do you believe me?" Sam demanded.

"Sure, I believe you. But a lot of boys knew he was going to fight you to-night. I'm just thinking how it would look to them."

"You can stop talking that way right now!" Gaybird protested.

Silvertooth sighed. "I reckon it might be easier to answer questions when you've got scars, instead of wounds," he said.

"I'd trade even for scars, right now. But who's going to swap me?"

"Maybe we ought to move along until they heal. Stretch out to-night, say. One of these days they'll find Casner laying in the sage and probably they'll figure it was Sam Cary that killed him. But it will be months before you show up again to answer questions. By that time, all you'll have is scars. Everybody's got scars. You can claim Casner never showed up. He was a brawler and a chaser, anyhow. A woman might have killed him."

"No!" Gaybird said tensely. "That's taking a chance. Let me tell Major Drew what happened. Why shouldn't he believe me?"

"Why should he? You're his pardner. Maybe you lured the sarge in here to keep his mind off guns. But he got around to hunting them anyway, and that was when Sam stepped in."

There was the racket of a gang of men coming towards the tracks. Cary's mind rose over the slogging misery in his hip to make a decision. They would ask the same questions and say the same things six months from now that they would to-night. But they would have no proof. In six months, witnesses drifted along, tempers lost their feather-edge, men's memories clouded.

Silvertooth flipped the tarpaulin over Casner's body, and from where Gaybird stood there was a choked sound of distress. The wagonmaster slowly shook his head.

"It's the best way, lassie. It's the only way. We don't care what anybody thinks about this—we know what Sam did was right. But we don't want Sam getting grey in the guardhouse while we convince them. Assuming we ever did. Stockwell would love this, I reckon. He'd chain us to Cheyenne for the summer, if it didn't end in a firing-squad. No. I can't see it any other way."

His hand pressed against his hip, Cary said: "I'll ride for the stock. John, will you . . . do for him?"

After he left, Silvertooth wrapped Casner snugly in the oiled canvas and kicked dirt over the dark stains on the ground. With the trooper over his shoulder like a bag of wheat, he started into the night. Behind him, he heard Dunavan's voice singing in a group of whackers entering the camp.

In the plum-blue darkness figures slipped back and forth before Stockwell's fires. Silvertooth skirted the camp widely and stopped to rest. Anywhere, he supposed, would do it. Then another idea occurred to him. It was a gamble, but the loss would be small if it failed. Presently he started north and west towards the railroad tracks.

XI

IN THE SILENT blackness before dawn, the Fort Greybull outfit broke camp.

With a grind of broad tyres rocking across the railroad tracks, the wagons pulled out into a long column. The sounds were heavy and muffled, of oxen lunging along swinging gaunt heads, of spokes and axles mumbling to themselves through the pale night dust.

Dawn came, and the sun discovered trampled acres of earth, naked of sage, where the freight camps had imparted substance to Cheyenne's dream of importance. Northward wound the reopened scar of a dying trail.

Before night, a train of wagons from Denver hauled in and possessed itself of Cary's old camp. Cheyenne took the whackers to her bosom.

In a week, Sam Cary's outfit made Fort Laramie and quitted it. North of Cheyenne, Laramie was sanctuary. Beyond Laramie, security was a man's own problem. The nearest walls, beyond burned ones, were at Fort Greybull, on the border, more than two hundred miles away.

Up to Laramie, it had been a shakedown affair. Now, working up the prairie-like bottoms of the North Platte, under a haunting cloud of dust, the train seemed to pull together. A primitive sort of despatch governed each action, from four o'clock rising to late afternoon squaring-up; and back of this tautness of order marched a shadow which was its cause, a shadow no one ever saw, but no one ever forgot.

Gaybird had not forgotten it. Yet it was as much a provocation to her as it was a threat. Through a hot morning she drove her own wagon, and wondered why she was not afraid. Now and then she glimpsed Cary, meeting a scout in the bright haze of summer distance to confer over some sign which might mean an encounter with Indians. He ran the freight company like an army. He tolerated no slackness of discipline, but out of his supervising ways came a feeling of security.

It made it possible for a girl to enter a canvas shelter and feel that she had locked the wilderness out. It encouraged her to watch for him in the evening as the wagons and trailers were shaped into a square corral, and wonder if his duties would make him late for supper.

Ahead of her wagon rattled the army ambulance bearing the envoy, Doctor Merritt, and his young wife. After a week Gaybird was not entirely satisfied with Mrs. Merritt. She did not always appear when it was time to wash dishes or set camp-bread. She was not wearing well, Gaybird thought.

Now she watched Cary jog down the staggered line of freight wagons, through the dust and cawing of axles. She reached for a handkerchief, to clear the dust from her face, and then she saw Sam pull in beside the Merritt wagon. With a small lift of her chin Gaybird glanced off towards the Laramie Mountains.

Seated in the army ambulance beside her husband, Dale Merritt had watched Cary approach with a quickness of interest. She had hardly seen him since they left Cheyenne, but she still recalled the quiet way in which he had handled Major Drew. She found him fascinating.

It was not fair to compare him to her husband, she supposed, since the doctor was utterly out of his element. She watched Cary guide his blue roan with his knees, lax in the Spanish saddle, his hand swinging a short length of rawhide rope. He could have been made out of the earth, she thought. Out of tough *parfleche*, out of buffalo hide and flinty gravel.

He stopped to inspect the loose sheeting of a wagon and came on through the heavy roll of dust. The dust was a compound thing. It was ground up by the wheels of the Stockwell train a few miles ahead. It half-settled, half-hung, to be churned afresh by the hoofs of their own mules and oxen. It was worse than the heat because the heat died at sundown. The dust was immortal.

Beside his wife, Doctor Merritt also watched Cary approach, with less enthusiasm. He shifted the reins of the four-mule team to one hand while he wiped sweat from his palm, repeating the operation with the other hand. A deep red had invaded his skin. His nose was peeling. He wore a handkerchief mask over his mouth.

"Blast him!" he said. "He could have spared a man to drive this thing."

Dale smiled. "You haven't anything else to do, Asa. You'd as well be driving."

"I could be out of the sun, at any rate." He watched her fingers touch her hair. "Primping," he said.

She laughed. "Oh, of course! For a man who wouldn't know the difference between a gavotte and a salad fork."

As Cary rode up, Doctor Merritt tugged his mask down and moistened his cracked lips. Cary smiled and gave them a salute. "How's the muleskinning?"

"You couldn't," Merritt said, "arrange for us to camp here until Crazy Dog pays us a call?"

"He'd pay one, sooner or later. Maybe not the sort you'd like." Cary nodded tersely at the thick dust. "Stockwell always would overload his wagons. We're overtaking him. That's why the dust is so bad."

Dale exclaimed in dismay, "Must we breathe clods all the way to your post, then?"

He looked at her thoughtfully. "There's an idea in that."

"You mean we might get ahead of him?"

"We could try. It would mean some driving for you," he told Merritt.

"I'll risk that," Merritt said grimly.

Dale Merritt watched Cary turn his horse. "But won't Mr. Stockwell object?"

"Probably," Cary said. "Tie down everything loose and check the wheel-nuts. We'll make Iron Pipe spring to-night—either just ahead of him or just behind."

Cary loped away. Doctor Merritt's gaze was not on the trader but on his wife. The tracery of excitement was in her face; the selvage of a smile on her lips.

Merritt felt a melancholy kinship with all men who took wives too young for them. He experienced anew the ancient and unreasonable jealousy, the conviction that every man younger than he was a rival. Had he himself been freer, less sterile emotionally, it might have been different.

With nostalgia, he thought back to the small-town medical practice he had deserted to take a diplomatic post in Washington—to impress Dale, as he hoped. He suspected that his whole life had been a yearning after proofs of his own competence. Medicine had drawn him because of its prestige. Satisfied that it was all hard work and difficult collections, he had courted the government post through a townsman who had gone to Congress.

And now fulfilment was upon him, and around him he saw, not fumed-oak conference rooms, but a brown and broken prairie peopled by traders and Indians. He carried an impossible portfolio, one no man could have satisfied. Back from Wyoming he would take renewed doubt of his own powers, in his eyes and those of his wife.

Merritt tugged the blue handkerchief filter up over his nose and stared grimly past the mules.

Cary let the horse loaf along the slow files of wagons moving under their load of dust and heat. To make the dust less intense, he had deployed the wagons two abreast. Their great wheels pulled up earth and dropped it back in a fine cinnamon sift.

A mile ahead, rocking and swaying across a stony ridge, Stockwell's train rolled on. The terrain was almost level, a high plateau sweeping on a gentle incline towards Laramie Peak.

It was a satisfaction to Cary to have caught up with Stockwell. It proved his contention that the trader would load a wagon until the hounds groaned. John Silvertooth had stewed for days over the midnight trick that had put Stockwell on the grass a half-day's travel ahead of them. Cary's lips took a slow smile. Silvertooth had been living for the time when they closed in. They were entering the desert now, every waterhole a murky seep that one night's use churned into a greenish-brown stew for the next train behind.

He found Silvertooth coming in with an antelope lashed across a pack-horse. Silvertooth had already discovered Stockwell's wagons. He was flushed with heat and anger, and savagely yanked at the lashings that bound the antelope.

"Something wrong, John?" Cary asked.

"Of all the dust I wouldn't care to eat, his'n's first."

"Reckon we could do anything about it?"

Silvertooth's glance swerved to him. "Maybeso. But there'd be a hell of a fight!"

Silvertooth loaded the antelope carcass into a provision wagon and remounted. They rode along.

"Not if we made a clean lead to the spring."

From a hogback, they observed the slow winding of wagons down a coulee under a weight of dust. "He's got a mile on us," Cary said. "We'd half kill the oxen trying to pass him in an afternoon. But we'll make dry camp to-night if he beats us in, and lose half the day to-morrow watering stock—if they'll drink the brine he leaves us."

Silvertooth studied the way the high-rolling plain, its spring green burned into summer tweed, tilted down into a basin cupping a muddy spring. Stockwell had taken the easiest course, but not the fastest. Finally the wagon-boss levelled his arm, stained with sweat in the creases of the buckskin.

"A man on a horse, ridin' that way, could spot him an hour and beat him in. I ain't sure about wagons. Them bulls would know they wasn't herd-bulls before we make 'er!"

"Then let's let them find out," Cary said.

He let the other train disappear before he turned the wagons single-file up a grassy draw. Stockwell's scouts ranged miles out: They would not discover the trick until too late. Pulling strongly, the oxen came to a windy eminence from which Iron Pipe Spring could be seen five miles north-west.

Lunging and swaying, the wagons held to the draws. But,

sooner or later, Cary realized, Stockwell must discover the banner of dust and realize what was happening. About four, when they were a scant hour from the spring, Silvertooth loped back.

"He's on to us! Them oxen are running like antelope."

Cary spurred back past the Merritts' wagon, telling them, "Hang on, now!" and came around behind Gaybird, tying his horse to the back of the dearborn. He swung up beside her and took the reins.

Gaybird took the opportunity to wipe dust from her face with a handkerchief. "Do you know what you're doing?" she demanded. "He'll fight before he gives up the lead."

"That'd be reason enough," Cary surmised.

In quick suspicion, Gaybird glanced at the Merritt wagon. As the wagon hit a stony rib, she clutched the seat with one hand, raising a handkerchief to her nose with the other.

"I suppose she talked you into it?"

"Mrs. Merritt?"

Gaybird said archly: "I imagine she'd think it thrilling to see men fight and wagons turn over. It would be part of the colour of the frontier. Unless she happened to be underneath one of them."

Cary smiled and rode with a lunge of the seat. "What's wrong between you and your red-head?"

"It seems to me the farther we get from a town, the more she wants the things she can't have. A tub bath last night! Fresh vegetables! I wouldn't have put it past her to suggest that we pass Stockwell to get out of the dust. Did she?"

"She didn't argue against it," Cary admitted.

Gaybird watched the cloud of dust riding above the hill which hid Stockwell's wagons. "You'd claim he was the shiftiest trader in Wyoming if he did this to you."

"He is. That's why I'm doing it to him."

"You're beginning," Gaybird announced, "to reason like a woman."

"Reasoning with women," Sam grinned, "is what brought me to it."

They made the last crest and topped over on to a long slope falling gently into the basin. Cary stood up to study their chances. The sunlight was off the valley. The trees around the morass called Iron Pipe Spring hid the water but gave it away. Invading the basin, a brushy arm like a mole-burrow screened Stockwell's wagons, but the tattered pennant of their dust flapped above it. Ahead and below, the Fort Greybull wagons avalanched down the long slope, at right angles to Stockwell's line of march. Cary noted where the clash would come. He saw how the wagons and animals would pile up in a wild free-for-all. It must be a clean-cut win, or it would be no win at all.

He held a bow for steadiness, and glanced back up the slope. Bull-teams lunged in and out of the massed boulders and sage clumps, sweeping the dust high and densely for the sunset to redden. Blacksnakes cracked and whackers shouted profanely, and in the blind fog of dust Dunavan's voice bawled: "Damn you, Belle—haw it over!" The basin echoed with this blunt-tongued uproar and the split-reed soprano of smoking axles.

Cary turned back, shaking his lines and shouting the greys into a shambling run. Gaybird clung to the seat, her black braids dancing. "Sam, you're insane!"

"No argument there," Cary said.

They flattened out into the basin. The crazy bounding of the dearborn slackened. One by one the bull-teams slung in behind. A rain-rut jarred Cary's right front wheel and glass shattered within the wagon.

The column of freight wagons wound across the hollow, and now, jolting behind three span of oxen, Stockwell's first wagon plunged into view. Two horsemen flanked it—Coy Mulland and Mark Stockwell. Stockwell shouted something and Mullan loped ahead to intercept Cary's train. Stockwell wheeled. He loped back along the lumbering cavalry of dust-veiled Schuttler wagons to give the animals the encouragement of a bullwhip.

Cary came to his feet, his arms thrusting forward to let the greys reach. Gaybird was frightened—cold and nerveless. She looked over at the Merritts' mule-drawn ambulance with its lanky, bandana-masked driver. Dale was clinging to the seat. Her face was alight with excitement. She waved at them. Gaybird sniffed. "If she knew what I know about wagons turning over!"

They saw Coy Mullan slashing in. His chunky barrel-body

erect, he took the run of his horse easily, and suddenly flung a blacksnake in a hissing arc and brought it about his head. His blunt mahogany features were savage.

"Turn them!" he shouted.

Gaybird put a hand on Sam's arm. Distantly there was a confused clatter, and looking back she saw an overturned wagon in Stockwell's train. She observed the grey smoke of smouldering axles on other wagons and heard the harsh cry of dry spindles.

Cary brought the wagons thundering straight at Coy Mullan, where he sat his horse just off the angle of the cottonwoods. The bullwhip swung slowly above the Montanan's head. She saw that the moment was a sort of contest . . . a test of whether Mullan could turn Sam, or Sam could turn him.

Suddenly she screamed. Mullan had flung the whip. It had come to life, arching and stretching and flinging its thick rawhide cracker against the shoulder of the nigh leader. The horse swerved, throwing the other off balance. Mullan hurled the whip once more and the horses lunged away.

The lines ripped through Cary's hands. He felt Gaybird clinging to him as the wagon rose on the nigh wheels. She screamed. Cary let the lines fall and seized the edge of the seat. He saw Mullan put spurs to his pony, evading the tangle as the wagon went over.

The prairie upended, ground was sky, the ordered pattern of the team was a wild circus. They were under the wagon-seat and articles were raining down on them. Cary anticipated the crushing burden of the wagon itself. Then he knew that the wagon was rolling away from them, bounding back on to its wheels. He saw it topple once more on to its side, where it remained. He crouched there with his revolver in his hand while Stockwell's wagons thundered past.

Among the trees, Silvertooth was closing the wagons in a ragged circle about the waterhole. Cary saw him take his pony along the line, waiting for the impact of the Montana outfit; but Mullan suddenly turned and arm-signalled the wagons aside.

Cary looked down, then, and saw that Gaybird's eyes were closed.

End of Part Three

Part Four

XII

AMONG THE TREES the dusk was deep, redolent of rotting leaves. Cary stood by the tarpaulin where Gaybird lay, watching Doctor Merritt examine a bottle he had taken from a brown cowhide portmanteau. He hoped Merritt's medicine was more skilful than he suspected his diplomacy was. Her skirts spread in a soft grey circle, Dale sat beside the girl.

"If you've anything else to do, Cary," Merritt said, "be about it. She's all right. She'll be around directly."

Cary thought briefly about vengeance, but lost the thought before he voiced it. He opened and shut his hands and looked down at her.

"She's not hurt," Merritt said wearily. "I've had less trouble with some prospective fathers than you're giving me."

Cary turned indecisively. Near by, men were fitting new bows to the dearborn. Stockwell and Mullan were still with the Montana wagons, which had gathered in the dusk a half-mile west. He moved to where a rank of kettles hung in a fire of cottonwood branches. Silvertooth was shaving saccharined coffee into tin cups. "That water hot yet?" Cary demanded.

"It's only been on two minutes," Silvertooth said.

Cary moved along, experimenting with the anodyne of activity, filling his pipe as he walked and trying to gather his thoughts. His mind fumbled. Under a tree he stopped to light the pipe. The tobacco was tasteless. He could taste nothing but a sick fear. He turned suddenly as Dale called: "Mr. Cary!"

Cary strode back and let himself on to his heels beside Gaybird. She was sitting up, a hand gingerly to her head. Merritt was talking quietly to her and administering a teaspoon of medicine. She took it, grimacing. Merritt said: "You took a bump on the head, young woman. And at that, you were fortunate."

"If you had the headache I have," Gaybird protested, "you wouldn't say that!"

Then she saw Sam, and reached quickly for his hand, as if the sight of him recalled all the terror of the last instant before the wagon went over. "Sam!" she said.

Cary placed himself where she could lean against him, filled with rough gratitude to Merritt, to circumstance, to luck. "Next time," he said, "I'll let you drive your own wagon."

"Next time don't try to bluff Coy Mullan," she said.

Cary said, in justification: "Well, our stock's on the water tonight." He held her hand roughly in his, wanting to say many things, but aware of the listening silence, and of Merritt's rutted face relaxed in a softness of humour. He stood up and reached his hands down to her. "Try your legs."

She let him walk her about. When they were out of earshot, near the blazing fires within the corral, she said: "It was almost worth it, to see you undecided about something."

"About what?"

"About me. I watched you for a while before they knew I'd come around."

Cary smiled. "That's prying into a man's mind."

She was silent for a moment and they watched a whacker cutting steaks off a hung quarter of the antelope Silvertooth had brought in. "Is there anything in your mind you haven't told me about, Sam? Anything I have a right to know?"

"If there is, it's got no right being there."

"But things don't always happen the way they ought to, do they?"

"No. White men marry squaws, and when they get townhungry and take them back, everything falls to pieces. And halfcivilized men like me take white wives to Wyoming, and the same thing happens."

"You're so sure I *am* civilized. I could still give a war-cry that would bring every man up working a ramrod."

"Don't," Cary said. "Be honest with both of us, Gaybird. Do you really aim to stay?"

"I don't know. I—I think so. That's being honest, isn't it? I want to see the Bighorns again, and the flowers along Young Woman Creek, and smell the wind loaded with sage. That's when I'll know. But I do know it's wicked to be only half married. And when I make up my mind about *that*, I'll tell you."

He saw the clean-cut resolution of her mind, a contrast to the humming-bird inconstancy of summers before. But she was still reasoning with emotion, and he was reasoning from observation and experience.

"I don't think it's any more wicked than mistaking obligation for affection," he said. "A post is a mighty tight society. Even marriages made in heaven sometimes blow up. But there's nothing to run to, not even a divorce lawyer. You're mortgaged to it for good."

Her face fell into soberness. "Now you've said it, Sam. Divorce. I hoped we never would. Whatever we did, I hoped we could find another name for it."

"Now," he said gently, "we're being sentimental."

She looked up at him, gravely smiling. "Then you're beginning to understand Gaybird Cary, at last. Sentimental . . . over small things and big ones. I'm glad you've reminded me. I might have got sentimental over you, as well as Wyoming. Just because you need a shave half the time and your sunburn only goes up to where your hat comes. Naturally I'd have got over it, but it might have been a painful convalescence."

She was full of the perverse mystery of her sex, he saw; he did not know whether she was hurt or angry. Her tight little smile did not tell. She turned her back and walked towards the fire. A moment later Cary heard Silvertooth carefully call his name through the smoky dust. He lingered an instant and turned.

In the early night he saw two men coming from the Montana wagon camp.

Cary slipped through a gap in the wagons, moving under the cottonwoods to where the dearborn was being repaired. Silvertooth waited there with Doctor Merritt and the others. Working up a large chew of Navy plug, Silvertooth growled:

"Mullan is coming to make his manners."

Cary rested his shoulder against the wagon-box and watched

the men approach. Stockwell, preceding Coy Mullan, strode through the trees with his hands shoved into his hip pockets. Cary heard the quick indraw of Mrs. Merritt's breath.

"Will you make them pay for the damage to the wagon?" she asked.

Cary kept his eyes on the Montanans. "In the coin of the realm," he told her.

Stockwell came into the ruddy area of firelight. The stain of weather was dark in his face and there were sweat-rings on his buckskin shirt. He was hatless, his dark hair crisp with perspiration. His brow was ribbed with harsh lines. He looked at Cary a moment and took his gaze to Gaybird as she came up.

"Miss Phillips," he said soberly, "I'd have given a span of mules to prevent this. You're all right?"

"Only because I'm indestructible," Gaybird declared.

"It wasn't intentional. Mullan's orders were to turn the wagons, and that happened to be the only way. We didn't start the race, you know."

"Didn't you?" Cary's shoulder came from the box. "You didn't start it by jumping the gun at Cheyenne, when we had every trail right?"

Coy Mullan moved up, his tough black brows joined. "Is there any rule to keep a man from putting out at night?"

"No. But I don't see why another man shouldn't pull his tricks in the daylight, if he chooses. I told you at Cheyenne to keep out of my way."

Mullan returned his stare brassily. "Who's getting in whose way?"

"Right now," Cary said, "you're getting in mine." He said it between lips pulled hard, and walked towards the wagon-boss.

"You don't want this," Mullan stated.

Cary kept moving, hearing Stockwell's angry voice: "Don't take it out on him, Cary." He was within three feet of the shorter man when he feinted at Mullan's belly and watched him blunder with a swinging right-hand blow at his head. It missed by inches as Cary leaned out of its way. Stepping in, Cary slugged him in the face. Mullan's head snapped. Cary prodded him stiffly in the belly and Mullan backed away with his shoulders hunched. He took several blows on his shoulders, and then, with vicious speed, stepped in to hammer at Cary's head. His fist slanted shatteringly across Cary's jaw. It turned Cary's head and caused him to stumble aside. Mullan surged in with his right fist back. He let the blow slam into Cary's mouth and the blood came saltily.

Cary had forgotten a lesson he had learned early: not to let your anger rule your head. He had carried the fight clumsily to Mullan.

He saw Mullan's face hazily, the eyes glistening with a brutal hunger. He saw him rock forward again and knew the fist was coming to his head, but he was powerless to duck. There was no pain in the blow; it was a dull force which killed all urgency.

He thought he had fallen. Then he became aware of hanging on to Mullan while the wagon-boss tried to shake him loose. Cary's eyes picked out Dunavan, standing by the wagon with a hammer in his hand. A sleek enjoyment was in Dunavan's face.

Mullan pivoted strongly and hurled Cary aside. The compact hardness of him was magnificent; he was muscle and wood. He plunged after Cary with his left hand reaching and his right fist cocked, and Cary moved away from him. Mullan struck and missed and was off-balance for an instant.

Cary lunged in. His long back muscles were in the swing he hurled as the wagon-boss lurched aside. Mullan grunted and blindly thrust at Cary as he came after him. He hacked at his face and Sam knocked the blow aside and turned him with a chopping punch to the jaw. He brought Mullan around against the wagon. He drove his fist up under Coy Mullan's jaw as though he were trying to lift him off the ground. Mullan's head snapped back against the wagon so that there was no give to the blow; the ache of it filled Cary's arm. He pulled back to strike again.

Then he saw Mullan's features soften in ugly and sudden sleep, and heard a formless word in his throat as his legs caved under him.

Cary turned, reaction weakening him. He saw Dunavan pivot and go towards the fires. He saw Stockwell regarding his fallen wagonmaster without affection.

In that instant things could be read in the trader's face—subsurface things. Cary felt the depth and breadth of him. He knew that he would sacrifice Mullan, or anyone else, to feed his ambition. He comprehended finally that Mark Stockwell was incapable of regarding competition as normal: to him, it must always be an affront, to be met as an affront was met—with enmity instead of rivalry.

Stockwell removed the cover from the water-barrel, dipped a bucket of water and sloshed it over Mullan. Mullan came round grudgingly. He frowned about him. His glance stopped on Cary. He said nothing, but reached up and tried to thrust away a headache with a fist against his forehead.

Stockwell said: "Go back to the wagons. Tell the men to outspan where they are."

Mullan got to his feet and shambled off towards the wagons.

There was the surprising sound of Dale Merritt's laughter. She stood back against a wheel with her hands holding the spokes, the firelight imparting a gipsy look to her face. "Things are so marvellously direct here! If Asa had handled that, it would have gone to the forty-second endorsement, and probably have finished in a war."

Merritt's sardonic eyes rested on the face of Cary. "You're assuming this won't, eh?"

"We've had the war," Dale smiled, her smile for Cary. "And we've won it. Or have we, Mr. Stockwell?"

Stockwell's broad shoulders moved. "Cary took us. But he'll race us again to-morrow."

Cary smiled. "Dry stock moves slow, Mark."

"Then the day after to-morrow. You'll race me every day until I get ahead of you again. This violates every rule of trail etiquette I know."

Cary laughed. "I didn't know you knew anything but 'get there first!' You can always strain your water through a dishrag like we've been doing."

Stockwell spoke flatly. "Give me credit for not liking a whipping any better than you, Cary. But also give me credit for having horse-sense. I knew you were close behind us, and I was glad of it. The day I sent Mullan to you in Cheyenne, he was to suggest that we travel together. This is Sioux country, and it's their summer of discontent. I'm suggesting to-night what I'd told him to propose—that we travel together."

"Why?"

"I've said why—security. Fifty wagons are better medicine than twenty-five."

Cary took a blue polka-dot handkerchief from his pocket and bound it about the bleeding knuckles of his fist.

"I'd rather know where my enemies are than have to guess at it." He turned to Silvertooth. "Bring the dearborn up as soon as it's in shape. The rest of you folks can wash up for supper."

Walking towards the trampled sump, west of the camp, he saw the dark sheen of the water, ruddied by the fires. He stopped near the herd and knelt to scoop muddy water with which to bathe his face. He heard someone behind him, then, and turned and saw Stockwell moving up unhurriedly, a pipe in his hand. He slowly rose and confronted him, while the trader found a match and struck it. Stockwell held it in the bowl of the pipe, and for a moment they were included in a close circle of orange light. Just before the trader dropped the match, he glanced up. He was smiling.

"It was too bad about Sergeant Casner," he said.

The cold unexpectedness of it struck Cary so manifestly that Stockwell chuckled. Cary stared into the harshly lined countenance. "What about Casner?"

"He's dead. You know that. Dead in the brush, with a knife wound in his breast. I wonder if they've found him."

Cary regarded him coolly. "You're making it more profitable for me to kill you than not."

"I thought you'd rather have me mention it out of the others' hearing. Mullan knows it, though. That's my insurance."

"Casner had it coming," Cary declared. "Did you send him down to the camp that night?"

"I followed him. He was talking about Gaybird in the saloon. I got to worrying about her."

"You should have. He was breaking into her wagon."

Stockwell made a gesture with his hand. "You say so. How does any one else know? I saw you fighting and I saw him killed, and the next thing I knew Silvertooth was dragging him into the brush. How do I know it wasn't an ordinary fight?"

"You didn't think I'd stand trial, did you, after feuding with him?"

Stockwell said: "No, I don't expect you would. You like to

make your own rules, whatever the game you're playing. If you were playing murder this time, it's about the way I'd expect you to play it. It's reasonable to think Major Drew would come to the same conclusion, given a couple of eye-witnesses.''

He drew on the pipe until it glowed, and then, expelling the smoke he said easily: "Suppose I water my stock to-night and we join outfits in the morning?'' He waited five seconds, and said: "Fine. I think we'll make good trail-partners. Both of us know how to play it cannily.''

XIII

IN THE HOT MORNING, under a sky like steel, Cary rawhided his outfit into shape. Afterwards, sitting his horse beside Stockwell's, he saw the wagons and trailers strung out impartially, a Greybull outfit and a Montana, letting every man consume his share of dust. Stockwell, favouring mules, had his long jerk-lines of dust-floured Missouri mules. The sun had gathered itself for a scorching day. The mountains were drowned in sulphurous haze. The peppery hills sidled off to the west.

The train made up into a ponderous column of fifty wagons, an offence to Cary's eye with its unwieldiness, to his throat with its blotter-dry dust. Coming off the rim of last night's square, the last of his wagons groaned into line. Stockwell swung away with a wave of his carbine. "A hundred braves will think twice before they tackle this outfit!'' Stockwell commented.

"A thousand won't,'' Cary said.

In the moment of riding forward, Cary saw the patched and dirty tilt of Stockwell's final wagon wallowing through the boggy spring branch. He hung there, scrutinizing it. He kneed the pony around and let it come up beside the wagon, touching the brim of his hat in a salute.

"Hello, Orrum. We get around, don't we, us gun-runners?"

Bill Orrum, who sold bad whisky and worse rifles, grinned at Cary. His lean, dark hand removed the red-bowled Cheyenne pipe from his teeth. "We do, now."

Cary's contempt for him was bitter as the aftertaste of long-swallowed greasy food. He detested the smell of his Indian tobacco, the thick shine of his pigtails.

"We find a pilgrim to sell our junk to on most any street corner, too, eh?"

Again Orrum bit on the pipe, adjusting the lines in his hands. "Don't get you, Sam."

Cary pulled the bullwhip from his saddle-horn. He made a cut at the green spire of a wild onion. It fell, cleanly cut.

"You and I," Cary said, "are going to look over some guns to-night. If we find any of them bad, I'll cut the living hide off you. I'll take your boots and your gun and leave you afoot."

Orrum saw the dangerous shine of Cary's eyes. He said again: "Cary, you're talking Blackfoot. Them were good guns."

"The one I saw on Major Drew's desk wasn't good. The breech was blown wide open. They found it by the body of an Oglala buck in the desert."

"Have I got to answer for every dead Injun in Wyoming?" Orrum complained.

"Only the ones who died trying to shoot Springfield-Allins. We lost a gun to a Sioux the night Silvertooth and I picked them up. This was the gun he stole. When he tried to fire it, it killed him. How many of the rest are going the same way?"

Orrum appeared stricken. "Sam, I vow before—"

"Were those guns new?"

Defeated, Orrum's glance wavered but came back. "Most of them, yes. The rest were A-1 salvage. I went over them myself."

"You didn't think to fire a couple of rounds in each of them?"

Orrum snapped his fingers. "By God, I'll tell you what! Some of them troopers don't know any better than to plug up a gun-barrel to keep the dust out. Makes it easier to stand inspection. It ain't all of them knows it rusts the barrel. Now, that buck must have got holt of one and forgot to pull the plug out! It would have blowed right up under his nose!"

Cary regarded him unenthusiastically. "Or maybe the rust was so heavy the ball couldn't pass through it. Either way, we'll find out. You'll fire them, whatever they look like."

He swerved the horse up the line.

Through the day the heat mounted. A sandstorm swept in from the Badlands and for two hours travel was halted. Men moved through a suffocating twilight of heated sand, handkerchiefs tugged to their eyes. Oxen found strange and stubborn madness in the blind purgatory of the desert storm, rebelling against handling, turning downwind unless they were chained to the wagon ahead.

The wind blew itself out; the sun floated in a dun fog obscuring the mountains.

For the first time that day, Cary stopped to talk with Gaybird. She had passed the sandstorm in the wagon, fighting the sifting grit that tried every seam. Now she came back to the wagon seat, her hair brushed and braided. Her smile chided him.

"I think you're growing fond of Mark. One minute you'd have no part of him, and the next he'd talked you into letting him travel with us."

"He's a trading sort," Cary conceded. "He traded me out of my best judgment."

He let her extract the meaning from it herself; tugging his stetson down, he rode ahead.

The wagons took their long nooning under a red bluff where the animals grazed on tough yellow graze merging in tufts between humps of buffalo grass. Creaking on, the wagons came in late afternoon to Cary's old camp at the head of Sage Creek, a lonely memory of cold supper fires, whitening antelope bones, and a warm pool of water among grey-green willows. Silvertooth took charge of the outspanning.

Cary singled out the arms-wagon in the half-mile stretch of groaning freight wagons moving up. He told the whacker: "Pull over here and wait."

When Bill Orrum came along, Cary signalled him to a halt. "Matt will take your wagon in."

Orrum raised his gun from the floorboards and jumped down, but Cary said: "You won't need that."

Orrum's eyes, the whites very white in his dark face, slanted to Cary and then shifted. He replaced the rifle. The other bull-whacker mounted the wheel to the box. The trader's wagon moved through the dust.

Cary took a painstaking moment to scan the red bluffs and the tawny reach of prairie on the west, looking for the faintest smoke of dust, the animal-movement that was not animal-movement. Satisfying himself, he turned, loosened a corner of the heavy canvas sheet, and furled back a deep sift of red dust. He pulled out a chest of rifles. Taking a claw hammer from the tool-box, he pried the lid from the chest and lifted a greasy Springfield off the rack. He opened a case of amunition and removed a handful of copper cartridges.

He said: "We'll fire three out of each chest. Put your lead into the bluff, yonder." He moved around to sit on the pebbly ground, carrying a cleaning rod and patch.

Orrum stood impassively, looking at the rifle. He opened the breech. Suddenly he glanced at Cary and loaded the gun. Cary saw the thin shine of perspiration on his face.

"I didn't say there mightn't be one or two bad ones. Safer to vise them against the wagon and pull the trigger with a cord."

Cary took a straw of sage in his teeth. "You forgot to tell me that when I paid you."

Orrum regarded him soberly a moment longer. He put his left side to Sam and raised the gun, the shot coming without warning. Dust blossomed on the bluff a hundred yards distant. Orrum handed the gun to Cary. Running the patch down the barrel, Cary watched him take a second rifle out of the chest.

The gun-barrel lifted strongly as the roar of the gun came.

Orrum fired the third gun and swung it to Cary, still smoking. He pulled down a second chest and pried up the lid; Cary saw him hesitate. Casually the gun-runner turned to open the third case, but Sam said:

"That was the case I was really interested in. There's only eleven rifles in it. It's the one the Oglala's gun came out of. The one that blew his face off."

Orrum turned back the lid and looked at the eleven rifles racked inside. He stood there in the late sun with his pigtails gleaming and his warped body still. He brought a gun out, rested the butt on the ground and examined the muzzle. Then in swift relief he looked at Sam. "There's a plug in her! Just like I said—the buck tried to fire it thataway." He drew the plug out, tossed it aside and upended the gun to catch a gleam of light through the breech.

Cary watched him, smiling a little. Plugged guns rusted fast, and these guns had not been used since the war. He saw Orrum bring the gun down. The trader grunted.

"Leetle rusty, at that—"

"Fire it. Let's see how rusty."

Orrum confronted him in quick and angry challenge. "I wasn't tricking you, Cary! I hadn't time to inspect them all; it was buy and git—a back lot deal. I judged you'd have enough savvy to clean them before you used them."

"Those guns," Cary said, "were going to stand between me and a wipe-out, if the Sioux laid siege to me this winter. Then they'd be for sale. You knew that. The Indians don't know about breech-loaders yet, and it may be they'll learn some manners when they find out what a Springfield can do. But if I had to clean rifles in the middle of an Indian attack, I allow Esconella would be wearing yellow scalps on his lance."

Emotion stirred muddily in Orrum's face. After a moment he faced away from Cary. He plugged a cartridge into the chamber. Cary observed that the follower went forward stubbornly.

Very suddenly then, Orrum dropped to one knee and his torso swivelled on his lean hips. Cary saw the clean glitter of the browned gun-barrel as it swerved towards him.

XIV

THE MOMENT LAY in Cary's mind like a jewel. It had the clean brilliance of danger. The shape of Bill Orrum was etched sharply against the pink bluffs. The Springfield gleamed. Cary had not trusted Orrum any farther than he would trust a sand rattler in his blanket. Yet he had not credited him with the courage to make such a play so close to the wagons.

In blind instinct, he smashed at the barrel of the gun. The vast roar of it shook him. But his hand passed short of the gun and he knew suddenly that Orrum had made a fool of him. The gun's arc had halted, still directed towards the cliffs.

Orrum was not looking at him. He was regarding something in the brush, and Cary observed a jack rabbit bounding erratically through the ragged heads of sage. Grinning, Bill Orrum glanced at Sam.

"There, now! You've spoiled my shot. You need a blow-off, Sam. You're jumpy as a cat."

"Around you," Cary said with wry humour, "a man's bound to be nervy. She shoots. Try another."

Orrum said: "I'll tell you what: I'll clean this case for you tonight. We'll go through the rest, but these are the only ones that I picked up used. I still say the Injun didn't draw the barrel-plug. She back-blowed on him."

Cary said: "That's what I thought, too. But I wanted to see if you were as sure of it when you were holding the gun yourself. Use plenty of soap on them, and don't grease them."

From Sage Creek the Bozeman road lurched north by ancient and deceptive landmarks. The route hung on a succession of rivers that were creeks, of creeks that were gaunt barrancas, of springs lost in sand; and all that could be counted on was the scorching honesty of the desert itself.

They had entered, without crossing a discernible boundary, the hereditary Sioux country, Sioux by right of conquest. Geographically vague, it was a sargasso of traditions and sacred grounds, where ignorant men could offend without knowing it. Cary's scouts now roamed more distantly, men weathered in smokes of Indian fires who knew every Sioux tribe and its habits.

Short of ruined Fort Reno, they lay over a day to wash and mend clothing, check up loose tyres and ferret out spoiling cargo. The forge fumed and hammers rang. The hunters had shot no game in a week, not daring to roam after distant herds. Corned beef and hardtack were the night and morning fare.

Cary watched, with a veteran's amusement, the emergence

from the greenhorns' chrysalises of a varied fauna of trail types.

His pride was Dunavan, taciturn, dogged, capable, and magnificently independent. Dunavan wore eternally his air of having been shanghaied, but under it Cary saw—or thought he saw—the man he had hired for a whacker's whacker.

Doctor Merritt was no surprise to him. He hated the trail with a comprehensive despite. At noon he lay under the ambulance in the sharp rectangle of its shade and his sardonic eyes hated the smells, the baking red buttes and the sand hills.

He watched Dale Merritt assimilating the things the desert offered, growing quieter and more brown, but containing her fears.

There began to be foundation for fears.

At Salt Spring, they found a tree with the bark peeled from it and a sign left on the wound. Cary knew this mark. He had seen it on a dozen trees the year the Sioux invaded the Crow country. He could not read the sign, but Silvertooth said:

"Uncpapas. That could mean one of Sittin' Bull's villages. They say he ain't much as a warrior, but he's a hellfire politician."

They were coming into the rumpled apron of the Bighorns, the mountains evident only in ground-swells that passed under the wagons. They found remnants of slaughtered buffalo and grey memories of fires.

Breaking out of the noon layover one day, Cary helped Merritt hitch his mules. Finishing this, he swung into his saddle and held by the fore-wheels of the ambulance long enough to give the envoy some cheer for the last, punishing hours of the day.

"Easier travelling from here on, Doctor," he smiled. "We hit Fort Reno to-night. Then we head up into God's country—water for shaving and maybe a break from corned beef and hardtack."

"I'll believe there's water in this country when I see it," Merritt replied grimly.

Dale said wanly: "And when we see it, we won't recognize it for mud."

"You'll recognize this," Cary promised.

Merritt tooled the team along through the rising dust. "Some time you might give me a tip or two on how to get around these head-hunters we're heading for. They say there's a way to make a fool of any man, if you have the key.''

"I wouldn't recommend making a fool of these people," Cary said patiently. "I'd try to put myself in their place. They've got their backs to the wall—the Bighorns—and now we're trying to take away the wall."

In terse inquiry, Merritt brought his glance to Cary's face. "If I'm not being inquisitive, whose side are you on?"

"Until the arrows begin to fly," Cary said candidly, "I'm on theirs. I'm for trying to buy trail rights from them for a decent consideration. What we want to remember, Doctor, is that when it comes to telling lies, we can always top theirs."

He felt his patience thinning for this dour man who could not understand that in the country of the red man, the white man was alien.

Dale was drawing something from a tapestry knitting bag under the seat. "Will you give another greenhorn some advice?" She tossed him a slightly wilted prairie blossom. "I want to know if that's what you call *kinnikinnick*."

Cary studied it in mock seriousness. "Not quite. *Kinnikinnick* is a mess of bark, leaves and dirt the Indians smoke instead of tobacco. So do I, when I can't get tobacco."

Dale laughed. "Asa, I've made a fool of myself. You see," she told Sam. "I botanize—collect flowers. Sometimes I press them. Usually I paint them in water-colours. It's quite fashionable in the East. I'd be the talk of Washington if I could go back with a collection of genuine Wyoming wild flowers. Would you have time before it's dark to-night to point out some plants to me?"

Cary glanced quickly at the doctor, who regarded his wife in slow gravity and then gave his attention again to the labouring mules. Cary hedged. "After the chores, if there's time. Doctor, I could show you some herbs that would match anything in your bag."

Merritt grunted. "For suddenness, perhaps. No, thanks."

Dale's eyes veiled themselves momentarily as Cary looked doubtfully at her, and she smiled. "After the chores, then."

•   •   •

In mid-afternoon they reached the shell of Fort Reno, on the Dry Fork of Powder River. The gap-toothed picket walls and burned structures loomed on a sagebrush bench above the river. The sun struck brassily on aisles of muddy water between sand bars. Where the land had not been cleared, sage and lean cottonwoods fringed the river.

Cary corralled the wagons on the flat ground between the old stables and the fort proper. He sent the stock down to the river to be watered. He was aligning oxbows against a wagon when Silvertooth sought him.

The weather had stained the face of the wagon-boss mahogany brown. His skin was grey with dust cut by rivulets of sweat. He carried a shard of pottery which he put into Sam's hand. Cary turned it over. Bits of burned meat clung to the rough terracotta. "Where'd you find it?" he asked.

"Inside the fort. There's the rubbish of a big camp. They must have spent a week. Ain't been gone three days."

"How many?"

"I make it a hundred and fifty."

Cary frowned and tossed the pottery away.

Silvertooth opened the grub box at the tail of the wagon and began taking out utensils. "Pretty soon," he said, "you've got to make up your mind what to do about Merritt."

"I ought to give him a map when we reach Fort Greybull and set him loose. If he's a peacemaker, I'm a bank teller."

Silvertooth kicked up a heap of buffalo chips and whittled twigs upon them. "Something else you've got to make up your mind about," he said, "is Gaybird."

Cary took out his case-knife, cut off a chunk of corned beef which he began to chew, and sliced more into the long-handled iron skillet. "What about Gaybird?"

"Nothing. Only that she's been in Stockwell's wagon ever since we outspanned. He's got an honest-to-God sewing machine in there. He's teaching her to use it."

Cary's hands slowed. Then again the knife moved, and he said: "That's her good luck. She'll have a trade, if the post fails."

"She'll have a trade," said Silvertooth, "but a filly like her ain't going to need one—I thought we'd met the wrong train when she got off that day.''

"How's that?"

Silvertooth's eyes were sly. "You hadn't noticed the change, eh? Maybeso you feel more like a father towards her."

Sam skinned grease from the blade and cased it. "No," he told him. "I don't feel that way."

"Well, if you hadn't noticed it, she's grown up. That's all. She knows how to pick clothes and she looks good in 'em. She ain't noways a squaw-girl any more. Being married, it ain't my place to notice how she's filled out, so I won't mention that." He stirred potatoes in the huge iron skillet. "Of course it all comes down to the fact that she's going to come around wanting that annulment one of these days. *Quien sabe?* It might be Stockwell she picks! She always did have a weakness for traders."

Cary made his hands busy, moving the skillet to a spot where the grease did not smoke. "She's got better taste than that."

"That a fact? When I went by the wagon just now I heard him sayin': 'You've got a real talent for this, young lady. But I think I ought to have a prize when I've finished teaching you.' "

"What did she say?"

"She said: 'Of course you should. I'll run up a shirt for you when I learn how to make ruffles.' "

Cary's eyes winced. He had noticed this interest of Stockwell's for Gaybird growing. He had waited to see him rebuffed, but it had not come.

He spoke slowly, then, staring into the fire. "I'd run him clean to Idaho if I thought she was interested in him. He's a four-flusher and no kind of honest trader. I can see trouble in this trail for her anyway, John. She's tasted the East. Folks with a fondness for cream don't get attached to skim milk again."

"Some of them never get the fondness, though. She ain't."

"That'll tell itself. Of course she's a woman, now. She'll be getting interested in some man. But then I've known girls of eighteen to fall in love with a horse."

"She was in love with a horse summer before last," Silvertooth reminded. "This is the season for men. But just being a man, and being around, ain't enough. A man's got to show interest to get interest."

Sam set an elbow against the felloe of a wheel, peering into the wagonmaster's sly and solemn countenance. "Who's wanting to interest her?"

"I don't know. I reckon nobody, maybe."

Cary looked away, then, moving presently to the skillet to fish out a chunk of corned beef. He said: "I reckon not," and took his rifle from the rack on the wagon-box. Against the warm evening wind, he sauntered past the wagons to see that the stock were cared for. But as he moved away he glanced back.

Silvertooth had exaggerated. Gaybird was not in Stockwell's wagon. She sat on a crate at the foot of it, a cumbersome sewing machine before her. She was a small form in a striped, full gown with an apron about her waist. Stockwell, massive in his taut-shouldered leather shirt and buckskin breeches, bent over the machine, guiding her hands.

Cary turned again and sidled down the pitch of faded grass toward the animals. He had thought himself under a calm and reasoned discipline. But suddenly emotion fountained through him and his arm went back to hurl the chunk of meat he carried at the broad rump of an ox. Then he wiped his hand on his thigh and stood motionless in the breeze hissing through the brush.

The virulence of his fury thinned. He saw exactly how it was with him.

He was in love with Gaybird, and with no fatherly feelings at all. He loved her the way any man loved any woman. That she happened to be his wife was merely an obstacle.

The problem was as ruthlessly simple as the most insoluble of problems often are: he was in love with a woman he had, in essence, just met. But Gaybird, he judged, must see him as a man she had always known—as someone older than she. Or, worse, as someone ageless, like a parent.

Gratitude was a fine thing, he thought, and she had more than enough of it. But it was no recommendation in a woman being carried over the wedding threshold.

He went solemnly on down the path towards the stream.

XV

NEARLY AN HOUR of daylight remained after supper. Day scouts ranged in and a quartette of horsemen, still chewing tough beef, rode out. At the wooden dishpan, Gaybird finished her dishes. She wore a striped dress that Sam had told her made her look like candy; it was roman-striped, full below, snug above. Her apron was a crisp accent for it. Wind and heat had richened her skin; her eyes were lighter grey, her lashes darker.

She rinsed the caustic dishwater from her hands and applied a lotion of glycerin and rosewater. But the skin of her hands remained slightly shiny, and she knew that in six months they would not be the hands which had turned the pages of text books. She sighed, feelingly but without tragedy.

Cary had been absent from their mess, but now he came up from the *bosque*. She watched him approach. It was unseemly in a young woman to be over-eager with a man, she knew. All right for him to discover that she was the proper woman for him, but not for her to attempt to tell him. So she smiled absently and said:

"I missed you at supper."

"They hadn't half-way got the stock watered. I'll borrow your buggy rifle for Mrs. Merritt," Sam mentioned.

She watched him take it from the seat of the wagon. Her back stiffened perceptibly. "What in heaven's name for?"

He shrugged. "Precaution. She's got it in her head to collect wild flowers. I'm going to point out a few."

Gaybird knew her face must look as stiff as rawhide. The rifle had been a present from Sam two summers before. She said: "Why, that's ridiculous! You wouldn't dare go far enough to find anything the stock hadn't trampled. She can find her flowers right in the corral."

"No, there's some things down in the bosky she might like. I don't mean to get out of sight."

Gaybird said: "I'd rather you left the rifle."

He halted. "Why?"

"The idea in giving it to me was for my protection, wasn't it?"

He regarded her thoughtfully. "That's right." Then an irrational lightness broke in him and he wanted to laugh. Instead he smiled and set it carefully against the wagon. "And I'll bet if you had to you couldn't break a vinegar jug at ten feet!"

Gaybird's chin tilted. But she was suddenly unsure what her voice might do, and she turned her back on him.

Sam laughed and strode off. The gun had been a mere notion, something to make Mrs. Merritt feel secure and important. If any Sioux were within ten miles, they were few enough to hide in a gopher-hole, or the scouts would have flushed them. But that feeling, of a light shining in him, of a small music-box tinkling, stayed with him.

Dale was waiting when he arrived at the ambulance. The doctor was off at his evening chore, pulling aching teeth and puncturing boils from sweat-gall and bad food. In this respect, a load had been taken from Sam's shoulders by his presence. Cary noticed that the vividness of the girl's colouring had been increased by the trail. She had the deep cocoa tones in her skin which weathered well. She had the green eyes to go with it and the rich, coppery hair. She had brushed it to a burning lustre.

"I'm sorry to travel so heavily," she deplored. She had laid out a flat wooden box, a drawing-pad, and a folding camp stool.

Cary took the stool and the wooden box. "Let's be glad you don't do your flowers in marble."

They moved down the meagre slope to the stream. A scout loafed out westward, the tail of his pony streaming, a distant, lonely figure against a florid evening sky. Cary turned upstream and they walked under the mountain ashes. In the night wind the feathery leaves whispered. A shoulder of cottonwoods bent with the stream. They rounded it and Cary halted to pick up a blossom. There was something elementally foolish in this which half-amused him.

"Evening star," he said. "Scarce in the desert."

She turned it in her fingers. "Then I may as well start with it. I like things that are scarce. The scarcer they are, the better I like them."

"Mrs. Merritt," Sam said, "you talk like a prophet sometimes. In parables."

Reproof pouted in her lips. "That's almost the only way a woman can talk, isn't it? Or she can be insipid, or bold."

He helped her arrange the stool, dipped a cup of water for her colours, and gathered a small bunch of flowers. The drawing-pad on her lap, she began to sketch. Cary sat against a rock to smoke. He was impressed again with the strangeness of her being the wife of a dry-minded man like Merritt. Then he heard her asking quietly, her eyes on her work:

"Do you like being a trader, Sam?"

"If I didn't, I wouldn't be one."

"I suppose you wouldn't. Most men seem to live in ruts they can't climb out of. But I think they feel safer in them. Still, you'll have to admit there are disadvantages to your life."

"Just one," Cary declared. "Sometimes I have to go into town."

"And you don't mind the dangers?"

"I'd be in more danger in Washington than I am here. I'd get run over by a runaway senator, sure as you're born."

Her brush moved meticulously. A quick glance darted towards him. "One thing you must miss. Women."

"An exploded notion. They're something else you can get used to doing without, like whisky."

"I don't know that I like being compared to whisky," Dale pouted.

Cary smoked his pipe. "You're both strong medicine, I've been told. Both habit-forming."

"Tell me something," Dale said. "Are you in love with Gaybird?"

Cary looked into his pipe. "She's just a child, isn't she?"

"A beautiful and mischievous child. I think she's playing you against Mark Stockwell. I noticed you went stock-tending while she had her sewing lesson."

"Gaybird," he said, "happens to be my partner, not my fiancée." He bit on the notched stem of the pipe.

"Sam," Dale said reproachfully. He looked at her. "I don't mean to intrude in anything you don't want me to. We'll talk about something else, if you'd rather."

"Motion carried," Sam said.

"We'll talk about how wrong women can be, then. I was wrong about being a country doctor's wife. It looked so dramatic, to a girl who didn't like being a grocer's daughter. But there's less drama to it than there is penny-pinching, trying to run a house on gifts of eggs and hams."

She rinsed the brush and applied new colour. "Then I was wrong about being a diplomat's wife. I made Asa take that political job, through a friend who went to Washington. But we landed in a Mexican desert town, instead of in Mexico City." She sighed. "In fact, this is the closest thing to excitement I've had yet!"

Cary struck the pipe against his heel and stood up. "I'd say, we'd had more dust than excitement."

Dale reached her hand and he helped her stand. For an instant she was close to him, her eyes holding his, a smile just behind her lips. "Does excitement always have to mean Indians?" she asked.

Cary glanced briefly down the river. Then he looked into the tawny oval face with its snug smile, its candid green eyes and its selfish, luxurious mouth.

"Mrs. Merritt," he sighed, "you're talking in parables again."

"But I'm really no prophet, Sam," Dale said. "I'm entirely fallible."

"Neither am I, but I'm going to prophesy that the doctor might think he was being dealt to off the bottom of the deck, if he were looking."

She relinquished his hand, still with that persuasiveness about her lips. She looked down at her sketch. "This is really one of the nicest specimens of wild-life I've done."

He looked at it. It was not professional work but it was skilled amateur. The colours were deep brown, rose and white against the green of mountain ash. The face was his own—long, hard-fleshed, dark.

He took it from her, thinking sadly of that somnolent man who was her husband. He slowly tore the page twice, dropping it on the ground.

"It seems to me the doctor might like evening stars better."

Her eyes clouded. "That wasn't very mannerly, Sam. What did you think I meant by it?"

"I don't know. I can guess what the doctor would think."

Suddenly a change entered her face, a rush of apprehension, and she turned. At the same moment, Cary heard the slow tread of boots. The lean form of the doctor came into view, moving along the path beside the crumbling bank. Dale picked up the stool quickly, closed the paint-box, and started towards him. Cary tucked his hands into his hip pockets and followed her.

Sunburned and breathing deeply from the climb, Merritt acknowledged them with a crisp smile. "Find what you wanted?"

"An evening star!" Dale exclaimed. "I made a wretched job of it. Next time I'll press it. Coming back?"

Merritt's eyes rummaged along the canyon side. "No. I'll stretch my legs a bit."

"Better make it quick," Cary advised him. "There were Indians here night before last."

Dale took her husband's arm. "Sam's right, Asa. Don't worry me by wandering about."

Merritt patted her hand. "Never worry over any man," he smiled. "It puts lines in a woman's face. And then—who knows?—perhaps she can't get another?"

Dale said: "Do hurry, then," and walked on.

Merritt moved along a little way and stopped under the trees. He turned to watch them, his wife and the trader, a slender feminine form and a lanky masculine shape with casualness in its movements.

Twenty years ago, he thought, I'd have outweighed him. But this was not twenty years ago. This was to-night, and Dale's eyes were so guileless he was certain they hid a deeper guile than any she had yet shown him. He watched them out of sight. Then he proceeded to the point where the rumpled earth showed him they had sat.

Then he saw the torn sheet of drawing-paper. Curious, he picked it up. It was no trouble to fit the pieces together. He regarded Cary's features without changing expression. His hands slowly made a packet of the drawing paper and he slipped it into his pocket.

He stood that way, his eyes lost in bitter reverie, until a falling pebble startled him. He faced around, half-frightened, his head full of the Indian tales the whackers told each other. A whistler squirrel popped into a hole.

His face sombre, he started slowly back to the wagon camp. Another sound came to him and he stopped, listening, and then with a frown moved on. Abruptly a far-off yelping reached him and this time Merritt's throat constricted.

He heard a shot. The report was followed immediately by a crisp rattling of other shots and the sound of men's voices raised in alarm. Merritt began to run.

End of Part Four

Part Five

XVI

As THEY RAN up the path Cary held Mrs. Merritt's hand, pulling her roughly along. On the bench he halted. The wagons lay to the left, a tilted hollow square against the broken walls of ruined Fort Reno. Within the corral, there was an uproar of running men and horses. Cary looked south and saw where the stock had been brought up from the wide, sandy stream on to the bench. Herders were desperately loping back to the wagons; the oxen and mules were on the move, streaming down the brushy mesa. Distantly he could hear the falsetto cries of Indians.

Cary said to Dale: "Your husband's coming yonder. Wait for him and head into the fort."

He ran on. At the bucking line of saddle-horses he found Silvertooth scrambling on to his calico mule. Bill Orrum rammed a bit into his mount's teeth and vaulted on to its back, disdaining a saddle. Stockwell and Coy Mullan had already moved out through the wagons to join the herders. Cary mounted and spurred over to where Dunavan was attempting to saddle a pitching bay.

"You won't need that. Take everybody into the fort. Then pass out the Springfields and shells."

Temper flared in Dunavan. He held Cary's bridle-rein. "Stay with the women? I'll be damned if I will, for any stiff-necked fool of a wagon-captain!"

Cary regarded him with a long and wondering stare. Dunavan's hand fell away. Cary said: "You don't have to be on salt water to mutiny. And the treatment for it is the same anywhere."

Dunavan's face slowly accepted the situation. "Have your fun, Cary. Have it this side of Fort Greybull, because you and me have got a date the day we reach the fort."

Cary saw Gaybird hurrying from the dearborn with her rifle. He spurred to her side. Picking her up he rode through the smoky walls. He looked into her eyes and they were wide and steady. "Never let a turkey gobble scare you," he smiled. "Stay with Mrs. Merritt. She'll need bolstering."

"Who'll stay with me?" Gaybird asked reproachfully.

"Dunavan. The best foot-soldier in the outfit."

Stockwell had the men assembled on the mesa south of the wagons. There were close to two dozen horsemen in the group when Cary joined them. A half-mile below, the Indians were driving the stock into the broad and dusky wash of the Powder. All the ponies were fighting fit, fired with the smell of danger.

"They've got every animal we own on the run!" Stockwell declared. He was burly and rumpled and greasy with perspiration. He looked the men over and his arm made a dividing cut. "You men cut ahead and drop into the wash. The rest of us will crowd them from the rear."

Cary pushed through to his side. "The devil with splitting," he said. "We'll cross here and watch for our break. If they try to cross the sand-bars we'll have them."

Stockwell's big frame was charged with an angry rashness. "If those critters get away, we'd as well all be massacred. I say we hit them now!"

Cary saw how the trader's righteous fury was duplicated in all the men huddled there. Even Silvertooth was red with his need for action. Yet he waited dutifully for Sam to have his say.

Into this quiet Bill Orrum drawled nasally:

"I go with Cary, or I go back to the wagons. I didn't grow these pigtails for no Injun to decorate his lance with." He winked at Sam and squeezed the belly of his horse with lean leather-clad legs, and rode to the edge of the mesa.

Cary spurred after him, thinking how friendship was a relative thing. The best friend he had at this moment was a man who had not thought it beneath him to sell him a case of rifles which could have cost his life.

Cary pulled in beside Orrum. They topped over on to the

brushy hillside. The sunset-tinted pall of dust drifted east from the trees; from it came the bawling of cattle and an occasional gobbling Indian yell. Cary put the horse into a jolting zigzag down the slope. Back of him, then, he heard the others running their horses, catching up. Presently he raised his rifle horizontally above his head. They halted. Cary told them: "Wait here." He jogged carefully on down the slope towards the sparse growth of cottonwoods. Now he made out the rumps of cattle and a flash of scarlet. He heard an Indian's prodding cry. He could see, on the opposite bank of the wash, a dismounted rider. He swung down and set his foot on the bridle reins, taking a wide stance and settling his boots in the gravel. He carried the carbine to his cheek. He locked the breath in his lungs and brought the dark silhouette into the pattern of his sights. Carefully he took up the trigger slack. The sun slugged at his shoulder. Dark fumes of powder-smoke burst from the gun-muzzle. He ducked down under the smoke and watched the warrior blindly turn to grope at his horse. The pony shied and the brave fell, rising and standing for an instant with a hand on his side before he toppled again on the sage-crusted slope.

Cary turned quickly and swung his rifle at the others. He heard a soft, thrumming sound like a guitar string plucked. The sound came from the brush along the stream; it was part and parcel of the pain which ripped at his side. With surprise he looked down at himself. A great triangle had been torn in his leather shirt. There was no arrow-shaft in his side, but below the ribs was a ragged flap of skin from which blood streamed in a glistening dark flow.

Brush crackled. A shirtless form came on to the back of a paint pony and lunged into the creek. Cary raised the gun again, but the steadiness was out of him. The shot kicked dust from the far bank. He bent over, his carbine falling, gripping his knees with his hands. After a moment, the other massing around him, he recovered his rifle and looked for his horse. Silvertooth peered at him.

"Better you went back," he said. "That ain't whisky you're spilling."

Cary shook his head. He spurred out of the group and let the horse pick its way across the sand-bars of the stream. They came out in a ragged line on the far bank, sidling along the margin of the trees. Below them and slightly south, the oxen and mules crashed along through brush and rocks under a cinnamon fog. The light was failing. Cary searched for sign of the warriors.

Orrum was at his side. Cary was giddy with pain and weakness. "Reckon this was a nuisance raid?" he said.

Orrum went slackly with the lunging of his pony through the brush. "Mought be."

"If they were looking for a fight, they'd have been in trim. The buck back there wore a shirt."

Orrum looked straight ahead and said nothing.

Cary was aware that his mind was not working. He said: "So the foam may be off it for them. How are we going to convince them they don't want those mules?"

Orrum said: "You're the doctor, ain't you?"

"I'd like to ramp down on them where the trees fade back, yonder. But I don't want to lose anybody over a few mules."

"Look yonder," Orrum said.

Cary followed his pointing rifle. On the east bank of the wash he discovered a brief file of horsemen slipping through the trees. The Sioux had abandoned the herd. Orrum said dryly:

"Good medicine to keep your eye on them."

"Take some boys and salt their tails," Cary grunted. "I'll start the bulls back."

In the windy dusk they brought the animals into the shelter of the wagons. Dunavan stalked out of the fort carrying a Springfield, a bandoleer slung about his neck. Dismounting, Cary saw Tom Kane, one of the scouts, loping in from the bench. Kane's moccasins struck the ground and he came to Cary with his mouth pulling wryly.

"They were in the bosky, Sam! I never seen them till they broke out. Don't know what they'd done with their ponies."

"Signal the others in," Cary said. "Then set a picket line a hundred yards out."

Skinners began to emerge from the broken gate of Fort Reno. Gaybird and Mrs. Merritt were with them, and Doctor Merritt. Merritt's astringent gaze found the blood on Cary's side.

"If you've anything to keep out the screw-worms," Cary said, "I'd be obliged."

Merritt glanced at the wound. He went to get medicines from his ambulance.

Dunavan appeared, his flat countenance rutted with dirt and sweat. He gave Cary a tight grin. "Well, gin'ral, did you cover yourself with glory?"

"And a certain amount of confusion," Cary told him.

"We had a little excitement here, too," said Dunavan. "A field-mouse ran out of the old grain shed and nearly frightened some of us to death. Maybe," he said, "you'd let me be horse-holder next time, now that I've served my time with the stablehands."

"Maybe," Cary smiled, "you'll get to lead a charge."

In disgust, Dunavan tossed the Springfield on to a tarpaulin and slogged off.

All this time Gaybird had stood by with nothing to say; but suddenly it came in a rush.

"You didn't keep a post all these years by letting a gang of green bucks snake up on you, Sam Cary! What's the difference this season?"

"Maybe I don't pay enough attention to my work," Sam suggested.

"Yes," Gaybird nodded firmly. "That might be."

She glanced at Dale and then went to clang a skillet into a dishpan and roll up her sleeves. At the fire, she made a pad of potholders and lifted a kettle of water from a hook. Her hands were trembling. Merritt stopped as she was pouring the dishwater.

"I'll need hot water," he told her. "Can you spare some of that?"

"Certainly," she said.

He went on. She saw him toss something into the fire as he passed it. Carrying the kettle towards the tarpaulin where Sam was seated, she stopped at the fire and glanced into the coals. A fat packet of folded paper slowly uncurled in the flames. She made out what appeared to be a portion of a man's face. She saw the shape of a man's jaw and ear, and suddenly caught her breath. She stared at Sam. Her gaze found Dale near him. She started to go on, but abruptly she hung the kettle on a pothook and called to Merritt. "The water is on the fire when you want it, Doctor." She hurried to her wagon.

• • •

Exhausted, Cary slept until midnight. Then he awoke, hearing guards at a fire drinking coffee. The black prairie sky shimmered with stars. Rifles glittering darkly, the sentries left the fire and silently moved through the wagons. A teamster in the squat blockhouse of the fort challenged them and one of them gruffly responded. They moved on down the bench.

Cary lay on one elbow, gazing at Gaybird's wagon.

He wondered if she had deduced anything about his and Mrs. Merritt's expedition from the doctor's attitude. Merritt had not said a word to him while he stitched and dressed the wound in his side. But afterwards he had said:

"Is this raid going to make it any harder to come to terms with Crazy Dog?"

"Probably easier," Cary said. "These were Uncpapa Sioux, from Montana. Either they were on a hunting raid or they'd been sent for by Esconella. Recruits for his hydrophobia army. No friends of Crazy Dog, either way."

Merritt said slowly: "Indians are a sneaking sort, aren't they? You never know what one is thinking. Or when he'll try to steal something that belongs to you."

The dearborn appeared lonely. It was small and frail between sets of wagons and trailers. It was like the contrast of Gaybird with the bullwhackers. Uneasily, Cary thought of that double-edged remark of Merritt's—not because of the sub-surface thing he had meant, but because you could not be easy in your mind if Indians were within forty miles. She had her rifle, of course, but she slept so soundly you could move everything out of the dearborn without her ever awaking.

He grunted and moved out of his blankets into the dry night cold, succumbing to his disquiet.

His boots made little sound. The brush had been cleared from most of the corral for fires. There was the sweet, dry smell of yellowed grass. Beneath their wagons, whackers slept in snoring exhaustion. One man, too tired or restless to sleep, sat up, smoking. He and Sam spoke briefly. Cary moved along, until the spring wagon was ahead of him. She had stretched a line from a bow to the freight wagon behind, hanging dish-towels and a few pieces of laundry on it: they would be dry by morning.

The wooden dishpan hung against the side of the dearborn.

He moved between the wagons to the outer side of the square.

Far out, he saw a guard relieving a man who had been on duty since sundown. Metal clinked crisply. Threading its dark sand-bars, Dry Fork whispered among the trees. Somewhere a horse rolled out his stiffness. Midnight, Cary thought, and all well.

A voice whispered near him and he pivoted, rifle swinging. Gaybird said primly:

"You're nervous, Samuel."

"Samuwell," he repeated. "You know I don't like that name."

"I forget sometimes."

"Only when you're angry."

He heard her part the canvas flaps and tie one back. A small nightgowned ghost with braids across her shoulders, she sat on the foot of her bed.

"*Are* you angry?" he persisted.

"Why should I be?"

He straddled the tongue of the freight wagon. "No reason."

They were silent, looking at each other in the darkness. "What are you up to, training around this time of night?" she asked.

"Restless. Those stitches Merritt put in feel like French knots instead of basting."

"Maybe it was his way of calling you Samuwell."

Cary's thumb rubbed the spur of the gun; he frowned. "I reckon it was," he sighed.

Gaybird exclaimed petulantly. "Why did you do it? If you wanted to be so ridiculous as to let a woman make a fool out of you, you could at least have been careful."

"Careful about what?"

"The picture, of course—and whatever it stands for. Oh, it's your business. But, of course, you know Doctor Merritt found it. I saw it in the fire before it burned."

Cary nodded slowly. "I figured it was that. Well."

"Well, what?"

Softly, Cary struck the tongue with his fist. "Dang the woman!"

"Certainly," she declared. "Blame the woman."

"The whole thing was foolishness! Merritt knew we were going, but he wouldn't go along. Then she made that picture of me instead of the flowers. I tore it up and threw the pieces away. That's the truth. We just sat there."

At the aperture Gaybird regarded the sky pensively. "So much can happen when men and women just—sit there."

"*We're* sitting," Sam said, "and nothing's happening. That's the way it was with us."

"*I* might believe you. But will Doctor Merritt believe Dale?"

"I wouldn't, in his place."

He rubbed the bronze frame of the gun with his sleeve. "Well, it'll work out." He rose.

As he stepped across the wagon-tongue, Gay demanded: "Why did you tear it up?"

"Why shouldn't I?"

"Were you afraid he would find it, and suspect?"

"Dammit," Cary said. "I told you we just sat! And we've never sat together before. I tore it up because it was foolishness and I didn't want it, and I didn't want Merritt coming across it."

"You are fond of her, though, aren't you?" He was a few feet along, but her voice followed him teasingly.

He came back and took her chin in his thumb and forefinger. He looked at the small, big-eyed face and said precisely: "No, I am not fond of her. I'm in love with my work. I'm married to a mule and a spring wagon. That's why I came out here with my wound giving me fits and the air knotting my joints. To see whether your wagon was all right."

He slogged off down the line, his shoulders set. When he had passed two wagons, he hesitated. He listened, his heart suddenly very still, not sure whether she had called him back or not. *She'll call again, if it was Gaybird*, he thought fervently, and he waited.

After a moment he heard a voice singing softly: "*Buff'ler Gals, Won't you come out to-night, Won't you come out—*"

It was the muted voice of the sleepless teamster. He went on, setting his boots doggedly against the ground.

At the dearborn, Gaybird waited a moment longer, hearing his footfalls and uncertain whether they were approaching or going away. *He heard! He must have heard!* she thought, and she held

her breath and clutched the canvas flap. But presently she knew
he was retreating, and she let the flap fall and tied it. She would
not call him again. No man deserved more of a clue to a woman's
heart than that.

XVII

OUT OF THE Badlands wind came to hiss through sage and rabbit
brush and whip hot, stinging sand through the wagons. For two
days it blew, capriciously, while the wagons groaned across the
hot current of it. One morning they discovered a ghost-like range
of mountains to the north-west. Snow-covered, the Bighorns
blended with the sky so that they appeared to be a low mass of
bright cloud. The wind veered north, whetting itself on the
snowpacks.

At Crazy Woman's Fork of the Powder they lumbered
through a wide alley of alkali water, sand-bars and black sedge-
grass. This was the entrance to the mountain country. Quickly,
now, the last landmarks would fall—Clear Fork—Rock
Creek—Lake Smet. Cary treasured the bright image of the pine
country. In two days they would make the sharp transition from
desert to pines, and out of the foothills one morning Young
Woman Creek would curl, looping gracefully around the log-
walled trading post, and for the last time the bullwhackers would
outspan, water stock, pack and repack.

By process of rotation, Bill Orrum had worked up to the head
of the wagon train. He witnessed the apprehension that made a
tighter society of the teamsters with every mile they advanced
along the foothills. He himself had lived too long among Indians
to be more apprehensive in one kind of country than another. Yet
this was a special year, a season for massacre. He would have
felt safer travelling with a riding mule and a pack-animal than in
this lumbering company of bullwhackers and muleskinners.

He was not, like Stockwell, chained to the train for security reasons. His only compulsion was to sell the wagonload of ancient smoothbore muskets he carried, and he began to be impatient to make his deal short of Montana. The rifles weighted him like an anchor, but Stockwell was still evasive about closing with him.

Orrum had scarcely talked to Mark Stockwell since the Uncpapa raid. Stockwell, he sensed, resented his having sided Cary in the matter of strategy. It seemed timely that the trader should jog by the wagon this mid-afternoon with his hat tugged down against the cold north wind and his carbine slanted across his saddle. Orrum kept his gaze on the trader's walnut features; but Stockwell declined to meet his eyes. He kept his thoughts locked behind a hard concentration.

He only half showed himself, thought Orrum, but Orrum was used to close-mouthed men and he could read the language of character as he read a trail. The slant of Stockwell's mouth disclosed a rankling dissatisfaction.

Stockwell's eyes were on the foothills ten miles west. He was staring attentively when the gun-runner said: "Got a minute, Mark?"

Stockwell looked around. "Just about. There's a herd of antelope over west. I'm one trader that's bellyful of jerky."

The mules humping up a long slope, Orrum struck a match for his pipe. "That was quite a ruckus the other night."

"Some of you made it into one."

"Don't blame Sam for being nervy," grinned Orrum. "They had a little taffy-pull down his way last year that still gives him the high-stericks every time he smells warpaint. Fetterman lost eighty-one troopers, didn't he?"

"Eighty and himself—still eighty when it came to Injun savvy."

Orrum pursed his lips and blew a thin pencil of smoke for the wind to shred. "Rushing after them bucks wouldn't have showed much savvy. You're a great one for rushing a thing, Mark. Rushed into trading about the same way, didn't you?"

Stockwell glanced closely at him. "No. Who told you I did?"

"A man that braces an oldtimer like Cary is either a greenhorn or an optimist."

"When it comes to me," Stockwell said, "I'm an optimist. I had a post on the Picketwire. Trapping went to hell and I came up here. Gold and silver are the caper now. I thought I'd done pretty well," he said. "The cash book's fat enough."

"How'd it look this time a year ago?" Orrum saw ill-nature darkening Stockwell's face, then, and he knew he had pushed him just far enough. "You know how it seems to me? Merritt's the man you want to worry about. Not Cary."

"How's that?"

"You get fat on trouble, Mark. Cary gets fat on peace. Merritt's a peacemaker."

A hard smile shaped Stockwell's mouth. "What kind of a peacemaker?" he snorted.

"He's got a good teacher. And Cary's just waiting to make the fort before he outfits for a trek into the Bighorns. And then where'll you be?"

Stockwell glanced back. Cary was not far down the line, working with a wagon which had pulled out for a minor repair.

Orrum sipped enjoyment from the pipe. "Cary and me are a lot alike. Set us down in the desert with a tin cup and a skinning knife and we'd haul in a month later, fat and sassy and loaded with trade goods. Just one reason we'd never make out as pardners. He hates me and I hate him."

Stockwell looked interested. "Why?"

Orrum lifted one shoulder. "Why don't I like sandstorms? They grate on my nerves. So's he."

He did not mention the afternoon in his camp near Cheyenne. He remembered how Sam Cary had taken him by the throat and struck him in the face when he paid him for the rifles. And he recalled a very small thorn that stung like a large one: Cary holding the strip of jerky he had given him, throwing it away when he thought he was not looking, because it was too dirty for a man like him to eat.

Stockwell said testily: "Well, I don't think I've got much to worry about, after the other night. Those Uncpapas aren't down here for nothing. Esconella's promised them heap scalps and powder."

"Be nice," Orrum reflected, "to be in Montana when they start shaking the skin rattles, eh?"

"How am I going to be sure of that? I'm not their keeper."

"You could be partways their keeper. There ain't nothing," Orrum said categorically, "that tickles an Injun like a new rifle. Even an old brass-bound Harper's Ferry. And them rebel Sioux are going to need guns, if they tackle a log-walled post. I could be talked out of these I'm carrying, I reckon."

Orrum saw then the same expression in Mark Stockwell's eyes which he had seen in Cary's the day he paid him for the guns. He wondered what made a man think he was any better than the men he traded with.

Suddenly Stockwell said: "It hasn't come to that, yet, and I hope it won't."

He swung his horse away, but heard Orrum remark: "From now until we hit Fort Greybull, there'll be Injun eyes on us every hour of the day. There was fifteen hundred that cleaned out Fetterman. I wonder how many'll hit us? If you want to make a trade with them, Mark, make it soon."

Near the foothills, Stockwell glimpsed the white rumps of antelope bobbing along. These days he distrusted every coulee and buffalo wallow. But the antelope ranged close. He had a hunger for fresh meat, and he remembered how Gaybird had said at the mess that morning:

"It's not gold that's building this country. It's corned beef!"

When he analysed what Orrum had been saying, his mind veered away. But the sight of Gaybird on the seat of the dearborn, handling her greys expertly, brought a slow crawl of gooseflesh up his back. She, and the other dozen-odd women of Fort Greybull, were the chief factor in Orrum's plan which he could not rationalize.

And beyond that she was a provocation to him. He was not used to being stood off by women, but he had had little enough encouragement out of Gaybird Phillips. The disturbing part of it was that it did not seem to be coyness.

As he pulled frowningly off the line of march, he turned in the saddle on hearing her voice. The rising wind sang across the pocket of his ear, but again he heard her call his name. He rode over and set the bit into his horse's jaws beside the wagon.

"Don't tell me," he smiled, "you've finished that shirt for me already!"

She had let the wind have its way; her bonnet hung by the ribbon, the dust dulling her burnished black hair.

"I've almost finished the cuffs," she said. "Did you want it with a dickey or a full bosom?"

Stockwell pondered. "I'd like to think about that before I decide." He smiled into the black-lashed grey eyes and tried to decide whether there was design behind her calling him.

"I notice you saw my antelope," she observed. "I'd give anything to be asked to the mess of a man who'd shot an antelope."

The trader let his grin come and said enthusiastically: "Be careful you aren't stuck with a promise, Miss Gaybird. I'm on the trail of an antelope fillet right now!"

Gaybird's glance touched Sam, down the line of wind-whipped freight-wagons. It came back valiantly.

"Would you like to make a bet with me?" she inquired.

"What's that?"

"That I drop my antelope before you do."

"If you can hit one from here," Stockwell declared, "you've missed your calling. You should be with the hunters."

"I wasn't meaning to kill one from here. I thought of going with you."

Stockwell solemnly leaned on the swell of his saddle. "If you meant that," he said, "I'd carry you in my arms or drag you on a travois. Which will it be?"

"I told you not to be surprised if I started wearing feathers in my hair. When I hunt with Sam, I wear deerskin trousers. You wouldn't be offended? Then if you'll persuade one of your hunters to trade places with me, I'll take his horse and go along."

Stockwell's eyes found Cary. He took a deep breath and said: "Pull out here and change. I'll have a horse for you in ten minutes."

The wind freshened, gaining force with the regular late afternoon breeze, hurling grit before it so that the advance was slowed. Alamosa Creek was only two miles farther. Cary kept the wagons shoving for it. In a few minutes Stockwell was back with Coy Mullan. Sourly resentful at the exchange, Mullan took over the dearborn and relinquished his horse. Stockwell shortened the stirrups. Gay had changed to a man's grey flannel shirt and deerskin trousers. She carried her .44 calibre buggy rifle.

As they were pulling away, Cary ranged in, a blue polka-dot bandanna pulled up to his eyes.

"If I'm not inquisitive," he said, "which one of you has lost his mind?"

Gaybird laughed. "We've lost our taste for jerky, that's all. Did you see the antelope?"

"Naturally. But they're drifting towards the foothills. They'll be out of range before you reach them."

Stockwell buttoned the collar of his shirt, smiling at Cary's pique. "We'd hardly be a mind to follow them to Cloud Peak. If we don't drop one this side of the hills, we'll give up."

"You don't really mind?" Gaybird queried.

Cary looked into her face, testily. He turned the roan. "Don't get out of sight of the wagons," he said crisply. He rode to the head of the train, keeping his gaze on the crossed braces of John Silvertooth, who rode his mule by the lead wagon. But he spat, once, with some force, at a rock.

A laugh in her eyes, Gaybird rode towards the hills with Stockwell.

"We'd best step it up," Stockwell suggested presently. "We don't want to pack the carcass too far."

Gaybird touched the bay with her heels and they loped along a side hill. He stopped on the crest to shade his eyes against the sun, searching north and south among the foothills. The wind blew so that he had to cup his hand about his mouth to make her hear.

"We'll get a shot at them from the next rise. Then we'd better go back. I don't like this wind."

Against the wind avalanching across the hills they descended to a shallow valley. Stung by driving sand, the horses restively whipped their heads. Stockwell grasped his rifle across the lock to keep sand from fouling the breech. A slotted dollar which hung on the lanyard of his stetson he slipped up snugly under his chin.

They jogged through black sage and worked into a cleft between two hummocks, coming to an apron sloping down from the hills. The mountains were now hidden in dust, but near them shapes moved in their direction.

Stockwell touched her arm, but Gaybird cried abruptly: "I see them!" She dismounted, letting him hold her horse. The wind was right. Moving with it, the antelopes would pass a few rods ahead of them.

Gaybird allowed the animal she had picked to approach into easy range. She raised the gun, then, but the wind blew against her so massively that the barrel wavered. Still holding her breath, she waited for a lull. She exclaimed in impatience.

Stockwell already had his gun at his cheek. His shot roared off and an antelope fell. He dropped the reins of Gaybird's pony and rode out to claim it. It lay slowly raising and lowering its head. He knelt to slit its throat and went to the skinning.

Gaybird rode up. "Cincinnati's ruined me," she said mournfully.

A biting cold sharpened the wind. It passed over them with a tumbling roar. Looking back, Gaybird could not see the gap through which they had ridden. She turned up the collar of her shirt, but shivered.

As Stockwell lifted the carcass on to the neck of the horse he suddenly halted and stood rigidly. He remained that way for several seconds. Then abruptly he said:

"Well, that's it." He mounted and gave her pony a whack on the rump which sent it loping down the long slope into the ragged clouds of dust. He did not look at Gay. He had his eyes focused on the blind shroud of dust and he crowded his pony hard. After five minutes she said:

"Mr. Stockwell, I don't think this is the right way."

"Neither do I," he said. "But we're not going to hunt for it."

He said that grimly and halted an instant to listen. He altered their course to the left, what she imagined to be about northeast, and they rode again at a lope. At last they came on to a hogback. A slope lay before them. Beyond it, they could make out nothing. The prairie was lost in a cold, sweeping fog of dust.

Stockwell took his case-knife and cut a slab of meat from the antelope, which he tied to the saddle with a rawhide string. He threw the rest of the carcass away then smiled at Gaybird.

"This comes of yearning for civilized doings. We'll have our antelope, but we may eat it raw."

She tried to keep her voice firm. "Are you lost, too?"

"Not exactly lost," he said. "I know where I am, but it's not where I want to be."

As he started on, she said: "Hadn't we better fire a gun? They'll surely hear us, sooner or later."

The trader's eyes evaded hers. "We'll try that later."

Terror lurked at her elbow. She raised her rifle stubbornly and cocked it. "Later will be too late. I'm going to fire."

Stockwell put his hand on the breech of the gun and shook his head, smiling a little though his eyes were solemn. "I wouldn't," he said. "I saw an Indian pony back there. I don't know where the buck was, but I have an idea he was following those antelope, too."

End of Part Five

Part Six

XVIII

THE WIND WRESTLED with the wagons as they sidled from the backbone of the ridge in the bosque of Alamosa Creek. Sharp hills crumpled north and south. The wind was a gigantic force rushing headlong from the mountains. It tore the canvas from a Murphy wagon and ripped it lengthwise before Silvertooth and a muleskinner succeeded in folding it. It thrust mercilessly at the wagons and the shambling mules and oxen.

Cary rode back from selecting the camp-site on the bank of the creek. A large and hoary cottonwood had nearly fallen on him. The growth here belonged both to mountain and prairie—cottonwoods and quaking ash, with a tough undergrowth of chokecherry and haw. A few yards back from the stream the ground was barren of all but sage. Here Cary shouted the wagons into formation beyond the range of falling trees. He had not seen such a wind in six years.

While he was finishing this chore he saw Coy Mullan removing the collars from Gaybird's team. He watched curiously. Then he rode over to discover why the Montanan had usurped this job which he generally saved for himself.

Mullan turned the horses loose. He stood awaiting Cary, a collar on each shoulder. His face was brick-red from the scour of sand. The dogged ill-humour he always showed Cary was diluted to-night with apprehension.

"Seen Mark?" he asked quickly.

"I saw him leaving to chase antelope. He must have—"

Mullan woodenly stared back at him. "I thought— I figured they'd tied on to another wagon and rode in—"

113

"You mean they aren't back—good God!" Cary said. He twisted to stare down the wind. "I reckoned they were back before the big blow started."

Mullan let the collars slide down and turned his head to regard the back trail, shrouded in a torn gauze of dust—cold, sweeping, impenetrable. He said thickly: "Blowing like hell—I said to myself it was plumb chancy."

Cary pivoted the horse on its hind legs and loped for the creek. Silvertooth was here, bossing the watering of stock. Cary drove up through the brush and trees, traversing the tangle of oxen, mules and horses.

"Have you seen them?" he shouted.

"Seen who?" Silvertooth demanded.

"Stockwell and Gaybird. They dropped out three hours ago."

Silvertooth closed his eyes for an instant, as if to see the problem better. "They'll be bogged in sand. Everybody with a horse had better get to riding."

Cary wiped his mouth with his palm. "Leave the stock with a couple of men and bring the rest to the south rim. I'll meet you there."

Silvertooth assembled every man who owned a horse or riding mule. They gathered near Gaybird's wagon and Cary came from studying the veiled hillside beyond the wagons. He mounted and looked for Dunavan. The Irishman's truculent face met his stare in the crowd of men who had straggled over with the horsemen. Dunavan was hatless and carried a coiled bullwhip over his shoulder.

Cary pointed at him. "Dunavan, it's you with the wagons again. Don't give me any talk! Keep the men under the wagons and on the look-out. Now, listen—all of you. This will be like a hunt in a cave. One man won't be able to see another, and we won't have any cord to pay out. Dunavan will fire a shot every two minutes. Doctor Merritt, will you help him load? We'll move until the reports fade. Then we'll leave a man there to fire at the same interval. We'll post three men that way. That will give us an area a mile wide and a couple of miles long we can cover. Range around all you like, as long as you can still hear a gun. But remember that if you get out of earshot, you're lost, too."

Dunavan had no answer for him, neither in his mouth nor in his eyes. But Cary saw a curious look of tranquillity in the homely features. He wished he were the kind of man you could explain things to. He would have liked him to know that there were men going out to search whom he would not have trusted with the care of the wagons.

The wind was an intemperate brawler, shouting and shoving at them. It grew colder and darker. They would not have over two hours of light. Presently, as they rode, a muffled rifle-report came from the wagons. They drifted a quarter-mile farther before Cary raised his hand. He posted a man here and they loped on.

In this way they posted two men. The wild-eyed plan began to seem feasible. It was not until a half-hour later, when the last relay was posted and he was riding alone through a screaming midnight of sand, that Cary began to accept the fact that a rider could pass within a hundred feet of him and never know it.

He stopped then and closed his eyes, praying in a tight and frozen way.

Dunavan waited until the horsemen had vanished into the blind dusk of the sandstorm. He stood looking after them, a knotty-shouldered, sandy-haired giant. Old sweat-rings, crusted with salt, patterned his grey cotton shirt. His large hand covered the breech of the side-hammer Sharps. As the time came to fire, he raised the gun in his right hand and squeezed the trigger.

Doctor Merritt took the Sharps from his hand and handed him the extra gun. His wife stood against the freight wagon near them, a mute horror in her eyes. Merritt pinched the primer on to the nipple of the gun, rammed home a charge and dropped a ball down the barrel. Dunavan shook his head.

"Save the lead next time. If I need a ball, I'll drop one in."

Watching the Irishman, Dale asked tensely: "Is there any chance of finding her?"

"Good chance," Dunavan stated.

Merritt glanced at his wife. "Worried about the girl, my dear? Or one of the men?"

Dale had had her share of innuendo ever since the night at Fort Reno, and she had a sudden, wild impulse to strike at him. "I'm worried about all of them, of course,'' she said angrily.

Dunavan fired another shot. He handed the gun to Merritt with a sardonic grin. ''Fine work for a man that's served in the infantry, eh? Shooting blanks.''

Merritt smiled. ''In my own way, I've been shooting blanks for years. It gets to be a habit.''

''A habit I wouldn't care to git.''

Watching him load, Dunavan said abruptly: ''Drop a ball in that'n. I'll be back in two minutes. Fire one if I'm late.'' He ran off through the choking dust to his own wagon, grubbed in a box and found jerky and hardtack. He seized his canteen, checked his powder- and ball-flasks and secured a rifle from a rack on one of the other wagons. He ran back. Merritt was preparing to fire the gun.

''Go on!'' Dunavan grinned. The doctor did, took the recoil with some surprise, and butted the gun against the ground to reload. ''Mrs. Merritt,'' smiled Dunavan, ''do you reckon you could load for him?'' Elation burned in his eyes.

''Of course, but—''

''No buts, Mrs. Merritt. Cary's jackassed me around so long with his if's and but's that they make me sick. You load for the doctor. I'm going for a hike.''

Merritt said forcefully: ''Man, you'll be lost! Why, you haven't even a horse!''

''A good foot-soldier,'' said Dunavan, ''has got no use for a horse anyhow. This is one fight I'm in on.''

Merritt called again, and then was silent as the big man strode away.

He heard Dale saying: ''It's time, Asa.''

Merritt raised the gun and fired. He turned back to her, a smudge of black powder under his eye. ''Does it still seem romantic to you? 'The Great Far West?' ''

''No,'' she said succinctly. ''It seems brutal.''

''And the men who survive are brutal, in their way. Cary, for instance. He's quiet and easy-going, but do you notice how they jump when he opens his mouth? Men like these don't jump for a man they think there's the remotest chance of their shipping. Soldiers don't mutiny, because they're afraid of the brass on their officer's shoulders. But a wagonmaster's brass is in his heart. There's plenty in Cary's. He doesn't have to hold Dunavan down, but he does, as an example to the others. He didn't have to whip Mullan, either, but he did—for the same reason.''

Dale lost a measure of powder to the wind. She put the spout of the powder-flask to the muzzle of the Sharps. "He whipped Mullan," she said, "because he'd made him less than his own master, for once. I thought he'd go crazy before Gaybird came around.''

"I didn't notice that. He seemed quite self-possessed.''

"He'd always seem that way, if you didn't look for the signs.''

"As an artist would?''

Dale's fingers hesitated as she raised the ramrod. She looked at him quickly. Then she thrust it firmly into the barrel of the gun. "I supposed you'd found the picture. I hope you haven't been so absurd to build a story around it.''

"I might not have, except that someone else seemed to be afraid I would, and tore it up.''

She met his gaze candidly. "That was Cary. He wanted me to do his portrait, to give to Gaybird. But then he began to worry about what you might think.''

Angrily, his long face rutted with harsh lines, Merritt laid his hand on her arm. He did not relax the pressure of his fingers until she flinched.

"My dear," he said sardonically, "you are undoubtedly the most artful liar the Lord ever put here to plague the soul of a man. But it seems to me Cary is the type of man to think of such a possibility first. It was your idea to paint him, wasn't it?''

She looked at the watch. "You've missed your cue, Asa.''

Merritt fired the gun. Dale took it from his hands and he picked up the reloaded musket. "All right," she said. "It was my idea. What of it? I painted Cary for the same reason I might have painted any other colourful desert type. In Mexico it was *cargadores*; in Wyoming it's whackers and skinners.''

Merritt's gaze pierced her arch coolness. His deep-socketed eyes had an angry thrust. "I wouldn't quite compare him to a peasant," he said. "Peasants haven't time for flirtations.''

She said angrily: "Flirtation! Asa, if you say one more word—''

Merritt let the muzzle of the gun touch her breast, a smudge of powder marking the cloth. "There's really only one more word to be said, isn't there?"

She pressed back against the wagon wheel, her lips bloodless. "Yes," she said. "That you apologize to me for this whole, ridiculous accusation. I'm standing out here letting the sand ruin what's left of my complexion, and you badger me like a naughty child."

"No," he said. "Children are only naughty about unimportant things. Your naughtiness involves things like a man's self-respect. You let me quit my practice for you. You prodded me into turning myself into a shabby political hack to give you the prestige a country doctor's wife couldn't have. And now I haven't even the satisfaction of being necessary to people! I'm a joke to every junior consul's clerk. And you cap it by making a fool of me in front of a company of sixty-five men!"

The gun-barrel was thrusting into her breast. Suddenly she cried out and slipped away. She dropped the flasks and began to run. The gun leaped in Merritt's hands. The report rolled briefly before it died in the wind. Dale looked back, clutching the side of a wagon. But the doctor had turned his back on her and fired between the wagons.

XIX

THE WIND RATTLED pebbles and tumbleweeds up the slope where Gaybird stood with Stockwell. The horses, tailed up to the wind, gave them some shelter. The trader retained both sets of bridle reins under his foot while he uncapped a canteen. Gaybird drank a little and returned it.

"You aren't so civilized," he remarked. "A city girl would have emptied it."

She smiled abstractedly. She kept remembering what he had said about the Indian pony.

Behind them, the shore of sage and rocks slid away to dissolve in fog. Stockwell offered a piece of hardtack. She shook her head.

Almost petulantly, she declared: "They should know we're lost by now!"

"Likely they do. But what can they do about it until the storm blows itself out? That'll be dawn. By then we can find our own way."

She made no reply. Stockwell reached back and fingered sand and perspiration from the inside of his collar. "Besides," he said, "if he were any kind of husband he wouldn't have let you go riding with a strange trader."

She was shocked out of her worries. "Husband? Where did you hear that?"

His eyes wrinkled in amusement. "I disremember. It's a story that went around. I never cared, one way or the other, until I saw you in Cheyenne."

"And why should you have cared then?"

"For my own good, I shouldn't have cared," Stockwell said. "But I do. I'd give half my trading post to hear you say you weren't married to Sam Cary."

"You aren't likely," she said, "to hear me say anything about it. It seems an awfully personal thing to be shouting in a sandstorm, doesn't it? What if the wind should die? They'd hear us all the way to Colorado."

"The way the wind is blowing, Wyoming must be in Colorado by now anyhow. Personally, I'm going to take a chance. I'm going to say that when we reach Fort Greybull, I'd give anything to have you go on with me."

He saw her lips begin to smile, wearily but with amusement. "I don't know whether you're being indecent or ridiculous," she told him.

Stockwell smiled. "I'm being practical. I know what you'll say—you own half the post. But you could sell your interest to Cary. If protecting an investment means anything, you'll do it. Not to mention protecting yourself. I've got a hope, Gaybird, but it's a little undernourished one. Still be a while growing yet. So I'm not talking about marriage right now. What I'm suggesting is that you get out before the tribes smear blood over this Bozeman road so thick the trail will run red for a century. There'll be a war fought here; a last-ditch war. The troopers will win, of course. But when?''

He had become very sober. He went on frowningly:

''That's the big question. The ones who guess wrong will die for it. That's why I'm saying—take your money out of the post, Gay. Invest in Butte or Bannock. But don't go too far,'' he implored, ''because a man can ride just so far with a box of candy on his lap.''

A little sadly, she said: ''I'm afraid I may go quite a distance.''

''You don't mean East?''

''Yes, I do. It hasn't worked out the way I'd hoped it would. Perhaps the country has disappointed me.''

''Perhaps,'' Stockwell suggested, ''someone else has disappointed you.''

Her glance was sharp. ''You mean Sam, don't you?''

''I might mean Sam. Assuming you two were married, it probably would seem unnecessary that he should spend so much time around the Merritt wagon.''

She was suddenly angry with him, but just then his whole face changed, hardening quickly, and she knew he was looking behind her. He took her hand and thrust the bridle reins into it. Taking them, she turned to follow his glance.

An Indian with his head tucked against the wind was riding from the twilight of driven sand. A red flannel headband crossed his forehead and a long rifle lay across his wooden saddle. The tail of a prairie cock fluttered on his head.

Drawing his rifle from the scabbard, Stockwell moved aside two yards and took his stance. He brought the gun up and took slow and bitter aim. Abruptly Gaybird gasped:

''No! Talk to him first . . .''

She could not become adjusted to this slaughtering of a people she had known all her life. The moccasins she wore had been made by Sioux; her leather riding habit had been tanned by a squaw's hands. Stockwell's vast contempt of the notion was in the disciplining gaze he gave her. Again he squinted across the sights. Tugging the ponies along, Gaybird reached him and lifted the barrel of the gun.

He wrenched away. "I know what I'm doing, Gay!"

The brave had seen them. He was within fifty feet, a young Oglala wearing high leggings and a breech-clout. Gaybird awaited him with her hand raised in the sign of peace. She said to Stockwell.

"He's wearing no paint and he hasn't even a lance. He's hunting, the same as we were."

"Hunting scalps or antelope, whichever comes to hand," Stockwell snapped.

Gaybird faced him. "If you kill him we'll all be sorry. Now, try to smile."

The Indian appeared to know he was at a disadvantage. Both his bow and dogskin quiver were on his back, his rifle was uncocked, while the white man was ready to fire. He sat his horse while Gaybird called to him again, using the Oglala tongue.

"I am the daughter of Silent-Walker, Crazy Dog's friend. We come with a peace-talker from the Uncle. We are lost from our train. We seek the camp at Alamoss Creek."

The Indian made no sign of understanding. Presently he called back: "Silent-Walker is dead. All white friends of Crazy Dog are dead."

"Silent-Walker's daughter is not dead. Long Rifle is not dead. Soon Long Rifle will come to Crazy Dog with talk of peace."

Stockwell made a sound in his throat. "If he's crazy enough to swallow all that, he's too crazy to guide us anywhere."

The Indian kicked his pony into motion. He was a young, hawk-faced brave with shallow dark eyes and raisin-brown skin. He had the strong physique of his tribe. Halting the pony near Gaybird, he took a wooden cup from his saddle and dropped it at her feet. Gaybird picked it up. She said to Stockwell:

"Heavens, what can I give him? It's a good-will present."

She found a small mirror in the pocket of her skirt. Stockwell growled: "Not a looking-glass, for the Lord's sake! They've learned to signal with them."

"They've also learned to primp with them. This is the best luck we could have had."

The brave handled the mirror. He grinned and carefully put it into his pocket. He said something, and Gaybird turned quickly, the force of the wind striking her in the face. It made her gasp as she told Stockwell.

"He'll take us to the camp."

For nearly an hour they trailed the Sioux. Finally he reined up. He appeared indecisive. Taking a new bearing, he veered left. For another fifteen minutes they worked along. The darkness thickened now; the cold increased, so that Gaybird never stopped shivering. Fear came with the cold; even Indians could be lost in sandstorms.

Suddenly the brave brought his horse around sidewise and turned his ear to the wind. Gaybird listened: after a moment there was the flat thud of a rifle.

The Sioux spoke to Gaybird. She fired her own rifle and there was another shot and then a faint shout. Swinging his horse, the Oglala crowded it up the bank. He waved his arm. "Your friends come." She tried to talk him out of going back, promising food and tobacco, but he shook his head.

Gaybird watched him knee the pony away from the bank, and then turned to cry into the wind.

There was a shattering roar behind her. She whirled. Lowering his rifle, Stockwell met her glance gravely, a big, tired, deeply burned man. He said: "I'm sorry, Gay. It was him or the whole train. He'd've brought them down on us sooner or later . . ."

She looked up and saw the empty saddle of the pony as it loped off.

When Dunavan strode up to her a few minutes later, she was seated on the ground, crying. The bullwhacker staggered a little as he slid down the bank. He had done all his searching without a horse and his great loose shoulders sagged. He looked down at Gaybird and squeezed her shoulder with one hand, and then looked up at Stockwell, who stood near the dead Oglala.

Stockwell's eyes stubbornly met the whacker's. "I had to kill him," he stated. "We met him in the foothills and he brought us in. But he'd've gone back for his brothers if I'd let him, now that he knew where we were."

"You mean you let him guide you in and then killed him?" Dunavan demanded after a moment.

Stockwell's brow corrugated with ill nature. "Don't talk like a pilgrim. If I hadn't killed him, we'd have had forty Sioux to kill before dark. Where are the wagons?"

Dunavan turned his back and walked to Gaybird. "Little lady," he said, "don't never go hunting with a greenhorn again. This is hell—pure hell."

XX

CARY HAD APPOINTED rendezvous for seven o'clock. That time came and they met where the third sentry was stationed. Their faces were raw with the burnishing of the sand and Cary saw that his rifle-stock had been scoured clean. There was no word of Stockwell and Gaybird. Cary counted searchers and they were all present. It was as he finished the count that a rifle hammered near by. But its direction was east; not north, where the sentry was stationed. They looked blankly at each other. Then there was a sudden rush to horses and they were all swerving into saddles.

At this instant a horse bucked through the driving sand. It was Stockwell's big bay. Just behind shambled a large, grey-shirted man who led another horse, and in the saddle of this one was Gaybird.

It did not register with Sam that Dunavan was supposed to be in camp. He did not hear what Stockwell, ruefully shaking his head, said to him. He saw Gaybird holding the saddle-horn with both hands and crying. He put an arm out and she leaned towards him. He caught her about the waist and lifted her against him. The wind blew her hair across her face. For a moment he held it against his face with his hand.

She moved, helping him to adjust her weight. She held on to him with both arms about his neck, murmuring something he could not hear. As he started back, she looked at him, her eyes filled, but her lips beginning to laugh.

"Why, Sam! You look almost—emotional!"

"Emotional?" Sam said. And then there was nothing in him but a fluid feeling of gladness. He held her with one arm and rode through the gang of men crowding before them.

Somewhere short of camp he got ahead of them. He rode into the wagons and bawled:

"*Safe!*" He let her stand by the horse while the teamsters came from the embrasures between wagons. A skinner brought coffee. Gaybird held the tin cup and tried to tell them what had happened. Sam saw her exhaustion and turned his horse over to a whacker.

He put his arm around her waist and led her along the wagons. Presently she stopped. "Sam, I don't want to sound like an Easterner, but I think you'll have to carry me."

He carried her past the sand-scoured freight wagons to the dearborn. It had been guyed to a cottonwood log to prevent it from capsizing. She let her head lie on his shoulder.

"Are you glad you found me?" she said. "You haven't said so."

"Any time I look emotional," Cary told her, "you can figure I'm glad about something. Or mad. Right now I'm both. When you've got your strength back, I'm going to spank you, the way your father would."

He carried her up the ladder and deposited her on the bed in the dark wagon. He stood there above her, his body and his mind at war. Something in him cried, *Gaybird, Gaybird!* He started to go to his knees beside the bed, but some essential logic turned him aside, to grope for the lamp.

He struck a match, screwed the flame down and set the lamp on the floor, where it would not tip over. Standing there, he looked unnaturally tall.

She lay with her hands under her head, smiling up at him. She was aware that she must look small and shapely and helpless in this position. She said: "Weren't you going to say something, Sam?"

"My immortal horse-sense," said Sam, "has kept me out of more mischief than any man's got a right to be kept out of. Sometimes it spoils my fun. But I always see where it was right, finally."

She hesitated, and then said quietly: "Perhaps this is our answer, Sam."

"Answer to what?"

"To where I should live. Could this be the country's way of letting me know I don't belong any more?"

Cary closed his fist and opened it and saw the fine grooves of his nails. "If you're going to go by the weather," he said, "to-morrow will be the finest day you've seen since you left Wyoming."

Gaybird smiled. He saw the clean whiteness of her teeth. "Sam, you're not arguing that I should stay?"

"I'm saying that you shouldn't hold the weather against us. They have weather in the East, too. But you're right. I'm glad you see it. The country hammers you into its own shape, sooner or later."

She was silent, thinking that a man must be obtuse who confused the effects of a sandstorm and a red-head. She saw him go to the ladder and step through. She said with a frown:

"Make Stockwell tell you about—about the Oglala."

"What Oglala?"

"He'll tell you. And don't let yourself be any more emotional with him than you've been with me, will you?"

There were all the tasks to sweat through which had been dropped earlier.

Cold dinner was eaten at nine o'clock, the wind, which was now dropping, being still too strong for open fires. In a small fire-hole lined with rocks, coffee was boiled for all hands. When Sam took coffee to Gaybird he found her asleep, all but hidden under her blankets. He watched her a while, full of the sharp sweetness a man feels who sees someone he loves snug and safe.

To-morrow. To-morrow, he thought, I can think it through. There won't be many more to-morrows, the way her thinking is going.

He joined the other searchers in the shelter of a tall freight trailer. Stockwell was talking loudly. The men slouched against the wagon or squatted, and one man sat with his back to a wheel. Somewhere Dunavan had found whisky. He tucked the bottle in his hip pocket as Cary entered the circle.

"I expect you'll be disciplining me for deserting my post?" Dunavan said.

"This isn't the army," Cary said wearily. He brought his hand out of his pocket and tossed something to Dunavan. "For valour," he said. Dunavan looked at the gold piece. "Bite it," Cary suggested.

Dunavan flipped it back to him. He wanted to say something devastating, but he was too drunk. He made a loose, jeering smile.

"To-morrow," Cary sighed, "you'll kick yourself across the corral for this. Stockwell, Gaybird said to ask you about an Indian."

Dunavan's eyes flashed to Stockwell in the sudden quiet. "Ah, yes! Mr. Stockwell's Injun. Tell him about your Injun, Mr. Stockwell."

Stockwell's face was ruddy with punishment of the storm. "I had to kill an Indian out there," he admitted. "I'll tell you about it to-morrow. I'm out on my feet."

There was a vacancy in Cary. "You killed a Sioux?"

Stockwell flared. "There ain't so few Oglalas hereabouts that one or two can't be spared."

John Silvertooth, having already heard it, gloomily watched their old dislike rising. "They ain't like coyotes," he said. "They don't just wander off and the village forget about them."

"Where'd he jump you?" Cary asked. His breathing was quick and shallow. He put a hand on the side of the wagon, his fingers gouging mutely at the wood.

"He didn't, exactly. We bumped into each other and Gaybird talked him into guiding us in. On the way they jabbered about how many wagons and men we had, and—Thunder!" he said, "if we'd ever made it to Fort Greybull after this boy went back for the rest—"

Cary's arm pushed Dunavan aside and he went for Stockwell. Caught by surprise, Stockwell took the fist on the side of his head. He went down among the legs and boots of the teamsters. Sam went in as though to trample him.

Silvertooth's body struck from the side and pinned him against the wagon. Dunavan and another man seized Cary's arms; Stockwell was up, throwing his hat aside and driving for Cary. Coy Mullan got in front of him, shouting.

Cary's fury leaked out of him, leaving him exhausted, flaccidly regarding the thing which had driven him to fury. So close to it! So close to smoking the peace-pipe with Crazy Dog, he and Merritt; so near to a real peace. And now a blunderer and a murderer had blown the whole thing to the sky. An Indian wasn't an Indian, to his tribe: he was a neighbor, a son, a husband. But as long as white men regarded them as half-tamed animals there would be wars.

Stockwell was tamed by the weight of bullwhackers. He strained, his face warped in irrational fury. Then the colour left his face and he was a turbid grey.

"All right, I killed a buck," he said. "It's always open season on us; but we've got to let them have first shot before we knock one over, eh?"

"He guided you in," Cary said. "He saved your life. You wouldn't have killed him, in Montana. Up there you'd have been the one they retaliated against. Down here, it's me."

Stockwell's anger showed flat and sullen. "When a man's been through what I have to-day, he doesn't worry much about whether he's in Wyoming or Montana."

"It's done," Silvertooth growled. "We'll know in a day or two how much harm's been done. The next move is theirs."

Cary pushed away from the wagon. Overhead, stars shone weakly. The wind was falling. To-morrow would be fair.

"No," he said. "The next move is ours."

Stockwell's gaze was ironic. "What's it going to be?"

"I wish I knew. But we won't leave this camp till this is squared. I can tell you this much right now: you're going to be in it up to your eyeballs."

XXI

CARY MOVED ABOUT the chilly dawn, adding his own small clatter to the sleepy camp-noises. A rosy haze marbled the sky. Through a gap in the wagons stock-tenders goaded weary oxen towards the trees. An axe bit cheerfully into a cottonwood log.

Dunavan, red braces crossed over his undershirt, sang in a cracked bass as he made repairs on a worn boot with a piece of wire.

> *"In Eighteen Hundred and Forty-one,*
> *I put me corduroy britches on—"*

A light breeze scurried by with breath of moist, dried grasses, and coolness. It was the apology of the prairie for its drunken uproar of the day before. Cary accepted it gratefully.

He liked the normality of this starting day. People and things ought to do what they did well. Breezes should bless and rain fall where it was wanted. Indians ought to hunt where they had promised, hunt in the joyful, childlike, bragging way of their race. *My brothers, there was evil magic in this wind. A white buffalo charged my horse. I threw my lance, and where his blood dripped* . . .

But the young brave lying on the prairie would not make his half-believed lies for the village, because a white man had broken the word of all white men who had agreed to let the Sioux hunt unmolested on the Bozeman road.

Crazy Dog, peaceable man that he was, would come out of his smoky lodge to balance the scales for this murder. And he would learn of it soon, for the brave would be searched for and found, near the fires of Sam Cary's wagon-camp.

Indian jurisprudence was elemental. An eye for an eye. That suited Cary, so long as it was the murderer's eye. But it did not suit him to have his own men bothered because of a Montanan's treachery.

He went gloomily about his chores, saw Mrs. Merritt appear from the ambulance and heard Gaybird stirring, and in a few minutes observed men abandoning their soft pre-breakfast voices and manners as the wagon-camp came masculinely to life.

An obscure impulse caused him to inspect his face in a mirror. He had not shaved since they hit the dry-camp stretches. The eyes of the watcher in the mirror disapproved of the reddish-brown stubble on his face, growing soft with length. They saw the fringe of untrimmed hair about his ears.

Cary turned away, frowning. Seeing Silvertooth carrying a blue tar-bucket to a wagon with a giant rear wheel slipped, he walked over and watched him swab the dry spindle. "Swap you a haircut and shave," he said.

"Are we laying over?"

"Might be."

Silvertooth had barber implements in his possible-sack. He brought them and a kettle of hot water and Sam sat on a crate. Silvertooth knotted a dishtowel about his neck and began to trim.

"Only two reasons why a bullwhacker would want a haircut," he said. "To please a woman or an Injun. You were whistling when you got up. And Gaybird's singing this minute."

"It's a beautiful morning," Sam pointed out.

Silvertooth's scissors whispered. "Then you're primping for an Injun. For such greasy specimens, they ask a lot of a white man. He ought to shave and keep his hair cut if he wants to talk to them. You're not fixing to talk to them, are you?"

"Somebody's got to. I'd rather I told Crazy Dog about this than that he told me."

Silvertooth's razor traversed his jaws with its papery rasp. Cary rinsed his face and heard Gaybird clanging a kettle to signal breakfast. They went to the fire, where she manipulated a giant skillet, smoking with corned beef and potatoes. Her brush had drawn the richness from her hair until the braids were blue-black.

After breakfast Dunavan sauntered over. "Some of us," he said, "have an idea them thimbles would last longer if we swabbed the sand out of the axles."

"Why don't some of you do it, then?"

The Irishman frowned like a man anxious to prove some point. "I had an idea Stockwell would be drifting across the wind yesterday, too, hunching away from the hills. But if I'd followed the orders of my betters, they'd have missed us completely."

"Dunavan," Cary said gravely, "did I ever say you weren't a man of ideas? It was a grand idea when you signed on with me. Just so our ideas don't conflict too often, you and I'll make out. Do you have an idea where we could find the Indian Stockwell shot?"

"If he ain't been drifted over." Dunavan's small, irascible eyes watched him curiously.

"Saddle a horse, then. We've got to do for him."

While Dunavan secured a horse, Cary made a circuit of his wagons, passing the word along to slip wheels and dig out the grit packed into the hubs. Doctor Merritt was eating in the shade of the ambulance, lank and unshaven. He had a nod for Cary, and that was all. If there were a key to the secret door called Asa Merritt, Cary thought, he must find it soon. But you could not help a man who refused to be helped. He thought of Merritt's bitter eyes brooding over the fragments of the portrait Dale had painted; his mind writhed away from the implications of it.

A trailer had split a tongue in the last rough mile yesterday. Cary watched the spare tongue unslung from beneath the wagon, while the blacksmith heated bolts. Moving along, he caught a flash of motion near the trees and saw Dale beckoning him.

Did a red-head never learn? he wondered. It was in his mind to ignore her. Then, glancing with close but casual inspection at the man beside the ambulance, he went to her.

"Not looking for a prairie flower to pose for you, I hope?" he said.

"It wouldn't be the same one, I promise!" Dale's smile came and went. There was a tight nervousness in her. "Sam, will you *please* say something to Asa about that picture? He's driving me crazy."

"Say 'something?' " Cary repeated. "It had better be the right thing, girl! I'd need to be a peace envoy myself, to handle this."

She raised her chin, a faint and petulant challenge in her face. "After all, you helped me get into trouble. It isn't too much to help me out."

Cary's eye underwent a chilling. "That sounds like something out of a back room in Cheyenne. You asked me to take you, Dale. Let's not forget that, nor who did the picture."

She glanced away, her hand slowly rubbing her arm. It had been a frightened gambit, and it dissolved miserably. "I don't blame you. But he frightens me! I'm sorry. Yesterday, after Dunavan left, he threatened to kill me—"

Cary held his breath and then gustily blew it out.

"He mustn't see us talking," she said hastily. "But I had to tell you. He told me he'd found the picture. He was determined to make something of it. I—I don't know what you can say. Just tell him I did it to tease you." She glanced back at the ambulance and caught her breath. "He's seen us! Say it was a joke, Sam— but then you were worried about what he'd think, and—"

Cary said gloomily: "Some advice, Mrs. Merritt: stick to wild flowers after this."

Dunavan and Cary rode through the yellow bunch grass. Tufts of graze stood on small islands. Where there had been no grass, the earth had been rabbetted away. Within a mile of the wagon-camp they found the Oglala. Half-buried in coarse sand, he lay on his face in a dry wash. Stockwell's bullet had caved in the back of his head. His clothing and ornaments were Oglala. That last, faint hope of Cary's evaporated—that Gaybird had mistaken for Oglala a warrior of another Sioux tribe, an off-limits hunter in Oglala hunting-ground.

They buried him and heaped round, washed boulders over the grave.

Then Cary stood by the grave, gloomily filling his pipe. "One dead Injun seems like a small matter to fight a war over, eh?"

Dunavan moved his shoulders. "We're running in bad company," he said. "That's the trouble with us."

"'The Alamosa Incident,'" remarked Cary. "Stay clear of incidents, Dunavan. That's my recipe for long life in the Indian country."

Dunavan swung on to his horse and put it up the rubbly shelf. He moved a few rods along to a low ridge, and Cary saw him stop, pulling sharply at the reins so that the horse turned broadside. He heard his voice in sharp and anxious command.

"Cary!"

Cary's horse lunged up the bank and stopped beside the teamster's, and sitting his saddle there, he watched them pour down a distant slope beyond the camps—hundreds of horsemen, vivid with the brilliant pigmentation of savagery and annihilation, a painted horde sweeping against the flimsy wagon-fortress beside Alamosa Creek.

End of Part Six

Part Seven

XXII

CARY WATCHED THE Sioux flood out over the prairie, their dust crawling up the sky behind them, the bright fabric of ponies and riders pricked by the flashing of steel. Overflowing into the dun bottomlands of the creek, the war party fluttered on towards the camp.

Cary and Dunavan jolted down the rubbly slope from the bench, cutting back and forth through boulders and clumped sage. The camp lay below and west of them, a close-packed square of grey tilts and weathered boxes. They could see whackers crawling into position beneath the wagons, rifles glinting through a gauze of dust. The corral was a vortex of milling cattle and running men.

Cary's ears picked up the blunt thunder of hoofs, the sharp animal yelping of the riders. *God*, he prayed, *God, if you're in on this, don't let a gun go off!* Give me ten words with this roman-nosed politician before the guns begin to blaze. . . .

Then for a while the camp was hidden by a timbered kink of the stream.

Looking over at Cary, Dunavan was obscurely angry. He saw nothing in Cary's features that he could call fear, and he was resentful of the fact that he himself, knowing they were riding to a pretty sure thing, was sick with unmanly anticipation. He had been through two attacks with the infantry, but never one that fell on you like this one, sudden as a dropped blanket. He did not want to die screaming. His prayer was for bullets in the belly for his enemies, a ball between the eyes for himself.

They came past a peninsula of tall cottonwoods and saw the Indians drawn up above the wagons. The camp seemed to sleep. The Sioux paraded their curvetting ponies back and forth with no visible plan, but Cary saw the order of it and picked out a little group of horsemen slightly ahead of the mass of warriors.

So they were not quite sure they wanted to fight. They desired to mill around for a while, get a white chief to ride out for a parley, and signal the attack by cutting him to pieces before the others.

Cary halted beside the wagons. He saw his teamsters and Stockwell's bellied down behind the wagon-tongues and wheels, and then a ripple of gay cotton cloth came along the line to where he saw his pony. Gaybird appeared at a slot between two of the wagons, carrying a rifle and bandoleer.

Cary spurred his horse around to cover the slot. "Get in your wagon!" he snapped.

She was tensely white, going to her knees beside a vittles box and laying the bandoleer beside her. "Sam, we'll need every gun in camp!"

"Not if you keep out of sight, maybe. Why parade the prize before them?" He saw her reluctantly rise and turn away. "Where's Silvertooth?" he called.

The wagonmaster responded from beneath a wagon. "Present."

"I'm going to make a dicker with them," Cary said. "That's Esconella in the ghost-shirt. Did you pass out the Springfields?"

"Aye. Them things are going to be third-hand before we ever sell them."

Near-by, Stockwell knelt with two rifles at his side and a pair of revolvers. Copper and brass ammunition gleamed in his hat, upside down beside him. Cary spoke as he rode past him.

"This is why I never shoot Oglalas out of season."

Stockwell's blunt brown features were slick with sweat. He said nothing and Sam turned to Dunavan. "You may as well drop off here."

The whacker snorted. "I'm in no hurry to hide, Cary."

"When you are, you won't find much cover out yonder." Cary let the pony carry him through curing yellow grasses towards the Sioux, Dunavan coming up beside him. The Indians had seen them now. Several made little lunging runs with their ponies, hauling them up and shaking lances at the two white men, and from the turmoil of horses five men, dismounted, moved forward.

"See him?" Cary asked.

"See who?"

"The boy in the ghost-shirt. That's him. That's Esconella."

A tall young buck stood out from the others, lithe and dark, with yellow-and-black bars of paint slashing his nose. He wore a breech-clout and deerskin tunic whitened with clay and ornamented with blue beads. It was a ghost-shirt, guaranteed to ward off arrows and bullets. The other men were shirtless, and Cary saw this with grimness: they were in fighting trim.

He reined in and raised his hand. Dunavan did the same, and the Oglala responded, holding a stout elkhorn bow in his hand. Cary saw that all the men with him were young. This was good, from the long-range point of view, bad for the moment. The war-party travelled without the sanction of the elders. But young blood was hot.

Esconella stared in haughty disdain, an arrogant young savage leading more men than many an old chief could summon.

In the Oglala dialect he declared: "Long Rifle's word spills like water. The Grandfather promised wagons would not enter our country."

Cary smiled. "Esconella's word spills too. Our treaty bars only buffalo hunters."

"A trader becomes a hunter when no one looks."

"I buy my buffalo robes from the Sioux, not from hunters. Are you here to trade?"

Esconella had the pupil-less black eyes of a lizard. He looked at one of his lieutenants, who shook his lance and brought the butt of it down on the ground. Cary observed the Oglalas stirring.

"No," Esconella said. "Make big hunt."

"Crazy Dog is not hunting with you?"

"My father-in-law is too sick to hunt. His legs are sick. We are afraid for him."

"Until he's dead, be afraid of him," Cary said. "Do you want to trade with us?" he asked again.

Esconella glanced at a blade-nosed warrior with a robe belted about his middle, and said to him: "Tell them we will go into the wagons to trade."

"I'll trade with the five of you," Cary declared. "The rest will wait where they are."

Dunavan breathed windily through his nose. Cary heard his saddle creak as he moved on it. He saw the dullness of anger film Esconella's eyes. Under the ugly dust of disdain he discovered the chined eagerness of the man. Prestige—he was starving for it. Scalps for his lance—yellow scalps to shake at lesser chiefs when he strode through their villages, proselyting warriors. Stolen rifles and knives . . . a thousand lodges calling him chief, chief among chiefs—it was the young boy's dream of being president, obscenely distorted. He had three red wound-marks on his body, but he could not wear more than a fistful of feathers in his hair, and the bonnet of a great chief must be heavy.

Esconella's expression was a dark taunt. "Are you afraid of us? Of your friends, Long Rifle?"

"If I were afraid of you," Cary said dryly, "then I would let you come into the wagons, because I feared to anger you. Would you let us come into your village? I say you will trade with us as you have always done."

The Oglala looked at the wagons. He weighed something in his mind. He said derisively: "Long Rifle's goods are cheap. We will trade with Owns Lance."

Cary knew then that he did not realize that Mark Stockwell, whom the Sioux called Owns Lance, was with him. He watched Esconella turn, the others turning with him and moving back to their ponies. Cary took a breath, knowing what might happen when he turned his own back.

"Let's go," he told Dunavan tersely.

They turned their horses and jogged for the wagons. There was a sound of weapons rattling, of pony hoofs behind them, but when they reached the camp and looked back the Sioux were moving up the bench in a sluggish tide.

Dunavan blew out his cheeks and touched his wet forehead with his palm. "Now I know where you got your ways of jackassing a man around, Cary."

"He hadn't made up his mind to it, that was all. Did you see their weapons? Columbus must have brought those blunderbusses. The older warriors have the rifles, and the way they got them is the way Esconella would like to. He's trying to nerve himself up to it with this cast-off army of his. He'll make another pass at a train one of these days—maybe ours—and if he catches us washing clothes or watering stock, he won't stop to feint. He'll have his rifles when he gets through."

Here, he thought, reviewing the camp from saddle-height, is the ultimate hunger of the trail—the lust for log walls, a barricade against the blind cruelties of the wilderness.

Of the Oglalas there remained only a memory of brassy dust drifting south, but the teamsters lurked anxiously at their posts, rifle-barrels propped on wagon-tongues.

Cary eased himself out of the saddle. Up the line he saw Stockwell, Mullan and Bill Orrum in a gesticulating congress. Silvertooth crawled from under a wagon, beat the dirt from his pants and shirt and turned to signal Cary. Sam overlooked him and walked by three wagons and a squad of dusty teamsters to come to the dearborn.

He struck the box once with his fist. "Gaybird . . ."

Hands, brown and slender, parted the puckered entrance of the canvas shelter and she stepped on to the ladder.

"You're an obedient child," Cary said.

She leaned forward to the support of his hands, her eyes faded by the sunlight on her face, her hair dark and clean. "You were sharp with me," she reproved. "You've no right being that way with anyone but a wife or a horse."

Her weight was sweet and light, and he held her a moment.

"I thought that seminary was going to educate you," he said, "and here I find you don't even know the fundamentals. You know how many men can dig a ditch in eight hours, but you don't know how many women it takes to start a war."

"How many?"

"One." His hands tried her weight, up and down, and his face went thoughtful. "It's an odd thing. If I knew what made women so important, I'd go to work on the cure for it. 'Old Doctor Cary's Proportionalizer. Restores things to their proper proportions, including women.' "

"Am I out of proportion, Sam?" He had let her down, but she stayed there, peering up at him.

"Sometimes. When you get lost in sandstorms, or fall under a wagon. I wish you'd told me before you came out how complicated you'd become. You used to be simple. You cried when you were unhappy and you laughed when you were having fun. I'll be all summer figuring whether you handle better with a spade bit or a snaffle."

"I think perhaps a snaffle," she suggested.

He pinched her chin. "You'd run wild. Now, flax down to business. I'm going to have a parley with Stockwell and Doctor Merritt. We've got to decide what's next. I think you ought to sit in."

She made her face sober, but the grey eyes kept their merriment. "As your partner?"

"As my partner," he said severely.

XXIII

NOONDAY HEAT, YELLOW flakes of it, sifted over the camp. The bleached earth radiated its cottony warmth, the heated air crowding close as he walked along. The line of saddle-ponies switched wrathfully at tawny flies. He found Bill Orrum drinking deeply out of a bucket, luxuriating in wasting water over his throat and shirt. The trader spat the last mouthful on the ground, where it broke into dusty fragments.

Cary had asked Stockwell, Mullan and Merritt to be under the cottonwoods off the north point of the wagons in ten minutes. He gave the same message to Orrum.

Orrum's bleached-denim eyes kept their distance. "I'm going to follow them Sioux a piece. They may be up to devilry."

"You can do that later. I'd like your notion of what to do about the dead one. You're in this as much as we are."

"Mebbe. Mebbe not. Got a notion to cut loose right now. This outfit's got the Injun sign on it."

"What sign would be on a lone wagon?"

"Injuns damn a man," Orrum lectured, "by the company he keeps."

Cary lifted his shoulders. "Fear or respect—either one will stand them off. Esconella would have struck to-day, if he hadn't been afraid. He's called out his blood brothers in the warrior societies and made his brag. He'll go back as a chief, or he won't go back at all."

"I don't like this setting around," Orrum drawled, "talking instead of travelling. If the bucks have rode south, I'm taking off."

His eyes still found other things to investigate, a tool-box laid open, a slender, grey-clad girl with black plaits moving gracefully towards the trees.

Cary said mildly: "We aren't having trouble over this, Bill. You're loaded to the axles with guns."

Orrum's eyes lashed around in surprise. "Who says?"

"I do. I investigated you one day. Those guns wouldn't be worth a damn to me, but if the Sioux captured them—" His finger tapped Orrum's taut, narrow chest., "We've got Wyoming in this train. For the next year or two she lives or dies by what happens to us. Two hundred rifles, plus our sidearms—probably three hundred or better. If the Sioux knew that, we wouldn't have a show."

"Some fellas," Orrum contended, "would think the guns were enough."

"It all depends on whether you have a chance to fire them. Have your scout, if you want, but don't try to leave the train."

When Cary left the wagons, later, he saw Orrum jogging away on his red mule.

A bucket of water with a dipper floating in it sat by the Y-trunked cottonwood where Gaybird, Doctor Merritt, Coy Mullan and Mark Stockwell were gathered. Stockwell greeted Cary ironically.

"Shall we start the meeting with a prayer?"

"It might be in order."

Gaybird stood apart from Stockwell. Her faint distrust of him had turned to a hearty emotion which was partly a thorough dislike and partly fear. A man who could murder a benefactor, as he had, could commit any crime. With a woman's instinctive pulse-taking of a group, she sensed a collision of wills between Mullan and Stockwell, a force thrusting from the trader, an obstinacy blocking it in Mullan. She saw it once when Stockwell eased himself down on the ground by the tree and the wagon-boss drifted towards the creek to scan the stock, and again in Mullan's refusal to meet the other man's glance.

Cary drank from the dipper. He fanned the excess out across the ground. "I wanted Orrum to sit in on this," he said, "but he's got some idea of scouting. Did he say anything to you about quitting the outfit?"

The creases of Stockwell's buckskin shirt were black with perspiration. His eyes were blandly disinterested. "I tried to talk him out of it. As far as quitting goes, that's on his head."

"And ours. Did you know he's hauling rifles?"

Before him were these two faces which lied so well—the rough, trail-burned countenances of Stockwell and Coy Mullan. He watched them both, hearing the trader's modulated: "No!" and then seeing Coy Mullan's face turn away as he rose from his heels. Mullan stuffed in his flowered calico shirt. Dirty and unshaven, he had the look of weathering badly.

"If you want my say," he growled, "we'll put out at noon and keep rollin', and the hell with Orrum and Esconella and talk!" He sauntered off.

Cary asked quietly: "What's wrong with him?"

Stockwell rolled a cigar between his palms. "Coy's missing town trimmings. A big drunk is all he needs. He'll simmer down." He lit a match and let it end its sputtering before he held it to the cigar. "It's hot," he sighed. "Too hot for talking. What's on your mind?"

Cary said bluntly: "I'm going into the mountains, to Crazy Dog's village to-day."

Gaybird caught her breath. "Sam—you're not serious!"

"We've got to make restitution for Stockwell's murder before they find out about it. I realized that this morning, when I thought Esconella had found the dead one. I don't want another five minutes like that."

"The army killed a couple of hundred last season," Stockwell said, "and you stew over one."

"One, with a bullet in the back of his head."

"Then be sure to make my manners to Crazy Dog for me," Stockwell shrugged. "Because I'm not going."

"No," Cary agreed. "You couldn't buy your way into this trip. When it comes to Indians, you're trigger-quick and gutless. You come into it with the gifts we'll take along. Tobacco and sugar. Buttons and ironware and needles. And a token of mourning, like that ring you're wearing."

Stockwell made a fist and inspected the ruby. His glance levelled at Cary. "You can take a couple of sacks of sugar and a hank of tobacco, if you want. The ring stays, and the ironware."

Cary looked at the too-careful face, with its thick reddish sideburns and the pottery-brown eyes under the dogged ledge of bone. He pulled a leather whang from the fringe of his shirt and began to chew on it.

"I saw some cases of reloading tools, too. One of those would do nicely for the chief. A packhorse-load of trade goods, and no skimping."

Stockwell smiled. "You mean I've got to pay the price, eh, just as though I'd murdered a United States soldier?"

And four of them there were thinking about a half-drunken sergeant in Cheyenne, lying at Cary's feet with a knife in his breast. For an instant Cary was stopped. Stockwell had hidden the weapon so well he had forgotten it.

It was Silvertooth who answered him.

"Except that a knife wound ain't like a bullet wound. A bullet wound shows. A knife wound might get mixed up with a dozen others, if the soldier got tangled with a train, say. If he was to get knifed and then be dragged on to the tracks under a couple of tumbleweeds, I reckon they'd have to hang a U.P. engine."

Exhilaration came up in Cary. He saw Stockwell's face go blank and then harden. With a grin, Cary thanked the wagonmaster for his ancient act of loyalty—planting Casner's body on the tracks that night.

He said: "I'll take the ring now. Then you can make up a couple of hundred pounds of goods for me to take in. Don't skimp, now."

Stockwell turned the ring on his finger. Abruptly he pulled it off and flipped it to Cary. He left the group. Silvertooth began to chuckle.

Merritt's eyes, black and dull as nail-heads, had watched the exchange closely. "What's this all about?" he demanded.

"Nothing. Except that you'll go along, Doctor," Cary said. "This is the best chance you'll ever have to come to terms with the Sioux."

Merritt glanced back at the wagons. Then he stole a glance at the mountains, and afterwards stared at Cary in astonishment. "You mean we'd be going into the mountains without escort?"

"Two would be as good as ten."

Merritt's face creased. Cary waited for his dignified hedging. But presently he looked up. "Perhaps you're right. It doesn't require a troop of cavalry to carry an olive branch. I suppose we'd leave to-day?"

"Sooner the better."

Gaybird came in angrily. "You don't leave at all! Sam Cary, I thought you were the Indian specialist around here. And here you are, ranting like a Congressman!" She turned heatedly to Merritt. "Aren't you a little old for bravado, Doctor? Of course Sam is too, but he seems to have forgotten it. No one would go into the mountains for any other reason than to show off."

Merritt's somnolent eyes smiled. "Men do insane things for many reasons. Duty happens to be mine—duty to myself and my mission."

In despair Gaybird accosted Silvertooth. "John, you tell them! Why, they wouldn't have a chance—"

Silvertooth patted her arm. "Lassie, there's a good chance. And it happens to be the only one."

Merritt's long thumbs rubbed his coat lapels. "How soon will we leave, then?"

"In about an hour. I'd like it if you took your medicines and tools along. You never know what you'll run into."

Gaybird recollected something the dormitory mother had said one day, when she was unforgivably homesick.

"For heaven's sake, girl, put your hands to work if you can't put your mind!"

Vengefully, now, she gathered into a large blue polka-dot handkerchief a housewife's kit for Sam. Needle and thread . . . a small block of wax matches . . . a stub of candle. If he loved her—really—how could he do it? Obviously he did not love her. The idea of love merely titillated him, so that he seemed to play with it sometimes. She tied the package angrily, but it was something so final that she slumped on to the bed and bit her lip. The tears mounted. A rigid pain clasped her throat. A woman lost something precious when she forgot how to cry easily, and Gaybird had not been able to cry womanly tears for years. But this time she felt the tears coming for sure, and when she least wanted them. She was panic-stricken. Already she could hear the men coming along the double-wall of wagon-boxes. She struck the bed in futile anger.

Now they were talking outside.

". . . Horse Creek, under Cloud Peak," said Sam. "Think about four hundred lodges. Sizeable. Sundown, to-morrow." He sounded infuriatingly calm. Nothing to worry about. Would nothing ever upset him? Nothing but getting lost, and you couldn't do that every day.

". . . Thought you said just the two of us," Merritt's voice rawly complained. "Well, Dunavan is a good man for a reconnaissance," Sam mentioned. "Teamed with the infantry and you couldn't budge him with a pry bar."

Men! she thought. Everything was an adventure, except to the girls they left behind them. She unearthed for herself the antique coin of feminine wisdom. Love was the whole pudding, to a woman; only the spice of it, to a man. Duty reared before Sam like a mountain. She could have levelled it with one kick.

Duty . . . she had accepted the word! And that only makes it worse, she reasoned. He was putting duty before her. The sour taste of what the poet was saying reached her: "*I could not love thee, dear, so much, loved I not honour more.*"

Tears overflowed the small dams of her eyelids. Her throat ached. Sam called to her:

"Gaybird? We're leaving now . . ."

She won a truce with her tears. She was able to say, "Take this along," and to place it on the step before she ducked back into the stifling tent.

His boots crunched. "Much obliged," he said. "It's arranged that John will take the wagons on to the post. Dunavan will go with us. Anyhing you'd like? Moccasins? Jewellery?"

"No," she managed to say.

The silence ached between them. "All right," he said. "Don't leave the train again, for anything. We'll see you in a couple of days."

His boots walked gently out of her hearing. The lump in her throat dissolved. She fell across the cot and wept.

A little after one, Silvertooth put the wagons back on the trail. The torment of wooden spindles punctuated the cottony dust with loud bickering. It was unbelievable that order could be manufactured out of so much disorder—hoarse bawling of teamsters' throats, massive yanking of tackle, lunge and stumble of heavy-footed oxen. Whips and leather lungs snapped the line into shape, scouts ranged far to east and west, and the dogged monotony of the trail settled as chokingly as the dust.

Bill Orrum loafed back into the train on his red mule an hour after Cary, Merritt and Dunavan rode out. He tied the mule behind his wagon. Having had his day in the van, he would travel for a time at the end of the line. He was in the cloud of earthy smoke at the rear when Mark Stockwell pulled in beside him.

Stockwell handled his horse cavalierly. Of his features, masked against dust, only his eyes were revealed, queerly enamelled against the grey of his skin.

There was little chance that the other whackers in Orrum's rank would hear over the rumble of the wagons. Nevertheless they talked in code.

"Still think you'll try it alone, eh?" Stockwell inquired.

"Bound to."

"Too bad there's no other way."

"I don't know what it'd be. I don't, now."

A few rods of silence passed under the wheels. "I don't, either." Stockwell agreed. "I have an idea things will get worse after this morning, rather than better."

All this, Orrum reckoned, was by way of last-minute nerving-up to a job. He would give better than even that there was brandy on Stockwell's breath.

He told him easily: "I aim to drop out sometime before night and keep rolling. Make camp late and take off early. I know a short cut through the foothills. I'll be in Butte before you're at Fort Stockwell. I'd like to be heeled when I get there, too. These customers of mine, now, don't always pay in cash money."

Stockwell made sure that the other teamsters were occupied with their bull teams. He put a slip of paper in the gun-runner's hand. "Give that to my manager at the fort."

Orrum tucked it into the sweat-band of his hat. "Thanks, Mark. May seem steep, but think of the risks!"

"You're right, it's steep. Smooth-bore muskets for the price of Spencers! Anyway, good luck! God knows you'll need a-plenty."

Orrum winked. "Fact of it is, I feel safer palavering with a gang of Esconella's bucks than I do training around with a hard-luck outfit like this. He was right polite with me."

Stockwell moved in closer. "That's Cherry Spring, now? Don't be in any rush to close with him. I'd like to clear Fort Greybull and be heading up into my country before the bucks get the guns out of the grease. Stall them a while, if you can. This is close timing."

Orrum snorted. "Stall, the devil! They get the guns, I get the tarnation out. They'll be dancing for two days, so you've got plenty of time." He smiled, half to himself. "Everybody to his own likker. They'll get down and knock their heads on the ground over some guns you couldn't pay me to shoot. I'll be investing half this money in a little French gal in Butte, but I bet Esconella wouldn't give four-bits for her and all her perfume! Well, Mark—"

Grinning, he extended his hand. They gripped briefly and the big trader swung hurriedly back into the dust. Orrum pulled his wagon out of line and pointed north-west.

XXIV

Dusk overflowed the Bighorns, puddling in the canyons of the foothills and staining the prairie coasting out to the badlands. That night, with twelve miles behind them, Cary camped on a green meadow, under fragrant pines. In five miles the desert had expired. A watered plateau with its apron fastened to the base of the dark hills had lifted them into the mountains.

After they ate, Cary extinguished the fire and silently moved camp a mile farther on. "No use tempting them," he said.

In the morning Dunavan and Cary talked it over.

"We should make the village before night, if they haven't moved," Cary declared. "As an infantryman, what's your opinion of how we should proceed?"

"Backwards," said Dunavan. "At least I'm with the grown-up men this time. It's a new caper, for me. Did you need somebody to wash the pots?"

"If you've been bragging about the kind of soldiering you did," said Cary, "it'll be worth our scalps."

Through the scented morning they penetrated a flinty highland of sparse timber and bleached grasses. They crossed ominous drag-marks of Indian *travois*. Countless creeks veined the flanks of the hills, icy bloodstreams of the mountains. A buzzard tilted overhead. They flushed quail and deer, and finally reached a windy junction of three valleys. Here, on a cold rib of granite, Cary and Dunavan discussed tactics. Cary heard Dunavan's ideas, and Dunavan looked astonished when the trader agreed that they should separate. It would be better to have a man across the crest of that ridge and the others on the opposite side, so that they would not be taken by surprise.

Dunavan waved his carbine and put his pony up the slope

towards the ridge. He crossed and sank from view. Cary loafed easily along the trail, his head never at rest, glancing right and left.

They rode for twenty minutes. Presently Merritt called: "Will you stop at the next stream? I'm dry."

Cary waved his arm. A fluting of green tokened a spring branch ahead of them. Cary swung down here and let his horse drink. He stretched, looked about him, and knelt to scoop water in the brim of his hat. The doctor dismounted. When Cary looked up, the hat-brim to his lips, he saw Merritt standing there silently with a pistol in his hand. The gun was directed at Cary's belly.

Cary let the water spill. He said quickly: "What's this?"

"This," Merritt said, "is the wages of sin. Was she worth it, Cary?"

The pure logic of it overwhelmed Cary. Merritt, contradicting everything Cary knew about him to endorse this sortie! Carrying his jealousy in his heart like a loaded gun, biding his time. . . .

"Was she worth it?" he said. "I wouldn't know, Doctor. I haven't had her."

An inquisitional anger spilled through Merritt. His voice tautened. "You haven't had her! By *heaven*, Cary! I thought I'd heard expert liars in Washington."

Cary began to rise, but Merritt snapped: "You'd better stay down."

"On my knees?" Cary smiled.

"No, I don't expect that. But I expect something like respect from my wife when I go back. I doubt that an amour was ever paraded more openly."

Cary said: "My God!"

The doctor was perspiring, his smooth skin limp, papery pockets under his eyes. He was all resolution and suppressed fury, which he seemed trying to liberate. "Would you like to tell me about the night at Fort Reno?" he asked.

"Have I got time?"

"You'll know when the time's up."

"I expect I will. I didn't know she was painting my picture, Merritt. I don't know yet why she did. But if she was painting, she didn't have time to get into any other mischief, did she?''

"You were gone close to an hour."

Cary sat back on the pebbly stream-bank. He regarded Merritt dryly, avoiding the bright focus of the gun-muzzle. "Since I'm already convicted, the defence might as well rest."

The doctor's hand trembled a little. "I don't like it any better than you do, Cary. Less, I think. A doctor gets used to trying to save lives. This goes against the grain. But I'm a man first and a doctor afterwards."

"A technical question," Cary said. "If you bungle it, do you fire again or attempt to save me?"

"I fire again."

"Good. From what I've seen of doctors, I'd rather have one operate on me with a Colt."

Merritt stirred, his face unhumorous. "If you're going to die protecting the lady's name, then—"

"Is there anything in it for me if I tell a good story?"

"Not a thing. It would make it easier for me, but that would hardly interest you."

"This is a damned shame," Cary sighed. "It's a shame for me, to begin with. It's a shame for the white traders and the Sioux. There's nothing between them and war, now. And it's a shame for you, because you won't get back."

"Anything else?"

"Yes." It was not easy to face up to that glinting gun-bore without flinching. Death was a one-eyed man with his eye on Sam's belly. "Yes," Cary sighed. "I'm sorry for my wife."

"Your wife?"

"Gaybird. We've been married for four years."

"I get a good story out of it after all, do I?" Merritt carefully shifted the gun to his left hand and wiped his palm.

"It was a sort of guardianship, after her father died. I couldn't adopt her, we found. The only way I could keep her out of an orphanage was to marry her. But it's been—well, subject to annulment, up to now. I was thinking it wouldn't be, by fall."

Merritt's fault, as a killer, was that he was too intelligent. He was amenable to logic. Sam saw him flashing back over the whole month on the trail, squeezing the juice out of each episode. "She wears no ring," he stated.

"Of course not. It wasn't meant to be a marriage. But the fact is, I've been in love with her for—dammit," he said slowly, "it's none of your business what's between us."

Merritt took a long, steadying breath. "It might be," he said.

Cary peered into the intent features. "I think she thought she loved me. But that was in Cheyenne, and I still figured she was a kid, and felt obligated to me. That would have been like her marrying her father. If I'm to be anything to Gaybird Phillips, it won't be that. I said she'd have her annulment, and I must have made annulment look so attractive by letting her see me in action that she's thinking about going ahead with it."

"I thought I detected a certain amount of affection between you," Merritt observed.

Cary wagged his head. "Of all the men to confuse affection and love, Doctor, you ought to be the last."

"Where does one begin and the other end?" Merritt scoffed.

"Do you mean, when does lead cease to be lead and become silver? It doesn't. They're two different things. Dale's a schemer, but I think when she married you she had affection for you."

"And now she doesn't even have that, eh?"

"No. She happened to be in love with you, too, and now that the affection is about gone, all that's left is love. Still, that's something."

If ever a man looked hungry, Cary thought, it was Merritt. His eyes were starving. His bitter smile came and he said:

"For a teamster, you're an interesting talker. Of course any man likes to talk about himself. How did you arrive at the conclusion that my wife had anything but contempt for me?"

"No one," Cary said, "not even a wife, will ever have contempt for you. People may hate you; you don't give them much chance to be friendly. But you've got a sort of bedside manner that lets you take over in a situation. Yet you've kept Dale at arm's length so long she's begun to try to take herself out of your life."

"Will you give me one inkling of her love for me?" Merritt challenged.

"Are you blind? The fact that she's in Wyoming. She knew it was dangerous, and yet she came with you. If she'd wanted to play it fast and loose, she'd have stayed in Washington."

Merritt's face weighed it. It silenced him. Sam shrugged.

"People ought to stick to what they're good at. You were a good doctor. But you threw it up to be a second-rate politician. And now that you're in a bind, do you know the one thing that's apt to get you out? Medicine."

Merritt's manner was changing from transitive to intransitive. Still the Navy pistol glittered in the cold mountain sunlight, and he was sustained by the same stiff dignity that was his backbone.

"I didn't ask you to bring your tools because one of us might get hurt," Cary assured him. "You're going to work on old Crazy Dog!"

Merritt shuddered. "So you mean to say you brought us out here on any such wild-goose chase as that? Man, there are seven thousand things that can cause paralysis of the limbs! One or two of them are susceptible to treatment."

"But this was the result of a shot. I thought maybe—well, it's a chance."

"You thought, maybe, I was God," Merritt grunted.

"I had a doctor staying at the post one winter," Cary said. "He worked on dozens of Indians. If there's a living god, to them, it's a man with a brown cowhide bag. Have you imagination, Merritt? Put yourself in the Sioux's place. A man comes all the way from Washington, not to make a treaty, but to make the chief well. The Grandfather—President Grant—had heard; he was worried. He sent his best medicine man. The white man's medicine brings the chief some relief. Maybe it cures him. Then, Doctor, he begins talking peace terms."

Merritt smiled wanly. "And do you know who would get the credit for all this?"

"Why, of course. Some politician. But you'll know. And so will Wyoming. The Indians will give you a tribal name: One-Who-Heals, something like that. They'll bring you tons of truck you've got no earthly use for. They did it to me for feeding a herd of them one winter, after hunters chased off all the buffalo. Junk! But I've never thrown away an ounce of it."

There was a loosening look about Merritt.

"Women are pretty strong medicine themselves," Cary smiled. "But you need to be your own man when you go to dickering with them. You want to respect yourself, to have something to fall back on if anything goes wrong between you and your woman. A trade; or another woman. That's been your mistake. She let you doubt yourself. Don't. Not for *any* woman.''

The gun dangled in the physician's long hand. He said: ''That wouldn't be a bad name for you, Cary. 'One-Who-Heals!' ''

''We won't know that until we see what you can do with the chief.''

Merritt asked, a faint, ironic smile on his face: ''Do I go back in irons, or do we go on?''

''We go on.'' Cary watched him turn away to pick up the reins of his horse, and he took the drink he had spilled before, and then walked to his own pony. He took a moment, before mounting, to wipe his palms carefully on his buckskin thighs. The perspiration made dark prints on the smoked leather.

The climb stiffened. There became increasing evidence that they were in someone's dooryard—someone who left shards of old pottery about, scatters of bright arrow-chips, bleached bones of antelope and buffalo. Yet they saw and heard nothing. A jay swooped low, disciplining them with its harsh cry, and Cary started.

The vestibule of Crazy dog's village was rotten with ambuscades. Cavalry would never pry him out. Infantry might, with five-to-one losses.

And now a horse clattered on the ridge, and a rider let his horse tumble down the slope, and Dunavan was plunging in with his tough features ropy with fear.

''In that tamarack, Cary! A platoon of the varmints, a-hoss-back and waiting!''

Cary squinted at the dark-green cones of timber masking the mouth of a canyon which funnelled in between two hills. ''All right,'' he said. ''That's what we've been waiting for, isn't it?'' He lifted his right hand ear-high and jogged toward the trees.

Now there was a flutter of colour and something arched from the trees. It spun and twisted in the cold mountain sunlight and struck the ground ahead of Cary. The feathered arrow-shaft slowly fell over. Cary halted. His belly-muscles wadded. Everything had been a prelude to this instant, all the weeks of dust and wind and heat, all the miseries of hoping and being doubtful. And now no man knew how the next few moments would go.

From trees the Indians began to file unhastily, solemn and businesslike. They were men toughened and tamed by experience. Sioux soldiers. Cary looked for Crazy Dog. The chief was not in the party, but Cary saw his son, Yellow Horn.

The Sioux drew up, robed and belted, sombre in manner, bright with ornament. Cary raised his hand again.

"How is my friend, Yellow Horn?" he greeted, in the Oglala.

The Oglala studied him while his pony shifted uneasily. "How is it that you come?"

"The Grandfather sends us. We come as an old friend and as a new one."

"What does the Grandfather wish?" Yellow Horn asked. "More buffalo to steal?"

The Sioux ringed them tightly. Cary knew these people; he knew they liked to smile, but none of the warriors were smiling. A brave thumped the rawhide *aparejo* straddling the pack-horse which carried food and gifts.

"He wishes to pay for the buffalo other men have stolen," Cary declared. "We bring presents. We bring the greatest medicine man the white man knows."

They stared at Dunavan and then came close to Merritt, gaping and pulling at his brown cowhide bag. He flinched; but Cary said casually:

"Easy."

After a moment Yellow Horn said: "Can he cure sick legs?"

"Maybeso Crazy Dog walks again."

Yellow Horn nodded slowly. "You come," he said.

Beyond the trees a trail lifted them through grey boulders and lodgepole pine to a hillside which sloughed off into a wide valley. Smokes rose lazily from many fires. It was like entering a vast and untidy fairground, only instead of tents there were hundreds of tepees scattered randomly. Dogs nosed about, yapping at them. Babies squalled and squaws gathered in groups and screeched at naked boys to keep back from the Long Knives. Hides were pegged on the ground under stirring mantles of flies. Yellow Horn stopped once and pointed at a fat white mongrel dog, and a squaw laid hold of it swiftly and struck it on the head with a rock. She dragged it away to a fire.

Merritt's face sickened. "Are we—expected to eat—?"

Cary grinned. "Best sign in the world. A dog-feast."

Before a ledge where a bullhide shield hung on a tripod, Yellow Horn slipped from his pony. He ducked inside, and presently came back to summon two warriors. They carried the paralysed chief out. He wore a bronze treaty medal on a rawhide cord about his neck. Weight had sloughed off his stocky frame since Cary saw him last. A white buffalo robe was belted about his middle and his heavy, plaited braids came forward across his shoulders. His face was wrinkled bronze with glints of black Indian eyes.

Cary spoke briefly with the chief. From his pocket he took the ruby ring of Stockwell's. Sitting propped against a boulder, Crazy Dog smiled and slipped it on to his finger.

"Long Rifle does not come to his friends often," he said.

"A trader is busy."

"Yellow Horn says the Grandfather sends his medicine man to cure me."

Cary put a hand on Merritt's shoulder. "He has cured many white chiefs. Maybeso his medicine cures you."

"We will go inside."

The lodge was stifling with its rancid-sweet odours of hides and sweat and food. The chief mixed tobacco, lighted a pipe and passed it. Between silences, there was talk. Then the elders rose again and all but Yellow Horn, another Oglala, and the chief left the tepee. Cary turned to the physician.

"All right, Doctor. This is your big play. He's your patient."

Merritt asked the chief to have the fire built up so that he could see better. He said to Cary:

"Can he tell me anything about this?"

"He was shot in a hunting accident. We'll say it was an accident. He hasn't walked since."

Merritt sighed.

He helped the chief turn over on his face and removed the belted robe. The firelight glistened on skin like discoloured brown metal. He touched a large scar on the man's spine. Cary heard the doctor murmur. He bent over, his fingers prodding gently at Crazy Dog's back. He sat back.

"What is it?" Cary asked.

"I'm not sure. I would say he has either a large concretion

alongside his spine, or the bullet is still there. But either way—I don't know."

Yellow Horn spoke to Cary. "He says the medicine man thought there was a bullet in him," Cary translated, "and they burned cow-dung over the wound to drive it out. But nothing happened."

"Surprising," Merritt remarked. His face was glum in the warm firelight. He groped in his bag and dispensed sulphate of morphia. Suddenly he smiled. "Nervous?" he asked Cary.

"Passably."

"You should be."

"Why?"

"Because we're working on ten-to-one odds. But there's always that tenth chance."

Suddenly Dunavan growled. "Here comes that squaw with a kettle! Have we got to eat that damned dog?"

"You'd pick a fight with a man who wouldn't drink with you, wouldn't you?"

Crazy Dog sat up again. They ate the dog-stew. Accustomed to Indian delicacies, Cary was able to eat his share. Presently, as the morphine took effect, Merritt prepared to work. "I have candles here," he said. "Will you men hold them?"

The operation was brief. The chief grunted occasionally. Merritt carefully laid on a handkerchief a lead ball. He blue-stoned the wound and fixed a dressing over it.

"All right," he said. "Let's take him outside."

End of Part Seven

Part Eight

XXV

CARY WATCHED THE warriors place the chief on the buffalo robe before the lodge. A staring pack of squaws, braves and children had collected. They spoke in soft, low rushes. Shell ornaments rattled and moccasins whispered on the bare earth. Merritt eyed them uneasily.

"If they're waiting for a miracle," he said, "they're going to be disappointed. After three months, it's hardly to be expected that he should take up his bed and walk. It will take some time."

"How much time?"

"Days . . . weeks. I don't know. I should think only a few days."

"But by fall for sure?"

"In time for the treaty commission?" Merritt smiled. "Yes. He'll walk by then, if he walks at all."

In the watchful silence, Cary brought the rawhide packs containing the gifts. On a blanket he set out dusky hanks of tobacco, bolts of red cotton, papers of needles and spools of thread. He produced loading tools and demonstrated them. Crazy Dog put the tools under his robe, his eyes gleaming. It was when he moved to do this that Merritt spoke suddenly.

"There's our sign, Cary."

In moving, the Oglala had spread his legs slightly and again drawn them together. Cary had noticed this without being impressed. But now the doctor said quickly:

"Ask him to bend his knees."

Cary translated. His back to the smoky boulder beside his

shield-rack, Crazy Dog placed his palms on the robe. His knees bent and rose four or five inches off the robe. Yellow Horn said something in a deep, excited voice. The dark eyes of the Sioux came to Merritt.

"Tell them," Merritt said, "he'll be able to walk within two weeks."

Cary let the moment stretch out, tightening, before he announced:

"In the time of the full moon, your chief will walk from his lodge to the river. When leaves fall, he will lead the hunt."

There was a great noise of Indian voices, the tribe breaking. The old chief's smile squinted his face and he beckoned to the doctor. Merritt squatted beside him. Removing his necklace of bear claws, the Oglala placed it about the doctor's neck. He spoke to Cary.

"He says you're the greatest healer the Sioux Nation has ever seen," Cary grinned. "He wants you to treat all of his people who are sick. That would mean about ninety per cent of them. If you were ever looking prestige in the eye, Merritt, it's right now."

Merritt looked about. Cary had the sudden fear that he would back out. That the smell and filth of the diseased would be too much for him. But a look of deep calm came to Merritt's face.

"You were right," he declared. "A man ought to stick with what he's good at. Tell them to go to their lodges. I'll visit them all in turn."

Merritt started his grand tour of the lodges, and Cary eased into his own business. He sat in the stuffy deerskin lodge with the chief and his old men.

"The medicine man was from the Grandfather," he told Crazy Dog. "The gifts were from the trader, Stockwell."

Quick, dark eyes were on Cary, keen as fleshing knives. "Owns Lance is not our friend. Why does he send gifts?"

"Owns Lance wishes to be your friend. He sends the gifts in grief, because he killed one of your young men. It was by accident."

Crazy Dog's breath sounded lightly between his teeth. "Owns Lance does nothing by accident. We thought Loud Bear died in the big wind. Why did he kill him?"

"He was afraid. He saw him in the wind and killed him before he thought."

"Why did he not bring the gifts himself?"

"Because he was afraid. Esconella frightened many of our men yesterday."

Crazy Dog shook his head. "The heart has gone bad in him. He has left the village of his fathers."

"He has four hundred men with him."

"He will find more. He has sent presents to the Brules and Uncpapas. The whole village of Two Elks has gone with him."

"But Crazy Dog is still chief."

The Oglala peered at him. "Crazy Dog is chief, as there is fire in flint. But first it must be struck. Without legs I cannot strike fire. If the white man's medicine is strong, Esconella will play with the boys again."

"If he comes back," Cary asked, "can you handle him?"

"He will not come back. He has sent my daughter back to my lodge. He has laughed at the Wind God. He is stubborn and stiff-necked. If he steals guns, he will be dangerous."

"If he does not steal guns, and the tribes do not take the warpath, will you talk peace with the white soldiers?"

The chief received it stolidly. "Why do they want to talk peace, when they will not keep peace?"

"They are sorry for the acts of white liars and thieves. They want to repay you for the buffalo they have slaughtered and the warriors they have killed."

"What is it they want?" Crazy Dog asked sharply.

"They wish to man the Bozeman posts again. To police traders and travellers, as well as renegade Indians."

"Will they pay for this?"

"They will pay."

Crazy Dog spoke to one of the Indians. In the lodge there was a thin strand of conversation, a word grunted, a sign made. At last he told Cary:

"We will make no promises. But we will talk when the leaves fall. If Crazy Dog is still chief of the Oglalas."

Night came before Merritt was finished. Cary noticed that the Oglalas kept sentries out. Esconella had left nothing with his tribe but the fear of him. Cary, Dunavan and the doctor spread their blankets outside Crazy Dog's lodge. Silence came. Mountain cold pressed sharply upon them. Small fires puddled the dark ground, expiring into coals; dogs relinquished their yapping and the last child ceased to complain. The camp slept.

Cary lay with his fingers laced under his head. He pictured the wagons forted up to-night on the lap of Red's Meadow. At noon to-morrow they would ford Silvertip Creek, and before nightfall they would make Fort Greybull, on Young Woman Creek. Cary himself hoped to make it by dark.

He thought of Gaybird that morning by the railroad tracks. Gently he handled the wafer-thin vision of her: Gaybird putting her hands out to him, her grey eyes dancing, her body young, impossibly fragile for such a country. Hers was the shimmering, uncapturable grace of a humming-bird darting in coppery rushes. When you captured such loveliness, you destroyed it. But the man who had it near him would be the luckiest man alive. The man who found reasons why he was not fit to accept it was a hypocrite. Sam Cary was done with hypocrisy. He would know where he stood.

From the blankets at his side, Merritt's voice came with the solemnity of a sleep-talker.

"It's here, Cary. It's all right here. They sent me out to make a fool of myself. Wyoming—the graveyard of diplomats. But I didn't make a fool of myself. By God, I didn't!"

With a packhorse-load of gifts, they left the village at sun-up.

The morning grew warm and green. Thick blackstrap odours of serviceberry and mountain mahogany rubbed from the brush as they rode. Working down from the crests, they followed bright streams shattering into foam on rocks. Their guide took them through a swift descent, finally pulling up on a timbered ridge above the grassy foothills. He pointed with his rifle.

"Half-day ride." The gun-barrel swerved southward. "Whackers sleepin' late!"

Cary studied the lean pencil of smoke rising from the hills. "No," he said. "My men would be nooning on Silvertip by now. Maybe Esconella?"

"Esconella rides north to meet Brules and Uncpapas."

"What's the varmint says?" Dunavan demanded.

"He says that the smoke yonder is our camp. He says it can't be Esconella, because he's north of here, waiting for the Brules."

"Are they going to spoil their record about never laying siege to a fort?"

"They've never finished one."

The guide riding back, they followed a canyon on to a grassy apron. As they drew near to the smoke, it became a meaningless smear, a grassy smudge against the sky. They angled up a grassy ridge, and Dunavan precipitously crowded past, eager and curious. They saw him pull up on the crest, staring down. He did not turn nor signal, but as they came abreast of him they saw the burned wagons and dead bulls below them, on a spring branch called Cherry Creek.

The camp was on the bank of the creek, a trampled acre of bruised grass and broken brush. In the centre of this area of rubbish and hoofmarks lay the remnants of a single wagon and trailer. The wagons had long ago burned out, but the smoke of foodstuffs and robes fumed in the wreckage. Arrows pin-cushioned the oxen.

They found where the bullwhacker had been stripped and pinned to the ground with stakes through his wrists. Skilled, curious knives had been at his body. The corners of his mouth had been gashed and his nose was cut off. His moccasins were on his feet but his leather breeches had been cut away.

How he had died, from which wound or from sheer pain, no one could have said. He was unrecognizable, but they had lived a month with that round-crowned stetson, with the greasy buck-skins and the quilled leather shirt, and they knew them instantly for Bill Orrum's. Nothing was missing but his black pigtails.

Everywhere lay remnants of gun-chests and ammunition cases, split yellow-pine slabs stencilled in black. A few paper cartridges lay about. Using a board as a shovel, Cary scooped out a shallow grave and Dunavan dragged the gaunt body into the trench, secured his clothing, dropping the stetson with its green headband across the mutilated face, the deerhide breeches on his hips. He held the Blackfoot shirt in his hands.

Paper whispered in a pocket. Cary pulled out a fold of writing.

"Mr. Williams: Please give bearer two thousand dollars in gold, for value received. Stockwell."

"For value received," Cary said. He and Dunavan gazed at each other, and Dunavan's face broke oddly.

"God damn it, Cary!" he said. "God damn it!"

Merritt asked quietly: "Will you tell me what it means?"

"It means that Esconella has his guns now. He's a war-chief, Doctor. A big war-chief. He has the guns. All he needs is the guts."

XXVI

SILVERTOOTH POKED ALONG at the head of the column, slapping at flies on the neck of his mule. They were in the meadow country, at last; the green country, the country of oceans of grass and islands of pine, of water you could drink without straining and grass that didn't crackle when you walked on it.

They had spent the night in Red's Meadow, that unbelievable park just a few miles from the desert. Then they had strung out again, nooned on Silvertip Creek and this late afternoon were working down through pine hills to the pale green valley of Young Woman Creek, the blue-black mountains at their back.

Silvertooth, never getting far from Gaybird's wagon, carried a worry or two. Last night Mark Stockwell had pulled out with his wagons. He was taking the short cut which lopped off a few miles but denied him the comfort of a day or two in Fort Greybull before the last fifty miles of his own trip. Bill Orrum had left earlier in the day on another cut-off. Their behaviour puzzled him.

From a high tuck in the hills, they had their first view of the fort.

It was a half-hour distant, still. Fenced by sharpened lodgepole logs, the buildings looked trim as match-boxes. Silvertooth waved the word down the line and loped out to look for his scouts. He had a treacherous desire to let down. He wanted to signal them all in: We're done, boys, draw your pay and spend it!

But he had been through too much on the Bozeman to be fooled.

After a time he saw Tom Kane, one of the scouts, sloping in from the north. Another rider suddenly slashed up from a coulee just behind Kane, and Silvertooth's heart squeezed. But it was not a Sioux! After a brief conference, the pair came in at a hard lope. Silvertooth waited.

The man with Kane was Coy Mullan. As they reined in on the green-granite-ribbed hillside, Silvertooth saw that the wagon-master's features were ashen. He rode with his revolver in his hand. He was out of breath. He waved the gun pointlessly and gasped:

"Damn the varmints! Damn them!"

Silvertooth struck the gun aside. "What's the trouble, now?"

Mullan stared with a sick fear. "One of the scouts flushed Esconella and a whole gad-blamed army in a coulee, waitin' for us! We've turned back. Got three-four miles, maybe, but they're ramping down on the train like the devil splitting kindling!"

"Same gang?"

"Hell, twice as many—three times! Mark's bringing them back to the fort. We're a mile and a half north, in the creek bottom." His throat clogged; he gulped.

Silvertooth scanned the foothills. "Join your outfit," he said suddenly.

He turned to fire a shot and bawl the warning. An outrider snapped his arm back and forth, turned and ran his horse at the train. The joints of the column slackened as the lead wagons stretched, like the couplings of a freight-train giving on a hard pull.

By standing in the stirrups, Silvertooth was able to discern a dirty-grey flow of canvas sheets in the bosque of Young Woman Creek. It was the Montana train, slicing back to the post. The wagonmaster began to slap the walnut stock of his rifle. He swore steadily. He had come to think of himself and Sam Cary as a unit. Neither one was much good without the other; at least he himself operated at reduced speed without Sam. He shuddered at the thought of the gigantic log-jam of Cary's and Stockwell's wagons crowding through the sally-port at once, should Stockwell make it back.

He groaned then, and turned away, and that was when he saw three horsemen sliding down a hill a mile to the rear. "*Injuns!*" The cry rang in his brain. But these riders came like whites, bent across their saddle-swells.

A hosanna went up from Silvertooth's lips. Sam—Sam and Dunavan and the doctor. Silvertooth triumphantly bore down on the train, no longer an old woman fussing with trivialities, but feeling himself growing.

They met at the rear and Silvertooth started to pass the word. "We saw them from the hills," Cary interrupted. "They've got the guns Orrum was carrying. Orrum's been murdered. Better cut loose the heavy wagons and bring the rest in. Merritt and I will take the women to the fort."

With an instinct for emergency, Cary had left the arms-wagon only half loaded. He whipped it out of line with its four-span of strong young mules and sent it on. He drafted a hunter to take Gaybird's wagon in, and put her on his horse behind him. Her skirts billowed at either side of the horse. As they rode, he glanced back. "You don't have to squeeze the wind out of me. I won't leave you."

She squeezed harder, closing her eyes. *Never, never*, her lips said.

They came off the last hill into the wide and indolent valley of Young Woman Creek. Near the western margin of it ran the creek in its entourage of cottonwoods and silver aspen, tender with new leaves. Hunters' trails ran down to a sandy ford about a half-mile from the post walls. Marks of travois scarred the meadow and hillsides, where Indian potato and wild onion had been dug. At the back of the fort rose a small hill capped by a high look-out tower. Beyond the hill was a reach of two miles of meadow, and then the hills again, stiff with timber.

They threaded the road through the trees, feeling the moist

coolness of the bosque. Berry thickets crowded close to the road and wild hop festooned the cottonwoods. They plunged through the stream. Silver spray drenched them. Gaybird's skirts ceased to billow; they modelled her legs glisteningly.

Shading with his hand Cary peered north-west. He made out the Montana train, lunging back to the fort. Beyond, on the slope of a distant hill, he discerned a blur of moving horses.

As they left the trees, Cary's post manager, Daniel Edge, came in sight beyond the haystacks. A two hundred and fifty pound man whose body turned everything he ate into fat, Edge swung his horse in beside them.

"A hell of a home-coming!" he shouted, his brown eyes vehement.

"You know about the Sioux?"

"The look-out spotted them. He made them at seven-eight hundred. I've got all the men on the walls."

"How many around?"

"Maybe forty."

For round numbers, Cary reckoned, a hundred inside the post if the wagons made it in, seven to eight hundred without.

They loped past the haystacks and outer corral. They crossed the mauled ground about the main gate. A square block-house dominated the north-west corner of the post, matched by a similar barn-like structure on the south-east. From loopholes in the blockhouse and along the walls, men were shouting at them. The tall gate made a two-foot slot. They crowded into the narrow, walled passage, where Indians were penned for trading in uncertain times. A sentry bawled and the inner gate grudgingly opened. They entered the post.

Cary felt Gaybird's arms relax. He heard her sigh. He explained it, too—the comfort of the walls.

The great, engulfing ocean of the wilderness could not break through the slim dike of sharpened poles. This square, no larger than a town block, had a cramped-down strength of many towns. It was a strong mix of abilities, cunning, and courage. Whoever broke that dike would not only let the wilderness pour in, but would release a barbarous energy on himself.

Across two-thirds of the enclosure fell the notched shadow of the forward wall. Log and rock buildings occupied the area to the right; the remaining space was an emergency corral filled with stock. Drenched and windblown, Gaybird held to the stirrup as Sam lowered her. Cary faced Dan Edge. "Get the women settled. Then get on the wall. If Stockwell beats me to the gate, hold him off. If the Sioux beat us both, lock the gates. We'll stand them off outside. We've all the rifles we can use, if it comes to a showdown. Trapdoor Springfields! You'll hear 'em."

Edge ducked his chin to his shoulder to wipe a droplet of sweat. Gaybird touched Sam's hand as he moved to ride out. "Sam! I keep thinking—if anything should happen—would we have to spend eternity in a sort of purgatory?"

Cary smiled. "Gaybird," he sighed, "I've been in purgatory. Whatever happens, one way or another, I'm coming out of it. Be a good girl and go along with Dan. Mrs. Merritt will join you. You can't have a light, but I reckon you can pray in the dark."

Wheels echoed hollowly in the sallyport and the Merritts rattled in. Cary struck the horse with his hat and went through the gate.

North-west, across the cropped meadow, he observed Stockwell's wagons muling through the upper ford. Spray splashed silver in the sunlight. A wagon was bogged in sand and the skinner was wallowing ashore to catch a ride. All the commotion of a full-scale retreat was there, teamsters standing to rawhide stumbling mules, freight sprawling out of lurching wagons, hubs grinding together as the wagons bickered for position.

Cary brought his gaze down the timbered stream-bed to where Silvertooth was dispatching the first of the Greybull wagons through the water. The wagonmaster lingered in the shallows, swinging his carbine.

Cary tried to measure the situation, but he could not reckon which train would reach the post first. A vermilion flake of colour twisted in the light on a near ridge, trembling like a dead sumac leaf. He knew it for a whirled blanket, counterpart of the white soldier's trumpet. Around it swirled a wave of acorn brown, blotting the young grass. The wave widened and swept forward, punctured with glints of steel—steel which had been files and dutch ovens until squaw-cleverness fashioned lance-tips from it; browned and blued steel moulded in Eastern factories for savage hands to master.

He sat rubbing the breech of his gun, waiting.

It grew evident that his wagons were going to have the edge at the gate. Rambling and broken, Stockwell's gaunt line straggled across the meadow. The vanguard of Silvertooth's disciplined column was already passing the haystacks. Cary took the coiled bullwhip from his pommel and moved out before the gate.

The wave of Sioux, offscrapings of four tribes, had dimension, now. It was a cloud painted gorgeously with red horsehide, with grey, green and vermilion blankets and buffalo-hide shields. A gigantic thundercloud to drench with its fury the wagons about to jam the gate of the trading post.

Cary moved forward. He and Silvertooth met briefly. "Take them in," Cary ordered. "Straight down the line till you hit the back wall. A jam will finish us."

There was a low, grinding echo of hubs from the passage as the first wagon went in. Up on the wall they were bawling encouragement. Team after team, heads low and swinging, the oxen streamed into the post.

The first of Stockwell's wagons rambled up, driven by a wild-eyed skinner with a tawny beard, a standing, shirtless figure hurling his whip. Cary moved into the way of the mules.

"Turn them!" he shouted.

The skinner's wide eyes stared. He lashed the mules again.

Cary hurled the whip against a leader's neck. The cracker drew blood; the mule lumbered against its collar-mate, and he gave it the whip again. The team fell away as the muleskinner shouted and jumped down.

Stockwell came loping along the line of wagons to plunge to a halt beside Cary. His face was crusted with dirt and sweat.

"They're on us, man! I had to leave some of my wagons in the creek. For God's sake, keep them moving!"

"Line them up before the gate," Cary said. "They'll serve as a final firing line."

Stockwell seized his shirt-front. "You aren't God Almighty! They can all go in, one and one."

Then he was looking at the paper Sam took from the bleached ribbon of his stetson. His eyes rushed back to Cary's face, a stark questioning in them. He knew then what had happened to Bill Orrum, and where Cary had found the paper.

"Bring your wagons around and overturn them," Cary told him.

Stockwell raised his hand in a half-gesture of protest, but let it fall. He jerked his head at Mullan and they swung back to take over the wagons. Cary retreated to the gate.

Wagon after wagon, they jounced on. If a man focused on them he could forget that half a nation of Sioux were streaming upon the post. It was a picture Cary would never forget. He would always remember how their horses stifled the bright little stream, and how the horde of them shook out over the meadow like an Indian blanket. He would remember the broken whooping, as their hands slapped their mouths. He would remember the way eight hundred running horses jarred the ground, the sensation that he was standing beneath a cliff, waiting for it to crumble upon him.

A little flight of arrows fluttered across the sky and dropped among the teams jamming the gate. An ox twisted to stare white-eyed at the feathered wand trembling in its side. The team wedged crosswise in the sallyport.

Cary saw the whacker drop from his wagon and try to force his way through the gate into the fort. He slashed at his face with his stetson. "Cut that bull loose and get your wagon inside!"

He dismounted to throw off the oxbow. They wrestled the animal out of the team. The wagons lunged on. Remounting, Cary saw that the bulk of Stockwell's line had formed raggedly in a flat crescent. Beyond, a trio of skinners who had abandoned their wagons in the stream were sprinting for the post. A warrior in advance of the others rode alongside and sank a war-axe in a teamster's head.

Through the turmoil of dumped freight and overturned wagons, the final wagon of Cary's string wallowed into the passageway. Above him, he heard the first crashing volley of fire from the walls. He vaulted into his saddle and loped out.

"All right—bring them in!"

Stockwell shouted the word to his teamsters. Snatching up horns and rifles, they sprinted for the fort.

XXVII

THE PASSAGE STRANGLED with the reek of rifles, long rays of sunlight coasting goldenly through the dust and smoke. Four of the post workers were hauling the gates to. Cary and three others waited, rifles to shoulder, for the last stragglers to sprawl inside. A hundred feet out, a shirtless skinner sprawled. A dozen Sioux rushed over him, mounted warriors streaked with yellow, black and vermilion. An arrow slanted in and lay in the dust of the tunnel.

The gates shouldered together. A moment later a thudding force piled against the logs. There was a high and muted fury of many throats. A salvo of rifle-fire rippled from the blockhouse. The thudding finished. Someone with his mouth against the gate began to moan.

They retreated, barring the inner gate. The post had come wildly to life. Wagons and bull-teams surged in dusty turmoil. Whackers dragging long plains rifles clambered to the roofs of buildings. The fore-blockhouse rocked with gunfire. A man on the catwalk below the greyed teeth of the wall sprinted low with a keg of black powder in his arms.

In all this hash of confused men and deserted animals, Cary glimpsed one man standing solemnly near the gate with a carbine crooked in his elbow and his hat on the back of his head, soberly inspecting the pageant. Dunavan had a big smut of powder across his forehead. Sam abandoned his horse in the corral and swung to Dunavan.

"Are you in this?"

"That gate won't hold long," Dunavan said.

"It won't have to. They won't get past the outer one. Get up there to the blockhouse and take over. I'll send up the Springfields."

167

The chaos of firing swelled again, smoke eddying from the tall slots of the blockhouses. A low, insistent thunder spoke of a battering-ram against the gate. On the wall, ramrods rose and fell.

Silvertooth was fighting to get the teams corralled; his voice complaining in bitter baritone curses. Cary thrust through the log-jam of tall wheels and weathered boxes, sorting among them until he found the arms-wagon. He gathered a crew to open the chests and carry armloads of greasy Springfields to the catwalk. He caught a case under his arm and ran to a building wedged into the south-west corner of the walls. Atop the married men's quarters, four men lay in an acrid fume of smoke, loading, ramming, firing.

Cary sprawled among them. He pressed his cheek to a rifle-loop and peered down. The horde of Sioux milling before the gate had swelled. The gate was bowing to the very weight of greasy flesh. In the thickening dusk, two or three hundred warriors fired up at the walls, while others hammered at the gate with cottonwood logs. The main force still lingered behind the wagon-boxes of Stockwell's ruined train, waiting for the rush when the gate went down. Their muskets flashed, flights of arrows soared into the fort; knuckles thudded red war-drums.

Cary nudged the barrel of the Henry into the loophole. A ball smacked close beside it, fanning yellow splinters over the opening. In that dusty turmoil of warriors, he looked for Esconella's white ghost-shirt. But the war-chief was staying back in the trees.

He gouged sixteen forty-four calibre balls into the horde of warriors, and sat back to fill the tube. A rifleman jolted off a shot and turned to grope for a shell. He ejected the smoking copper case and slipped a new cartridge home, and then in sober amazement looked at Cary.

''Greased lightnin'!'' he said.

The firing fattened, as other Springfields came into action. Wounded warriors dragged themselves away from the walk; a gang of Tetons carried a wounded chief back to the wagons. Horses were down and others pitched wildly through the bitter twilight of black powder-smoke. The attack slackened for lack of impetus.

The firing from the walls subsided. The Indians had given back. Single shots rang through the smoke drifting from the walls. Dunavan's voice mounted peremptorily.

"Doctor Merritt! A man's wounded up here."

Somewhere in the grey dusk the envoy called: "I'm coming, man."

Cary slumped back, and could not ease the crabbed grip of tension.

Dusk flooded Young Woman Valley. A rusty green stained the sky above the marbled Bighorns. From the litter of wagons, hissing swarms of arrows arched; rifle-fire crusted along the ground and winked out.

Dark came on. The angry legion began to work into bivouacs, warriors from each tribe and village guarding their identity. Fires blinked, glistening bodies slipped back and forth, working up to a dance. Skin rattles shook. Through a fibre of writhing bodies, Cary saw something that lay gauntly, pin-cushioned with arrows—one of the skinners who had not made it in.

He smoked a pipe, glancing from time to time towards the creek. A faint fog of stars misted the sky. At eight o'clock he shoved himself up. He struck the pipe against his hand.

"Four-hour watches," he said. "They won't attack to-night, but they'll be crawling up for the dead and wounded. Let them have them. It may be all they'll want. But if they get too thick, watch out."

He descended from the wall. A cramped little city, the post lay in a silent paralysis. He opened the door of the mess-shack and shouted for the cooks. He had coffee and venison put on for half the crew, and then strode along the wall, calling men down.

In the blockhouse, he found Merritt finishing with the wounded skinner. A winy stain drenched the linsey-woolsey of the man's right thigh. "We'll carry him to the powder magazine," Merritt said. "It will do for a field hospital."

Cary went ahead. He sounded the signal on the thick portal. A small stone cell, the magazine was buried to half its depth in the earth. After a moment the door opened an inch and a gun muzzle gleamed darkly. Then Gaybird cried out and let Sam push the door open.

Dale Merritt crowded through to clutch the doctor. Ignoring her, Merritt directed the litter-bearers inside.

"They've pulled off for the night," Cary said.

Dale turned quickly. "But surely they won't attack again? Haven't they had enough?"

"Jericho had walls, too," said Cary. "You ladies can sleep in your rooms to-night, but you'll come back here at four o'clock. Food will be ready in a few minutes."

Daniel Edge walked to the mess with Sam and Gaybird. He wiped his mouth on his sleeve, an over-heavy man with a sea-walk. "The Pilgrims never had it harder," he said bitterly.

Sam and Gaybird sat across a long table from each other. A distant surf sounded in Cary's ears, remnant of the firing. Gaybird was soberly occupied with her thoughts.

"Tell me about Crazy Dog," she said finally.

"I'd rather tell you about a girl I know."

"Would I like her?"

"She's a humming-bird in armour. Even a thousand Sioux can't upset her."

Her chin began to tremble then. "You'd better tell me about Crazy Dog," she said.

"The chief's going to walk. Merritt took a bullet out of him."

"And he'll come to Laramie for the parley?"

"He said he'd be there."

"Then there's still some chance . . ."

A rifle exploded in the night—and echoes cascaded through the post. It was silent again. The Pawnee cook brought steaks and coffee. Sam regarded her with a sober smile.

"Will it be worth it, Gaybird? We may never see the time when you can ride out without wondering what's behind the next ridge. Will anything be worth that?"

"I've never seen it any other way," she declared, "and it's always been worth it."

Afterwards, with Gaybird in her own room behind the commissary, Cary made a slow tour of the post. It was now past ten. Each roof had its silent watchers. The blockhouses had their sharpshooters who smoked quietly with rifles across their knees. He mounted the wall. In the fore-blockhouse the smoky darkness was restless with low talk and snoring. Shells and burned primers crunched under his boots as he crossed the floor. He kicked a bucket of water, and swore under his breath. The air was choked with tobacco fumes. He put his palms against the wall and peered through a slot.

He thought he saw a wagon moving. He heard Dunavan growl.

"They've pulled away half their dead. They may quit when they git 'em all."

"Keep thinking it, if you want. It's as good a prayer as any."

Coy Mullan's voice said testily: "I never seen the Injun yet that liked climbing while he was being shot at."

Cary put his back to the wall, thinking about the wagon. "We can't shoot at a thousand of them at once, if they swarm together."

"What'll they climb on? Ladders?"

"No," Cary said. "Wagons . . ."

The blockhouse was quiet. Someone grunted and shifted his position, and a muleskinner growled: "Wagons. Yes. That'd be the caper."

Mullan rose from a corner and stood by the trapdoor. He was silent for a moment. He said roughly: "I'll go down and have a bait. When you've time, Cary, I want to talk with you."

You want to tell me it was all Stockwell's fault about the rifles, Cary said to himself. You didn't know he was planning it, until it was too late.

"When I've got time," he said, "will be when the Sioux have left. Send up a bucket of coffee."

Reliefs came. Carrying their rifles, the men descended the ladder. A last man slouched in beside Cary as he stepped on to the catwalk.

"We did have a date at Fort Greybull, didn't we?" said Dunavan. "This is Greybull, now, eh?"

"We did have."

"There's been times you were thirty seconds from a ball in the back. That's happened, in the army. Only I fight from the front. Why did you think you could handle me like a green-horn?"

"One of us," Cary said, "had to handle the other. You'd have been handling me before we reached Fort Reno. It's a point with you not to be handled by anybody. You must have gone crazy in the army."

". . . I bought out after six months. Then—my God!—I ran into you. Was it any business of yours how I drank and worked, so long as I got my chores done?"

"There's only one commodity I can make money out of," Sam told him. "Men. All the trade goods in Wyoming won't do me any good if I can't move my wagons. Some men can pack goods with less loss than others, and now and then a man can pack a wagon, whack bulls, and fight Indians, too. I don't know why I picked you for one of those. Silvertooth told me I was crazy. I picked you the same I'd pick a horse—no offence—with the heart more than the head."

"What do you like in a work-horse? Something that leads well?"

"Something that doesn't fight the bit. You fight the bit because you think discipline is beneath you. Dunavan, it isn't beneath anybody. The sergeants you fought with were under discipline to the shavetails. The shavetails answered to the captains, and back in Washington there's a general with poor digestion who's under discipline to every man and woman in the country."

Dunavan peered solemnly into Cary's eyes as though to be sure he was not being joshed. He asked scoffingly: "Who do *you* answer to?"

"To you. And to all the other men I'm supposed to move through hell without getting the smell of fire on them."

Dunavan shifted his rifle. He looked down, suddenly. He muttered, "Well, that's one way of looking at it." Solemnly he went down the ladder.

Cary remained in the blockhouse until three-thirty, sleeping a little. There was the depressing air of an army hospital ward. Most of the men lay on the floor, turning much and sleeping little, their breathing heavy. A teamster startled them all by coming out of a nightmare with a yell and lunging to his feet. Someone threw a dipper of water on him and he sank down, shaken.

Dawn would begin about four-thirty. One hour . . . Cary checked the ammunition, took a last look at the Sioux camp and sensed a throb of movement in it. He left John Silvertooth in charge and went down to rouse all the relief men.

As he descended the ladder, a rifle-shot tore the pre-dawn silence. He stared at the corrals, from which the shot had come. A sentry shouted and there was a bristling of guards along the walls. But in a moment someone called:

"Go back to sleep. Owls ought to know better than to roost on walls anyway."

The man sauntered from the rear of a storehouse which backed up to the corral. He halted, leaning against the poles and ejected a shell from his rifle. Cary moved from the ladder and went along the corral fence until he reached the man. It was Mark Stockwell.

Stockwell slowly thrust the bolt of his rifle forward and they regarded each other in the tingling grey of early dawn. "Won't be long now," said the Montanan. "I wonder how much of my freight will be left?"

"It doesn't seem to worry me," Cary said.

"You're nursing your suspicions for all they're worth, aren't you?"

"Found a hole to crawl through?" Cary asked. He saw him clearly—saw the tough, aggressive mind which would wriggle out of any trap. He was a nice balance of magnificent greed, of lack of squeamishness and of egotism—the kind of far-sighted egotism that sometimes got a man's profile on a coin or a postage stamp, and sometimes got him hanged.

Stockwell said: "Orrum was a damned fool. I warned him against leaving the train, but he was in a hurry to see that French girl of his in Butte. He had a load of old Harper's Ferry's I was buying from him. I dickered for those Springfields once, too; remember? I told him to leave them at the post and my manager would pay him."

Cary did not reply. Stockwell stirred under his regard and demanded testily: "Well, what did you think?"

"You know what I think. I mean to put you in the guardhouse when we get through this. You'll go back to Cheyenne in irons. You can handle your own men better than I can or I'd have locked you up before now. And we need your gun. We need every gun, to match the ones you put in their hands."

Stockwell said: "I'd like to see any ten of you put me in irons."

"You will."

Cary walked away from him. At the rear blockhouse he made his inspection. He located Dunavan in the mess hall. He sat down across from him with a mug of coffee. Dunavan's eyes nestled in tired, puckered flesh. His face was surly, as a good foot soldier's should have been.

"I'm going to leave you in charge of the yard," Cary stated. "I want the freight dumped from eight or ten of the wagons and a barricade made out of the boxes. Lay them out to face the gate."

"What makes you think they'll come in that way?"

"Because if they start moving wagons up to the walls, I'll open the gates."

Dunavan pressed his fingers against his eyes. "I'm tired. I don't hear things right. You said. . . ?"

"I'll open the gates. Let them in. If they storm us at too many points we can't stop them. They'll be all over the post, setting fires."

"And how in thunder do you think you're going to stop eight hundred at one spot?"

"With fire power. It's the only way we can hope to. You don't have to kill every man in an army to lick it. If we can pile them up shoulder-deep at the entrance, the others are going to lose heart. Especially if we can make a liar out of Esconella, with his bullet-proof ghost-shirt."

"Let them in!" Dunavan muttered, peering darkly into his coffee-cup.

Cary rose from the bench. "Maybe we won't have to. But if we do I want the wagons ready."

A rifle roared. Another hammered out its horde of echoes; then a crackling of shots from the south wall broke out. Cary shouted to the room: "Get to your posts!"

XXVIII

Outside, a murky light seeped from the sky. Tongues of fire licked through a slot in the blockhouse. A guard bawled:

"They're bringing up the wagons! Let's have some of you coffee-swillers up here."

Cary went back to the blockhouse. From the ladder, he looked down to see Dunavan impressing teamsters into service. A man shook off his hand. Dunavan struck him with the back of his fist and sent him reeling towards the wagons. Cary climbed into the dim reek of powder-smoke.

The dregs of night lay over the fields. Through river mist he discerned the gaunt shapes of freight wagons moving down both sides of the post. One was already against the sallyport. There was no evidence of bull-teams. A dozen Sioux could push a wagon without difficulty, lurking on the off side so that they were protected from rifle-fire. Yet the main horde of Oglala, Brule and Uncpapa warriors remained among the vestiges of Stockwell's freight.

Rifle-fire rippled up and down the walls. The wagons came on, ghostlike in the dawn. Inside the post, a wagon went over with a splintering crash. Cary turned to study the yard. One or two wagons had been unloaded and moved into place about fifty feet from the inner gate of the sallyport. Dunavan had now given up unloading them and his workmen were pushing them into place loaded and overturning them with a bull-team.

Cary turned to Silvertooth.

"Take over the walls, John. Hold the men as they are until the attack begins. I figure it will be at the main gate. When it comes, take most of the men to the front and pour it into them."

Crusty with fatigue and tension, Silvertooth growled: "You seem damned sure they'll play it your way."

"I aim to make it so attractive they can't pass it up. What's more tempting than an open gate? But we knock them over as they come through."

"And what's more suspicious! Esconella's a fox, not a fool."

"This is going to be convincing."

He descended the ladder and slung off to the rear posts to pass the word. Oxen and horses surged anxiously about the corral as he strode by.

He headed for the rear posts, but in the shadows back of the commissary, he stumbled over something. He caught himself and looked back. Puzzled, he returned to the man who lay against the log wall. This man's cheek was against the earth. His arms were drawn under him and one leg was pulled up. Cary pulled him on to his back. Coy Mullan looked up at him with filmy blue eyes. His throat had been torn by a bullet and there was a grisly display of cords and muscles.

He hoarded something in his hand—a clutch of buckskin whangs, a handful of fringe torn from the yoke of someone's shirt. Cary regarded him grimly.

Owls ought to know better than to roost on trading-post walls, he thought; and wagonmasters should know enough not to question their employers' motives. Coy Mullan had learned this too late.

A man of ideas, Dunavan had placed crates of hardware in random fashion just within the inner gate. The warriors who rushed through it would not come on a straight line. Their charge would be slowed and blunted. Cary made a hand, helping to over turn the wagons. Between the boxes they threw up a shallow earthworks. A pattern grew: a wide half-wheel of wagon boxes confronting the gate; crates radiating from the hub like stub-ends of sunken piles. A second, paralleling ring of boxes began thirty feet behind the first; the final firing line.

Crates of shells were split open and scattered for ready loading. Cary was sweating. He came face to face with the question of whether he had forgotten anything . . . any *pons asinorum* of military strategy which might backlash on him.

Dunavan was manning the boxes with teamsters as fast as the wagons were overturned. Axes made rough loopholes in the bottoms of the boxes. As Cary brought up a crate of shells, Dunavan growled:

"I'd like to meet the fella who said Injuns don't besiege."

"After to-day, maybe he'll be right. Or it might be that white men won't build forts any more. You'll stay with the second rank. Pick off any who get past us, and move over if we have to pull back."

He found Daniel Edge. "Dan, I've a chore for you."

Edge blinked slowly and pulled a forearm across his forehead. "I know. I reckon that's what I get for bein' fat."

"That's what you get for being fat and trustworthy. You won't go soft?"

"God keep me from it. And God help all of us, Sam."

Edge laboured slowly past the commissary towards the powder magazine. Sam saw him pat his shirt pocket, like a man leaving on a scout, who checks to see whether he has his matches.

She came to him then in a little cameo of vision, smiling and sweet, sitting on a wagon-tongue as she brushed her blue-black hair. It struck him bitterly that nothing should be so hard as this, nothing so lonely and full of consequences.

And now Silvertooth came to the window of the blockhouse and roared down:

"Something's up! Esconella's ranging up and down the line. Make your play, if you're going to."

The darkness of the powder magazine was warm and thick as smoke. Gaybird sat on a pallet against the wall, a bucket of water where she could reach it at her right, a rifle on her lap, the wounded man at her left. There was an odour of sickness and medicines. That, and the monotonous, snoring moans the man made, burdened the darkness.

It was tiring to have the eyes opened, focused on nothing. It was more tiring to squeeze them shut. While she sat there, she worked on knitting she had brought from her wagon. Her needles made a tiny, good-natured prattle.

Sound suddenly pricked through the stone walls, like a distant crackling of flames. Gaybird's heart compressed.

There was a scratching sound and light broke dazzlingly in the room. Dale Merritt was on her knees a few feet away, holding a dripping wax match in her fingers.

"I won't sit in the darkness like—like a criminal waiting to be executed!" she cried. "Why did they have to put this man in with us? Why—"

Gaybird said firmly: "Put the match out!" She was not looking at Dale, but at the crates and kegs of shells and powder.

Dale struggled up. "I'll not put it out! If we've got to stay here, I'll know whether it's rats or Indians I hear!"

She faced Gaybird furiously. Gay quietly raised a dipper of water from the bucket and hurled it. The light was extinguished. Dale began to sob.

"Just sit down," Gaybird told her, "and think less of us and more of them out there. That isn't so nice, what they're doing. Much less nice than waiting."

At the same time, she was not so sure. Now that the rifle-fire was a full-throated roaring, she had to cease knitting. Her fingers were unsteady. The wounded man began to mouth a word, over and over. She gave him water.

Then she sat back and thought of Sam. She wished she had done one thing last night: given him the ring and asked him to put it on her finger. But it had all been too confused for sentiment, and now, perhaps, he might never do it.

Dale was whispering: "But they can't get in, can they?"

"I don't know. I don't think so."

"If they do, what will happen? I mean—what do they do to—to women?"

"Sometimes they make slaves of them. They don't covet us as one might think. They have contempt for white flesh."

The strong-hearted lie. What *did* the braves do? And what did the squaws do, drunk on jealousy and cruelty? She was not sure, because men did not tell such things to women.

The door sounded to the signal knock. Quickly she crossed the dark floor to open it. The cold, grey dawn seeped in. Fat Daniel Edge stood there smiling, a short axe in his hand.

"Ladies," he said heartily, "we thought you might be wanting company. I see you brought your knitting, Gaybird. Sam said to be sure you put heels in his socks this time. You left them off, last time, you remember."

He came in, closing the door on the shocking thunder of the rifles. They heard him cross the floor towards the powder kegs. The axe made a single, sharp smack against a keg, and a piece of wood fell to the floor.

Dale said hastily: "You may sit over here by me, if you want, Mr. Edge. There's a pallet."

Dan Edge seemed to yawn. "No, I'll be quite well right here." He made himself comfortable on the split-open top of the powder keg.

Cary took his horse from the line and loped through the wagons, striking Dunavan on the back as he passed. He found Tom Kane, the scout, and shouted:

"Come along!"

The gate bars were dressed eight-by-eights. The two men lifted them out of the iron hasps. The gate swung slowly outward. Cary mounted again and looked out. He had again the feeling that the dammed-up fury of the wilderness must rush into this gap, forcing it like a hole in a dike. In the grey dawn, he witnessed the pre-attack skirmishing of the Sioux, the little pointless rushes, the rattled weapons and curvetting ponies, which corresponded to a white man's spitting on his palms and settling down to work.

Esconella, distinctive in his white ghost-shirt, a red blanket across his lap as he sat his pony, had discovered the open gate. He sat utterly still.

Between the gate and the wagons lay the body of the murdered teamster. He was naked, and bristled with arrows. Cary said to Kane: "Back away, now, and get to your post. Let the first man through—it had better be me."

He spurred the horse out of the post and crossed the torn, bloody ground before the gate. The silence of the walls ached in his ears. He loped for the corpse of the muleskinner. Reaching it he swung his pony broadside to the Indians and slid off on the post side. He crouched beside the dead man, not touching him, not looking at him! There was nothing he could do for the dead man, but there might be something the skinner could do for him. Recovering your dead—there was something an Indian could understand.

Then a yell like the scream of a mountain lion came from a bronze throat. A gun cracked. Peering under the barrel of the horse, Cary saw the line begin to melt towards him. Ponies and mounted warriors oozed through gaps in the wagons. Clots of horsemen flowed around the ends. The wilderness had found the hole in the dike.

Cary lunged for the pony. With his hand on the saddle-horn he felt it quiver. He heard the *pop* of an arrow entering the tough little body. The horse sank down, biting at the feathered shaft in its side. Cary turned to run.

The Springfields began to shout, throwing out their dirty-black smoke and the shuddering explosions of sound.

Behind him, the line was shredding, the faster ponies racing ahead of the others. As he reached the gate he turned to raise his carbine. A breech-clouted warrior carrying a musket and a bullhide shield led the pack. Sam put him on the tip of the Henry and fired. He felt the quivering of earth under the horses' hoofs, and just as he turned into the gate he saw the Sioux throw his hands up and leave the wooden saddle.

Cary ran through the cold sallyport and entered the post. Crates studded the ground like stumps. He dodged through them to the first line of wagon-boxes. He sprawled behind a box and came into a kneeling position with one foot kinked under him. He raised his gun to steady it against the grey wood of the tailgate. He was gasping for breath. His hand pulled at the loading lever, inching it down, thrusting it back, until angrily he smacked it home and circled his finger through the trigger-guard.

There was the boom and echo of rifles along the catwalk. Riflemen jolted to the kick of the guns. Suddenly a man ran from the blockhouse and came half-way down the steps, to sit down and wait, his rifle trained on the crates.

The flat hammering of pony-hoofs filled the passage. An Indian was shouting soprano invective. The sallyport seemed gagging on its gorge of Indians and horses.

A naked Sioux with rifle and reins in his left hand and a coupstick raised in his right lunged out of the passage. The teamster on the steps got his shot in an instant ahead of the others: the Oglala dropped the rifle. The other balls struck him simultaneously, changing the look of his face and breast. His pony swerved and kicked out at a crate. The next horse ran broadside into him. A rifleman knocked its rider on to the ground.

It was suddenly as if a dam had broken. Cary felt his body know itself. He was in the path of a flood. It boiled with a flotsam of horsehide, of copper skin streaked blue and red and green. Lances, bows and rifles tossed and thrummed and roared.

He found himself firing. A hot shell stung his cheek. A hand which did not seem to be his slapped the loading lever down and up. He was firing into the howling vortex of ponies and riders. The quadrangle was choking on them. Scores . . . hundreds . . . you could not fail to hit.

A splatter of colour broke off and bubbled through the boxes, getting behind his wagon: a half-dozen Sioux had broken the first line of defence. They swung and charged back, and one of them fired a musket and a man was shouting.

My arm, my arm!

Bullwhackers were sprawling everywhere and their shots were a stuttering clap of thunder. There was not an Indian on his pony an instant after the six broke through. Someone flopped on to a scrambling brave and a skinning knife fell.

Cary's eyes lingered on a grey stone structure beyond all this, tucked in behind a building at the rear—the powder magazine. I hope she can't hear. I don't want her to have it to remember. And she must remember, she must be able to look back on this day. It will not all end for her before the sun climbs the wall.

He looked back. Another dozen Indians could not be packed into that shouting square. Crates were overturned and spilled. Blankets, white crockery and jugs of vinegar tangled the ponies' hoofs. Horses lay on their backs, screaming and kicking at the air. A bitter smoke wound through the buildings. The fort was a travail of dying.

The cauldron was filled. The pressure in back was greater than the restraint of the wagon-boxes and rifles, and in an instant it would boil over on the riflemen.

Cary lurched up, shouting: "Back up! Keep firing!"

They gave back stubbornly. Some of Dunavan's men retreated to the porch of the commissary. A tall Oglala with an eagle-bone through his top-knot and a knife in his teeth rushed a teamster. A double-bitted axe met him. The Indian went down in full run.

Hunched behind the box, Cary reloaded the Henry. He raised it again and dully chose a target. Then something in the crowd of warriors screamed for his attention.

"*There he is!*" Cary yelled. Clay-whitened, its stippling of blue porcupine quills just visible, Esconella's ghost-shirt was struggling forward. A lance flashed, fluttering a fresh scalp as the point came down into the body of a teamster caught in the muck of Indians.

Then the shirt again came ahead, twisting through the mob, seeming truly to be magic. Rising slowly, Cary went to meet it.

Esconella guided his horse with his knees. He held the lance high, blood dripping from the point. Arrogance burned in his face. This is his day, Cary thought; his hour. The first warchief to overpower a fort! Across his face yellow-and-black bars shone greasily. His eyes found Cary standing beside the wagon-box. The moccasined heels struck the pony's ribs. He leaned forward, his arm carrying the lance back.

Cary raised the carbine and pulled the trigger.

The hammer fell without a sound. He looked dumbly at the gun. Empty. He swore and dropped it, reaching blindly for his Colt, but Esconella was over him, driving the lance in. He felt the point tug at his armpit and go through his shirt. Something sleek and sharp chattered across his ribs. His hands closed on the shaft of the lance. He hauled back and the Sioux released it. The lance fell. Esconella reached for his revolver—Bill Orrum's Colt—but Cary was lunging in to seize the Oglala's leg and drag him out of the saddle. The roman-nosed warrior was on top of him as they went down.

They were on the ground. Cary's hand closed on the rancid mat of hair. He held the lean head down and rolled over to pin the twisting body with his own. Gory fingers closed on his throat. His free hand groped at his hip, searching. Now it closed on a smooth, corrugated cylinder of bone and he pulled his case-knife free. He let Esconella see the knife. He felt the fingers leave his throat, and drove quickly. The knife struck Esconella's collar bone; it slanted off into his throat. Sam struck again, and a third time.

He stood up and dragged the chief's body behind the wagon. He cut the bloody shirt from it and found a discarded rifle to hang it on. Jamming the gun between the spokes of a wheel, he let the shirt dangle where the Sioux could see it.

Up on the catwalk there was a wild yelling. The old, primitive story was still good business, Cary reckoned: chief slaying chief.

A brave discerned the shirt and rode forward to recover it. Bullets began to hit him; he kept coming, but within reach of it a final ball slugged him aside. He was down in the roll of hoofs and dust.

Heated to smoking, the Springfields still rammed their machine-made bullets out; the queer bolts lifted and copper shells slid home, and chunks of fifty-calibre lead roared out in a fog of brackish smoke.

It was coming home to the Sioux: these were fifty men with the fire-power of two hundred. Esconella had lied to them. There was no magic in his deerskin tunic. There was no wisdom in his strategy.

Cary saw the beginning of the pressing back. With a full magazine he stepped into the interval between the rings of wagonboxes and commenced firing. Sweat trickled saltily into his lips. This was a cowpen slaughter. They were not fighting: they were running, riding, crawling back to the sallyport. There they ran into the glut of braves still dreaming of scalps and high deeds.

Cary brought the rifle up again and frowned across the sights.

Indians did not comprehend surrender, but they understood retreat. You retreated when the hearts of your gods turned bad. You retreated when you had to climb the backs of your own butchered companions to get at the enemy. Nearest the gate, the bucks fought back into the passage. Among the wagon-boxes, marooned warriors battled with clubbed rifles and broken lances. It was a massacre from mythology.

Cary had had enough. He raised his arm. "*Hold your fire!*"

But no one heard him. The rifles continued to roar.

The sun came up, as if reluctantly, to peer through the smoke and dust. A torpid reaction had rotted the life of the post after the retreat. Across Young Woman Creek, a mauled army of Sioux lurked among the trees, waiting for nightfall, when they could recover their dead. If the white man comprehended the etiquette of warfare, he would place the dead and wounded on the ground before the post.

Grey with powder-grime, Cary saw to the caring for of the wounded and told off a dozen men to carry the dead outside. As the wounded were cared for, they were laid beside the dead.

He remembered Coy Mullan. Now that significance came back to such small things as a single murdered wagonmaster, he remembered Mullan . . .

He had seen Mark Stockwell helping to carry a wounded whacker into the dispensary, but he had not seen him since.

Cary went past the commissary and turned into the alley between the long building and a storehouse. A cold night gloom clung close to the ground. He saw Mullan's body. Pressed against the unbarked log of the commissary was another figure. He drew his Colt. The man held Mullan's right hand in both of his, but he dropped it quickly and rose to his feet.

They were face to face, fifteen feet apart. Stockwell was a grey, hunched figure without a hat. He made a hopeless gesture.

"Done for Coy, they did," he said. "Shot in the throat."

"Yes, before the fight started," Cary said. "I saw the fringe in his hand. You should have come back for it before his fingers froze."

Stockwell moved away from the wall. He said: "You . . . damned . . . fool!" A dark gleam of metal showed the upward movement of his hand.

In the alley there was one great throb of sound, a single, stunning heartbeat. Then sound flowed out both ends of it and Cary was alone with a man who lounged woodenly against the wall and dropped his gun, and sank to his knees.

XXIX

DARKNESS CAME DOWN White Woman Creek and shapes moved on the meadow. Pickets observed them from the walls. In the dispensary someone lighted a lamp. Doctor Merritt had been asleep with his head on the table. He looked up to see his wife placing the lamp before him. She appeared very thin and pinched, but she had brushed her hair and changed her gown. She came across the scrubbed, wet floor.

"Asa, you must come to bed. You're exhausted."

He shook his head. "Dead."

"We have a nice room next to Mr. Edge's. I have some marvellous beef broth for you—and real coffee!"

Merritt leaned forward; he looked as though he were falling out of the chair. But he put his palms on his knees and slowly levered himself on to his feet. "All I want is sleep. All I'll ever want. I've been riding or fighting or doing surgery for—how long? Two days? That's a long time for a little Washington politician."

She held his arm and smiled at him, more in coaxing than in persuasion. "And still, we had good times in Washington, didn't we?" she said. "And we shall have again. It's all very well to be patriotic, but we've earned something better than Wyoming. We're going home, Asa!"

He was silent, looking about the cramped little chamber. Behind this minute surgery was the infirmary; he would be back here a dozen times to-night. Yet there was a species of comfort in the thought. These men, when they summoned him, were a continent removed from dissimulation. When they said, "*I need you*," they meant it.

"I won't go back to Washington," he said. "I'll send my report from Fort Russell."

Dale's hands dropped away. She looked at him like a child meeting punishment. "You'll go back to your practice?"

"I am thinking," Merritt said, "of contracting to the army. There are forts in this country without a single surgeon."

Men were coming across the ground from the commissary. Someone spoke drunkenly and dragged his feet.

Dale's lips parted. Her face grew lax and her hands clenched the folds of her gown.

Merritt stood up, smiling. "If it's prestige you want, my dear, I'll be the most important man in the post. I'll wear a uniform. You'll be Mrs. Doctor Merritt, and no officer's lady would dare give a tea without inviting you."

Two men ascended the steps and crossed the porch with a third man half-carried between them. It was Tom Kane, the scout. Kane's face had been mauled. All three of these men gave off vapours of whisky.

"A little disagreement," said one of the teamsters. He helped seat Kane on the table. "This fella was recruiting a company to mine gold. He tried to get Dunavan to make a hand, and Dunavan whipped him. He promised the same to any other man who tried to leave before the end of the season. Funny thing, because Dunavan was only drinking beer."

"Not so funny," the doctor murmured.

After he had pulled together a cut in the man's eyebrow and mended his lip, he let him go. They heard the trio leave; then the doctor backed down the flame of the lamp, left it on the table and took his wife's arm. She did not move. Merritt regarded her and said gently:

"Of course I wouldn't make you stay. If you don't happen to like this country nothing can make you."

Something about her at that instant—some softness of indecision—made him think of the first year of their marriage. Dependency in a woman was a fine thing.

"Do you want me to go back?" she asked him.

Merritt held her hands, slowly shaking his head. "I think you know what I want you to do."

Dale came against him and began to weep.

It was late when Gaybird found Sam in the armoury. He had come and gone for hours, elusive as quicksilver.

Now he was fitting the Springfields into wall racks, except for a few chests stored against the wall. The stocks had been rubbed with linseed oil and the browned steel had a moist lustre.

"I think you're in love with them," she said.

Cary padlocked the retainer and dropped the key in his pocket. "I brought them up here to sell," he said, "but I'll hang on to them now until the army comes back. That may not be long."

She watched him move cases of ammunition about. He frowned over the arrangement. "Maybe those ought to go into the powder magazine."

"I'm sure I wouldn't know," she said.

Cary saw, without appearing to, that she wore the candy-striped gown she had worn in Cheyenne. It gave her the silhouette of a handbell, a slender stem above, a generous flare from the waist, her slippers just visible. She wore a narrow blue sash and a velvet wristband, and he detected a richer scent than the decorous rose-water fragrance he associated with her. An out-and-out French perfume.

He set one case on top of the other. "I was worried that there might be rats down there this morning."

"No," she said.

He inspected a gun-crate, saying gruffly: "These will have to be nailed down against the dust." Her slippers were silent on the floor, but her dress and petticoats rustled tartly, and just as she reached the door Sam said: "You've put your hair up."

She turned. Her chin was up as well as her hair. "Braids are for girls," she said.

Sam went to her. "And is there anything wrong with girls?"

"Some people seem to think so."

He reached up and found the bone hairpins which made a coronet of her rich, dark braids. He drew them out and let the braids fall forward over her shoulders. He ran his hands down them. "That's it! You looked like a business partner that way. I almost forgot to tell you about the upstairs room your father had," he said.

"I suppose there are guns stored in it, too?" A smile brushed her lips. The lamplight uncovered a flush in her cheeks.

"Guns? There's a new goosefeather mattress on the bed and a crockery bowl and pitcher. I put down some Indian rugs last spring."

"Well, that's nice," she said. "For you?"

"For us," Sam said.

Gaybird bit her lip. Sam picked her up, the silken, rustling froth of her skirts billowing about them. She was pulling something from the bosom of her dress, reproving him. "Sam! This is indecent. There!" She put the ring in his hand.

Cary laced the ring carefully over her finger. "Didn't I do this once before?"

"But you didn't finish the ceremony. You didn't kiss me."

He kissed her, swaying slightly, their eyes closed. She took a deep, trembling breath when his face moved away. Sam reached for the wall-lamp without taking his eyes from her, and holding it by the ring he carried her into the dark vestibule.